D1111042

As You Wish

From Robin Jones Gunn

ROBIN
JONES
GUNN

As You
Wish

CHRISTY AND TODD
THE COLLEGE YEARS

BETHANYHOUSE
MINNEAPOLIS, MINNESOTA

Published by Bethany House Publishers
A Ministry of Bethany Fellowship International
11400 Hampshire Avenue South
Bloomington, Minnesota 55438
www.bethanyhouse.com

Printed in the United States of America by
Bethany Press International, Minneapolis, Minnesota 55438

Library of Congress Cataloging-in-Publication Data

CIP data applied for

ISBN 0-7642-2273-2

ROBIN JONES GUNN loves to tell stories. Evidence of this appeared early when her first-grade teacher wrote in Robin's report card, "Robin has not yet grasped her basic math skills, but she has kept the entire class captivated at rug time with her entertaining stories."

When Robin's first series of books for toddlers was published in 1984, she never dreamed she'd go on to write novels. However, one project led to another and *As You Wish* is Robin's fiftieth published book. Other series include THE CHRISTY MILLER SERIES, THE SIERRA JENSEN SERIES, and THE GLENBROOKE SERIES. Combined sales of her books are over two million, with worldwide distribution. Many of the titles have been translated into other languages.

Robin and her husband, Ross, have been involved in youth work for over twenty-five years. They have lived in many places, including California and Hawaii. Currently they live near Portland, Oregon, with their teenage son and daughter and their golden retriever, Hula.

Visit Robin's Web site at *www.robingunn.com*

To my husband, Ross.

I made a wish, and you came true.

And to our son, Ross, and our daughter, Rachel.

We wished together, and then there was you and you.

CHRISTY AND TODD
THE COLLEGE YEARS

1 Todd, you are really bad at keeping secrets, you know."
Christy Miller let go of her boyfriend's hand and stopped in the middle of their trek across campus.

"And who says I'm keeping a secret?"

Todd Spencer's wide grin and dimple were sure signs to Christy. "Your face told me. All you have to do now is fill in the details. With words, preferably."

"I'll tell you over dinner." Todd motioned for her to follow him.

Christy stood steadfast, folded her arms, and asked, "Where are we going to dinner? The cafeteria isn't open until Friday."

"I know. Just come with me. I made reservations at a quiet little out-of-the-way place. Come on."

Christy raised her eyebrows skeptically. "You made reservations?"

The hot Santa Ana winds that pushed their way from the desert to the southern California coast every September grabbed the ends of Christy's long, nutmeg-colored hair and drew the strands across her cheek like a veil. She brushed back the wisps from the corner of her mouth and noticed that Todd was looking at her "that way" again.

She had been home from Switzerland less than a week, but already Todd had looked at her "that way" at least six times. Maybe seven. His silver-blue eyes seemed lit by some inner candle, and she felt as though he was waiting for her to come closer and make a wish before the flickering light went out. Each time Christy had seen that look, she had turned away.

This time she paused. *He's waiting for me to tell him I love him.*

When no words came from Christy's lips, Todd held out his arm to her and in his easygoing manner said, "Well, actually, I sort of made reservations. Come on. You'll see."

Christy responded by slipping her arm around his middle. Todd put his arm across her shoulders and drew her close. They walked across the campus of Rancho Corona University in perfect step.

What's wrong with me? I know I love Todd. Why won't those three simple words find their way from my heart and burst out of my mouth?

They entered the open plaza at the campus's center just as the sun slipped behind a clump of rustling palm trees. Filtered beams of amber sunlight sliced through Todd's short, summer-blond hair.

"Over this way." Todd led Christy to the edge of the large fountain in the middle of the plaza. Since classes didn't begin until next week, not many students were on campus. Todd and Christy had the plaza to themselves.

"Do you want to sit here?" Todd asked. "Or over on one of the benches?"

"This is fine." Christy sat on the fountain's wide edge

and crossed her long legs. "What about our dinner reservations?"

"We have some time," Todd said. Then he quickly added, "Doesn't this fountain remind you of that one we saw last summer?"

"Which fountain? One of the dozen in Salzburg that Katie liked?"

"No, I was thinking of the fountain in Rome," Todd said. "Or was it in Milan? I don't remember."

Christy smiled. "When I close my eyes, this spot reminds me of the train station in Castelldefels."

"Spain?" Todd asked. "There weren't any fountains at that rundown train station in Spain. That place was a wreck."

"I know. But close your eyes. Listen. It's the palm trees. That's what reminds me of the train station in Spain. That rustling sound."

Christy watched Todd close his eyes and tip his chin toward the sky, listening. "Reminds me of Hawaii," he said, opening his eyes and looking at Christy.

The sound always made Christy think that the trees were clapping. Now she heard the echoes of Hawaii along with Todd. "You're right. It sounds like a whole row of hula dancers swishing their grass skirts."

"Hula dancers?"

"Yes, hula dancers. Tall, slender hula dancers."

Todd laughed. "Very tall and very slender."

A gentle breeze swirled around them, spraying the evening air with a mist from the fountain. Christy tilted her head. "So are you going to tell me your big secret now? Or do I still have to wait until dinner?"

"Oh yeah, my big secret. What was it I was going to tell

you?" After a thoughtful pause, Todd shrugged. "Guess I forgot."

"You did not." Christy playfully grabbed Todd by the shoulders and threatened to push him into the water. Todd responded by taking hold of her shoulders. "If I go in, you're going with me."

They laughed and play-wrestled until Todd's upper-body strength from his years of surfing enabled him to overpower Christy's best efforts. He pulled himself upright and, with his left hand, scooped a handful of water to splash her.

"Hey, don't start something you can't finish," Christy teased, lightly splashing him back.

"Oh, you think I can't finish a water fight?" Todd scooped up another handful of water. "Just watch me." He splashed her again and again, his laughter dancing around her, riding on the waterdrops.

Christy's next scoop of water was the biggest yet.

"Okay, okay," Todd spouted, laughing and coughing. "You win. Truce."

Christy blinked the beads of water from her eyelashes and brushed them off her cheek and chin.

"I got the position," Todd said out of the blue. He used his T-shirt sleeve to mop his wet face.

"What position?"

"The position at Riverview Heights Church. They hired me this afternoon as their youth director. That's my big secret."

"You're kidding! I thought you said they were going to hire someone who had graduated already."

"That's what I thought. But they had their final meeting last night and voted. I'm the guy."

"Wow," Christy said. "That's really great, Todd."

"They said they liked that I could lead music as well as teach the Bible studies." Todd stretched out his feet in front of him and added, "I told them all about you, and they asked if you would be willing to teach the junior high girls' Sunday school class."

"What did you tell them?"

"I said you would."

"You said I would?"

"Yeah. I told them you were the best teacher on our missions team to Spain a few years ago and how you helped out at an orphanage this past year in Switzerland. They can't wait to meet you."

"Todd, you told them I would teach Sunday school?"

Todd turned his full attention to Christy and seemed to try to read her expression. "You've taught Sunday school before."

"Preschoolers."

"Oh. Well, you were a counselor at summer camp a few years ago."

"Those girls weren't even in middle school yet."

"Have you ever taught junior high students before?"

"No, never."

"Well, you'll love these girls. And they'll love you."

"Todd!"

"What?"

"Why didn't you at least ask me first? I mean, what if I don't want to teach the junior high girls?"

"Why wouldn't you?"

"I'm not saying I would or I wouldn't. I'm saying you should have asked me first before agreeing that I would make a commitment like that. It sounds like they hired you because they thought they could get three employees for the price of one—a youth director, a music leader, and a girlfriend Sunday school teacher tossed in for free."

Todd straightened himself and looked confused. "You think people should get paid for teaching Sunday school? Is that it? You want to be paid?"

"No, of course not. You're not hearing what I'm saying. I just . . . it seems that . . . well . . . ."

"What?"

"Todd, I think you should have let me think about it before you went ahead and made a commitment for me."

"Oh." Todd nodded slowly. "You're right. I apologize. I spoke for you instead of letting you decide. I shouldn't have done that."

Christy shifted uncomfortably. "I didn't say I absolutely wouldn't consider maybe sometimes teaching or at least helping out."

Now Todd was the one who sounded exasperated. "Are you saying you will teach or you won't?"

"I don't know. Let me have some time to think about it, okay?"

"Okay. Take all the time you need. Decision making has never been your strong point, has it." The thought wasn't spoken as a question but as a statement. Christy hated to admit it, but the remark was true. Still, it felt like a slap of cold water.

"Todd," Christy stated firmly, lining up her thoughts and preparing to defend herself. "I think that—"

Before she could finish, Todd said, "Hey, our dinner is here."

Christy looked out at the parking lot and saw a young guy walking toward them wearing a red-striped shirt and carrying a pizza box.

"Are you Todd Spencer?" he called out as he approached.

"Yeah, that's me. You're right on time. Thanks." Todd paid for the pizza and took the box.

"Have a nice night," the guy said and then jogged back to his delivery car.

"This is what you meant by having reservations?" Christy asked. "This is your quiet, out-of-the-way place?"

Todd grinned. "Cool, huh? Just the two of us. Perfect night. Great atmosphere. It's not exactly the Island of Capri, but we have hula-dancing palm trees for our dining entertainment."

Christy stared at Todd. She didn't know if she should be charmed or bummed.

"I ordered their monster combo." Todd opened the box. "Looks like they went a little heavy on the onions and bell peppers. You can take off anything you don't like and put it on my half. Do you want to pray before we eat, or should I?"

"I think you better," Christy said.

She did her best to hide her feelings, which still stung from Todd's comment about her inability to make decisions. Yet the hurt hung over her like a shadow for the rest of their time together. She only ate two pieces of pizza and silently listened as Todd filled her in on more details about his new position.

When they walked back, hand in hand, to her dorm room, Christy said, "Sorry I got so stressed about the Sunday school thing."

"Don't worry about it," Todd said. "I'll be back on campus Friday to move into my dorm room, and we can talk some more then."

"Okay," Christy said. "Call me when you get here. Katie and I can help, if you want."

He stopped at the front door of Sophia Hall and leaned over to give Christy a soft kiss. If he was upset or disappointed with her, it didn't show in his words or in his kiss. "See you Friday."

Christy found her dorm room unlocked and Katie, her red-haired best friend, standing precariously on a chair, trying to squeeze a small stereo speaker onto the top of their built-in bookshelf.

"Oh, good, you're back." Katie gave the edge of the speaker a whap with the palm of her hand and commanded it to stay in place. "Where did you and Todd go to eat?"

"He made reservations at a quiet, out-of-the-way place." Christy flopped on her bed.

Katie stopped to stare. "Are we talking about Todd Spencer? Your Todd Spencer?"

"Yes. It actually was very creative. He ordered a pizza and had it delivered to the fountain in the central plaza, if you can believe that."

"How romantic!"

"It would have been if I wasn't such a bean head."

"You? A bean head?" Katie climbed down from the chair but still was eyeing the speaker as if commanding it to stay in place.

"Yes, me. What is my problem?"

"Which one should we discuss?" Katie made herself comfortable on the foot of Christy's bed. Katie was always ready for a good evaluation session.

"Forget I asked that."

"Oh, come on. Give me a hint. Why did Todd come all the way here tonight?" Katie's perceptive green eyes examined Christy's expression. "Let me guess. He drove an hour and a half from Newport Beach because he missed you so much, right?"

"Not exactly." Christy told Katie about Todd's new position as youth director at Riverview Heights, including the parts about Christy teaching the junior high girls' class and Todd's comment concerning her inability to make decisions.

"Well, that is true, you know," Katie said. "I mean, you have gotten a lot better about making decisions and everything, but I don't think you should be upset with Todd for saying that. It was an observation, not a criticism."

"Well, I am upset. I feel like crying my eyes out."

"That's probably because of the jet lag. You were in Switzerland for a year, Christy. Your body has had only a few days to adjust to the time change. Give yourself a break. That's why we decided to move into the dorm early, remember? You were the one who said you needed a chance to adjust to all the changes."

"Arrrrgh!" Christy pulled a pillow over her head. "I hate change!"

"Now we're getting somewhere." Katie grabbed the pillow and used it for a backrest. "Remember, flexibility is a sign of good mental health."

"Oh, please!" Christy yanked at the pillow. "Give me back my pillow."

"Only if you promise you'll work on a better attitude about Todd's new job. This is what he wanted, you know. It's perfect for him."

"I know. It is."

"It's a real job." Katie handed the pillow to Christy. "A career. A ministry. Something permanent. This isn't like all his random jobs over the years."

Christy made herself comfortable. She knew Katie was determined to shower her with advice. Resistance was futile. And even though Christy wouldn't admit it, deep down she wanted to hear what Katie had to say.

"This is it, Chris. This is the final stretch for you guys. It's possible that both of you could graduate this year."

"Only if I can figure out what I want my major to be." Christy sighed.

"You will. When is your appointment with your counselor?"

"Friday."

"That works," Katie said. "You can sleep all day tomorrow to get over your jet lag. On Thursday you can find a job, and on Friday figure out everything with your classes and your major. By the time Todd arrives Friday afternoon, your life will be in order."

"I wish," Christy said. "It's not always that easy, Katie."

"And it's not always as complicated as you make it. I mean, can I just say that it's obvious God is doing all His God-things at the right time so you and Todd can get married and get on with your lives together?"

"Katie, you're assuming an awful lot."

"Assuming a lot? *Moi?*"

Just then someone knocked rapidly on the door. Katie hopped up and swung open the door. The visitor who came floating in wore a glowing expression. Her wild, curly blond hair cascaded over her shoulders.

"And just where have you been, Little Miss Happy Heart?" Katie asked.

Sierra Jensen, a fun-loving, free-spirited freshman, gave Katie an impulsive hug and then flitted over to Christy and gave her a hug. Sierra had been roommates with Katie and Christy two years ago when they had met on a missions trip in England. Despite Katie and Christy being older than Sierra, they were all close friends.

"I've been to the chapel." Sierra twirled dramatically. She spun around to Katie's beanbag chair and lowered herself with a poof.

"I take it you saw Paul." Katie pulled up a chair. "What happened? Did you guys have a chance to talk?"

"Yes. Everything is wonderful now." Sierra fiddled with the dangling silver earring in her left ear.

"Details, please," Katie said. "Don't leave anything out."

"Well," Sierra began, "you both know how everything was so disastrous with Paul a few hours ago."

"Slightly," Katie answered for both of them.

"Everything is perfect now. We talked and prayed together in the chapel, and it's like we're starting our relationship all over. We both have the same understanding and expectations, and it's just right. Not too fast, not too slow. Just right."

Christy smiled. *I remember a few brief seasons when I felt that way about Todd. As much as I said I didn't like it at the time, those stretches—when we knew our relationship was in a holding pattern while we figured out who we were and what we were going to do with our lives—were comforting and settling. So why am I nervous about making the next round of decisions in our relationship? I wish I could figure out why I feel this way.*

Sierra pulled Katie's beanbag chair closer to Christy's bed and wiggled herself into a comfortable position. "After a whole year of Paul's being in Scotland, now he's less than an hour away. And we're both in the same place in our understanding of our relationship. Finally! No unrealistic expectations. I can't believe how I was starting to make everything so complicated."

"Did you hear that?" Katie gave Christy a motherly look. "Why would you want to complicate things with Todd when it's all finally coming together so naturally?"

"And did you hear what Sierra just said about unrealistic expectations?" Christy countered.

Sierra's expression turned somber. "Everything is okay between you and Todd, isn't it?"

Katie answered for Christy, "She's afraid of the future."

"I am not," Christy snapped. "I'm just not ready to talk about getting married."

"Who's talking about getting married?" Sierra asked.

Katie raised her hand. "I am."

Sierra's eyes opened wide. "You, Katie? Who are you planning to marry?"

Katie laughed. "I'm not talking about *my* getting married. I was talking about Todd and Christy getting married. It was the topic *du jour* right before you knocked on the door. It's the next step for Todd and Christy, and she's afraid to make such a huge decision."

"Katie, that is not what I said, and you know it."

"Okay. What did you say?"

Christy sighed. Part of her didn't want to discuss this with Katie and Sierra right now. However, another part of her had longed for the closeness of good friends while she was in Switzerland. She had even written in her diary how much she was looking forward to settling into Rancho Corona University so she could spill her guts to Katie and be open to her best friend's advice. Having Sierra to talk to, as well, was a bonus.

"Okay, this is the whole thing. Just listen, please. Both of you. I promise I'll listen to your advice, but first let me say what I'm thinking."

Katie and Sierra leaned forward, their expressions open and warm.

"This is what I know for sure. I know I love Todd."

"But you haven't told him," Katie jumped in.

"I said let me say everything first."

"Oops." Katie covered her mouth. "Sorry. Go ahead."

"I know I love Todd, and yes, I haven't been able to tell him yet. I know he loves me. He has told me he loves me at least a dozen times since that first time in Switzerland this summer. But, you see, to me there's something really deep and final about telling him I love him. It's only a tiny step away from saying I promise to be committed to him. Forever."

"And you don't feel ready to say that to Todd?" Katie surmised.

Christy looked at her hands. The overhead light in their room caught the corner of the gold ID bracelet Todd had given her years ago when he had promised that, no matter what happened, he would always be her friend. She ran her finger over the word "Forever" engraved on the bracelet.

Sierra jumped in. "Does it feel too final to you? Are you thinking that the moment you tell Todd you love him he'll say, 'Then let's get married'?"

"Maybe. I don't know."

"He's not going to propose to you on the spot," Katie said.

"And what if he does? Why wouldn't you want to marry him?" Sierra asked. "Haven't you been thinking that was the direction your relationship was going all along?"

"Yes and no. Sometimes I think I'm ready to marry him

right then and there and never look back or have any regrets. Then other times I look at him and I think, 'Who is this guy?' There's so much I don't know about him."

"So? Give yourself some time to get to know Todd better," Sierra said. "That's what Paul and I are doing. Not that we're even thinking about marriage. Neither of us is. We have plenty of time to get to know each other as friends without any pressure to make it more than that."

"Right," Katie said. "But Christy and Todd have already been through that phase for . . . what? The last five years?"

Christy nodded.

"It's time for them to make decisions, and sorry, Chris, but I have to say this. Todd is right. Decision making has never been your favorite thing."

Christy didn't feel as wounded when Katie said it. She actually found it easier to agree and slowly nodded her head. But something more lay behind her uncertainty over Todd, and she felt she was on the edge of formulating that very important thought.

Katie turned to Sierra and continued her analysis of Christy as if she weren't sitting there. "Christy likes things to be planned and in a logical order. You know, 'First comes love, then comes marriage, then comes the baby in the baby carriage.' "

Sierra chuckled. "That is the way it works best."

"If only a detailed tour book for relationships existed!" Katie spouted. "Todd and I discovered when we were traveling with Christy in Europe this summer that the best way to travel is with a plan and a tour book to guide you. You miss too much along the way otherwise."

"Oh, so are you now admitting publicly that having a plan is a good thing?" Christy said.

"I told you that in Europe." Katie raised her voice.

Sierra jumped in. "But I don't know if love can always be planned and logical."

"Right," Katie agreed. "Nobody can make guarantees about the future. We have to take what we know and act on it at the moment, trusting God for the outcome."

"I don't know if I agree with that," Christy said. "I think we're responsible for our actions all the time, including the possible results of our actions."

"Yes, but," Sierra spoke in a firm tone, "there has to be a balance because we're not in control of our own lives. God is."

"And we shouldn't be afraid of the future," Katie added.

"It's like that verse in Proverbs 31," Sierra said. "You know, the one that says, 'Strength and honour are her clothing; and she shall rejoice in time to come.' "

"I memorized that one last year," Katie said. "Only my version said, 'She can laugh at the days to come.' "

Christy pulled back and became somber. The important thought she had been formulating was rising to the surface and bringing sadness with it.

"What are you thinking right now?" Katie asked. "Your face clouded over like a thunderstorm."

"You and Sierra think of laughing and rejoicing at the future part of that verse, but I worry about the strength and honor part of it. Committing myself to Todd is a huge decision. If I marry him, we'll be together for the rest of our lives. I don't want to let him think I'm ready to make such a major commitment until I'm sure I'm ready."

"But you do know that you love him," Katie reminded her.

"I think I know that."

Katie dramatically grabbed her hair with both her hands and acted as if she were going to pull it out. "You said a few minutes ago that you knew you loved him!"

"I know. But try to understand what I'm saying—"

"I do. I get it." Sierra stepped in. "I think I get it, anyway. You're saying that you know you love Todd, but you don't know if it's the same kind of love, or a deep enough love, to be certain you're ready to commit yourself to him for the rest of your life."

"Exactly," Christy said.

Katie burrowed her head in her hands and seemed to be taking it all in.

Sierra's summary of what Christy was trying to say had somehow allowed the important thought she had been formulating to become clear. "That's it! This is what I've been trying to figure out." Christy leaned forward and paused, making sure she had Katie's full attention. "I want you both to tell me the truth. Tell me your honest opinion."

Sierra and Katie both waited.

"Do you think it's possible to finally decide that you really, truly love someone but not end up marrying him?"

The room went still for a moment while the three friends exchanged glances.

"Yes," Katie said, her expression completely serious for the first time all evening. "I think it's possible to realize you love someone as deeply as you know how to love and not end up spending the rest of your life with him."

Sierra slowly nodded. "I think so, too."

Christy felt her vision blur with uninvited tears. "So do I," she said in a whisper. "And that's what I'm afraid of."

CHRISTY AND TODD · THE COLLEGE YEARS

2 Christy stayed up until after two in the morning talking with Sierra and Katie. When Katie rose shortly before noon and said she was going into town to get something to eat, Christy told her to go on without her. Then she did something she didn't think she had ever done before—she slept all day and all night.

On Thursday morning Christy woke with a horrible headache. She ate a soggy breakfast burrito Katie had left for her with a note saying that Katie was shopping with Sierra. After a hot shower that did her little good, Christy went back to bed, where she fell into a deep sleep for the rest of the day.

When she woke, it was almost dusk, and she felt more coherent than she had in weeks. Maybe even in months, as if she had broken through the exhaustion barrier.

Christy had just pulled herself out of bed and was stretching, when Katie came in holding a bag from the deli in town. "Hey," Katie said, "she lives! She breathes! Does she want to eat?"

"Yes, I'm starving. Thank you so much. Thanks for leaving the burrito for me this morning, too."

"No problem. You must be feeling better."

"I do. I feel normal again. No, better than normal."

"That's good to hear. I was beginning to worry about you."

Christy reached in the bag and took out one of the turkey sandwiches. She closed her eyes and said a quick prayer of thanks before taking a bite.

"You look better," Katie said. "I think those extra weeks at the orphanage in Switzerland really did you in."

Christy knew Katie was right. Her year in Switzerland had been good in many ways, but her life had been nonstop, requiring a great deal of her physically and emotionally. She gave of herself to the children at the orphanage, often for more than thirty hours a week, as well as maintaining a full schedule of classes.

"I know," Christy agreed, settling cross-legged on her bed. "You're right about the orphanage. Those kids broke my heart every day. I really felt empty by my last few weeks there."

"Are you glad you stayed through the term?" Katie asked.

"What do you mean?"

"When Todd and I were there in June, you had that big breakthrough revelation about how you weren't suited for crisis maintenance-type work. You know, all that stuff you were talking about when we were in Amsterdam. How you were going to change your major but you still thought you should stay in Switzerland to finish the program. Are you glad you stayed?"

Christy nodded, her mouth full.

"I know you felt you needed to keep your promise to the orphanage and to the university in Basel," Katie said. "I

never told you, but I admired you for making that decision."

"Thanks."

"I've been thinking about all the stuff we talked about
the other night. You're good for me, Chris. You cause me to
think things through rather than impulsively run ahead.
Sierra and I were just saying how we both have a problem
with being too spontaneous."

"That's why you're both good for me. I need you guys to
tell me to lighten up sometimes. I wish I'd gone shopping
with you. I haven't been to a mall in more than a year."

"I think getting some sleep was more important for
you," Katie said. "You honestly look a whole lot better."

"I feel better about everything, too. It really helped to
talk with you and Sierra the other night. I think the most
important thing I can do right now is to take each day as it
comes and resolve each decision as it comes."

"The Sunday school decision was the final phone book,
wasn't it?" Katie asked.

"The final phone book? What does that mean?"

"It's my new theory. You know how I told you that one
of my many fascinating summer jobs was delivering phone
books door to door?"

Christy nodded.

"Well, I learned the very first day that I could only carry
eight phone books at a time. If I tried to pick up one more,
I ended up dropping all of them."

Christy didn't see Katie's point.

"You were already carrying a lot when Todd dropped the
Sunday school question on you. Think about it. You had jet
lag, you had decisions to make about your major, you were
worried about finding a job, you were confused about why

you didn't feel ready to rush into a lifetime commitment with Todd, and then—bam!—the Sunday school decision was the final phone book."

"Kind of like that saying about the straw that broke the camel's back," Christy said.

"Exactly. Only, the things you're carrying aren't little straws. They're all heavy like phone books. You can carry a couple of them at a time, but when you hit your limit, it feels as if you're going to drop all of them."

Christy leaned back and felt herself breathing more easily than she had for several weeks. "You just described perfectly what I was feeling."

Katie beamed like a proud sunflower. "No extra charge for the advice. I wondered if you were going to have a meltdown a couple of nights ago when we went to the store and you were about to cry because you couldn't decide which laundry soap to buy. I'm glad to hear you say that you're going to take each decision separately, one at a time."

"What about you?"

"What about me?" Katie had gotten up to turn on her stereo and pulled a stick of gum from an old Muppet Babies lunch box she kept on the corner of her desk.

"Didn't you have an appointment with the counselor today?" Christy asked. "Or did you have to reschedule it?"

"No. I went into town to get breakfast with a bunch of people, and then I met with the counselor at ten. Sierra had an appointment with financial aid, and we went shopping after that."

"Did you end up changing any classes around?"

"No, I'm sticking with botany for my major. I told the counselor my goal in life was to create herbal teas, and he came close to laughing aloud."

"Didn't you tell him about the herb garden you started on campus last semester and the experiments you did?"

"No, I'll wait to tell him about that after I complete a successful experiment."

Christy grinned. She remembered an e-mail Katie had sent last spring with the hilarious account of her first attempt to serve herbal tea she had grown and mixed herself. The experiment resulted in two out of five students in her chemistry class breaking out in hives. The other three complained of stomach pains. Apparently Katie was the only one in the class who didn't suffer any kind of reaction.

"By the way," Katie said, "your aunt called this morning while you were dead to the world and wanted to take you to lunch. I told her you weren't available today."

"Very kind of you, Katie. And true. Thanks."

"You might not thank me when you hear this part. She said she would be here at noon tomorrow to pick you up for lunch, and if you had anything on your schedule, you needed to change it because that was the only time she was available."

"Oh. Did she say what she wanted?"

Katie laughed. "Does she ever? I mean, does she need a reason to step into your life at any moment and take over?"

"She's probably upset that I haven't called her since I got back. When I asked my mom about Bob and Marti last weekend, she said she hadn't seen them or talked to them since the Fourth of July."

"That's a little unusual, isn't it?"

Christy shrugged. "My mom and Marti aren't exactly the closest sisters that ever lived."

"They're certainly the most opposite," Katie commented.

"You know, maybe one of the good things about Switzerland was that my aunt was thousands of miles away instead of an hour-and-a-half drive."

"Do you want me to come to lunch with you tomorrow?" Katie asked.

"Yes! Would you?"

"Of course. Free food. Why wouldn't I come to offer my moral support?"

Christy thought a moment and added, "It's not because I'm intimidated by my aunt, you know."

"Oh no," Katie said with a sly grin. "Never."

"It's because your being there will take off the edge, if you know what I mean. I want you to come because then I know it will be fun."

"That's me, all fun all the time." Katie tossed the crumpled deli bag toward the trash can and missed. She got up and placed it inside. "I'm going to the baseball field. Do you want to come with me?"

"The baseball field?" Christy thought that was an odd place for Katie to want to go to. Then Christy remembered. "You still searching for number sixteen?"

"His number was fourteen, and yes, as a matter of fact, I thought it wouldn't hurt to revisit the place where we met last June."

"What was his name again?" Christy asked.

"Matt."

"Matt what?"

"That's all I know. I told you I hadn't found out his last name yet. He's Matt, number fourteen, the best baseball player Rancho Corona has ever seen."

"You know," Christy said, pulling on a pair of jeans and a T-shirt, "I'm surprised you haven't employed your extraordinary detective skills on this guy yet."

Katie shook her head, making her red hair swish in trademark Katie fashion. "No, I'm really determined to let God be in charge of my nonexistent love life. If He wants to bring somebody into my life, He's going to have to do it in His time and His way. True, I've thought about Matt an awful lot in the past 104 days since I met him."

"One hundred and four days, huh?" Christy laughed.

"Yes, but I'm not going to push to make anything happen." Katie pulled a worn baseball cap over her silky red hair and tucked the chin-length strands behind her ears.

"However," Christy teased, "you still believe it's okay to just happen to be at the right place at the right time to help God along in the sovereignty department."

"Exactly."

"I'm ready," Christy said, slipping her bare feet into her leather sandals. "Let's go be 'available' for God."

"Don't mock my methods." Katie closed the door behind them. "I'm really trying, here."

"Yes, you really are trying, aren't you?" Christy suppressed a laugh.

"I'm not talking to you anymore, Christy."

The two friends exited their upper-classmen dormitory and headed down the road toward the center of campus, both still grinning. Christy felt relieved that she and Katie were back to normal in their friendship and that the jet lag blues hadn't gotten the two of them off to a bad start this year. That was one of the things she had long appreciated about Todd's easygoing personality and Katie's bouncy personality; they both let Christy go through her loopy moods without changing their friendships.

Christy and Katie walked past several trucks that were

backed up to the main walkways of each of the dorms. Dozens of arriving students energetically unpacked their meager worldly possessions. Christy was glad she had moved in early and had the days she needed to adjust and to sleep, which probably wouldn't have happened at home in Escondido.

Moving in early had been her dad's idea. He had said he could either move her in right after she returned from Basel, or she would have to wait until Saturday afternoon, which wouldn't have given her much time to settle in before classes started. She knew her parents also had hoped it would give her a chance to find a job on campus, and she felt bad that she hadn't pursued that yet. That was one of the "phone books" she had been carrying around.

"I love this weather, don't you?" Katie apparently had forgotten that two minutes ago she had said she wasn't going to talk to Christy. "I love it when it's still warm and breezy like this, even after the sun has gone down. It feels like Indian summer. Maybe I'll invent an herbal tea and call it 'Indian Summer.' What do you think?"

"I like it," Christy said. "I like this time of year, too. This dry, windy heat always makes me think of new beginnings because the weather was like this when my family moved to Escondido. That's when you and I first met, remember? It was at that sleepover the first week of our sophomore year in high school."

"I will never forget that night." Katie's laughter took off like a hoot owl headed for the moon. "Remember when we tried to TP Rick Doyle's house, and you got caught, and he chased you down the street at midnight?"

Christy had to laugh. That was still among her top ten

most embarrassing moments. "I wonder what ever happened to Rick."

"Why do you say that?" Katie's laughter vanished.

"Because the last time anyone saw him was more than a year ago at Doug and Tracy's wedding. Did you talk to him then?"

"No, did you?"

"No."

"You're not having dreams about Rick waltzing back into your life or anything, are you?" Katie asked cautiously.

"No, of course not. I just think it's too bad that we're all together again, but he's just out there."

"Rick always was sort of 'out there.' "

"I know. But I kept hoping he would figure out his life and be one of the gang."

"You know what your problem is?" Katie said and then plunged ahead before Christy had a chance to answer. "Your problem is you have too much mercy. That's why being with those kids in the orphanage killed you and why out of the blue you would start wishing happiness on a guy who was a jerk to both of us. Rick deserves whatever he gets."

Christy stopped walking a few yards from the baseball field. "You're still mad at him, aren't you? You haven't forgiven him for the way he led you on at the Rose Bowl Parade on New Year's all those years ago."

Katie shrugged.

"You need to forgive him, Katie. Let it be what it was. Learn from it and move on."

"He was my first kiss, Christy. Tell me, how does a girl forget the first guy who kissed her?"

Christy let her tender, blue-green eyes scan her best

friend's expression before answering. "You don't ever forget."

"Exactly." Katie took off, walking at a fast clip.

Christy caught up with her. "But you can forgive him for hurting you, Katie."

"I have. I do." Katie paused. "I will. But enough of Rick Doyle, okay? I'd like to move on to Matt, number fourteen."

Christy glanced around the baseball diamond as they approached it. The two of them were the only people in sight. "Doesn't look like anyone is practicing tonight."

"I didn't think anyone would be practicing," Katie said. "I just thought . . ." She paused and stood still for a long moment. "I don't know what I thought. Let's go to The Java Jungle. I don't know why I had us come here."

"The Java Jungle?" Christy questioned.

"That's the new name for the coffee shop on the lower level of the student center. I saw the sign today. I guess no one liked the old name, The Espresso Stop."

Katie pointed out the new sign after they had hiked across campus to the student center. The large complex housed The Java Jungle, the student mailboxes, and a large lounge area on the top level. When they entered, Christy noticed more students were in the lounge than she had seen on campus the entire week. The place was beginning to feel more like a university than a ghost town. The cafeteria, which had been dubbed The Golden Calf, would begin serving meals for the first time in the morning. That meant Christy finally could stop spending her limited funds every time she wanted to eat.

They entered the coffee shop and stood in a short line to order something to drink. "My turn to pay," Christy said.

"I have money with me," Katie protested.

"But you bought the sandwiches."

"Actually," Katie said, "I got a two-for-one coupon on the sandwiches when I filled my car at that little station at the bottom of the hill."

Rancho Corona University was built on top of a mesa, and every time the students wanted to go into town, they had to go down the hill. Christy was sure Katie knew where all the gas stations were because she was so fond of her new car, a bright yellow Volkswagen Thing. It reminded Christy of a cross between a Jeep and a dune buggy. Katie seemed to enjoy making sure the gas tank on her "Baby Hummer" was always full and the windows free of smashed insects.

"Okay, then we're even," Christy said. "Be sure to thank Baby Hummer for me."

Katie motioned to a booth that had just been vacated in the far corner. "Why don't you hold that booth for us? What do you want to drink?"

"Lemonade."

"Lemonade?"

"Yes, lemonade. I don't want anything hot to drink. A good, old-fashioned American lemonade sounds good to me."

"Okay, one lemonade." Katie headed for the end of the line as Christy slid into the booth by the side window. She looked around and realized she didn't know a single person in The Java Jungle. It felt odd starting all over again in a new school. She was more grateful than ever that Katie was there. And Sierra and Todd.

Friends make all the difference in life. She thought of her two roommates in Switzerland who were both from Germany. They were nice roommates, but Christy couldn't keep up with their social activities and had spent most of her free time alone in their room. She liked the solitude after the noise of the children at the orphanage, but now that she was back in southern California, Christy felt ready to reinvent her college experience, spending lots of time with her closest friends.

I wonder if that's another reason I reacted so strongly when Todd said he had volunteered me to teach Sunday school. Maybe I'm afraid my free time will be devoured if I commit myself to a group of younger kids again. I'm not ready to do that. I need time with my friends.

Just then Christy noticed a tall, slender guy entering The Java Jungle. A wonderful, warm feeling came over her.

Matthew Kingsley! Look at you! My mom was right. You are all grown-up now, aren't you? There was no mistaking the Wisconsin farm boy she had known since childhood, the guy she had developed a huge crush on in elementary school.

Matthew's brown eyes scanned the room from under his baseball cap. Christy hadn't seen him since her grandparents' fiftieth wedding anniversary three summers ago. She watched Matthew, wondering if he would recognize her right away.

Matthew's gaze passed over her at first. Then he did a double take and grinned before charging across the room toward her. A firefly sort of fluttering started in her stomach and came out in a lighthearted giggle when Matthew greeted her with an awkward hug. His shoulder smashed her left ear in the quick embrace, and she noticed he didn't smell too fresh.

"You're here." Matthew slid into the booth next to her and grinned.

"I'm here," Christy repeated. "And so are you. How are you doing?"

"Great. Just got in. I've been driving since five this morning. It's so good to see you, Christy. Did your mom tell you I called Monday?"

"No, I've been on campus all week. I haven't talked to her. Are you hungry?" Christy realized she sounded like her mom. It was the lingo Christy had grown up with on the dairy farm in Wisconsin. Whenever one of the men came in from the field, food was offered.

"No, I ate already. I'm trying to find my roommate. He said he would be waiting in here with our keys, but I don't see him. It's the same guy I roomed with last year. Pete Santos. Do you know him?"

"No, but my roommate might. She seems to know everyone." Christy turned to see that Katie was at the front of the line, paying for their drinks.

Matthew looked out the window and leaned closer to Christy to get a clearer view. "There he is. Hey, Pete!" Matthew tapped on the glass. The guy turned and motioned for Matthew to come outside.

"I should have known he'd be talking on his cell phone," Matthew said. "He should have that thing permanently wired to his head. He's on it all the time."

Christy looked away from the window and saw that Matthew was staring at her.

"I wish I didn't have to run off," he said with an honest expression. "But I left my truck in a no-parking zone." Matthew rose and gave Christy's arm a quick squeeze. "How about if we meet for breakfast? We have a lot to catch up on."

"Sure," Christy said and then quickly corrected herself. "Oh, wait, I can't. I have an early appointment in the morning."

"Lunch?"

Christy shook her head. "My aunt Marti is coming to take me to lunch."

"Then what about dinner? Six o'clock? Meet in The Golden Calf?"

"Perfect," Christy said. "I'll meet you there."

Matthew paused a moment and said, "It's great to see you, Christy."

"You too," she said.

"Six o'clock tomorrow," Matthew repeated.

"Six o'clock."

He took off, and Christy watched him stride through the crowded café, waving to several people as he went.

Matthew Kingsley. Who would have guessed that we would end up at the same college?

Christy was still smiling softly when Katie arrived at their booth. "I just saw a guy from my hometown in Wisconsin," Christy told her. "And if you can believe this, I used to have a huge crush on him."

Katie placed the tall lemonade in front of Christy and, ignoring her comment, said, "Well, you're not going to believe what I just did. Go ahead and thank me now."

"Thanks for the lemonade," Christy said.

"No, not the lemonade. Thank me now because I just found a job for you. On campus, even."

"Where?"

"You have to thank me first."

"Thank you, Katie."

"You're welcome." Katie settled into the booth and took a slow, leisurely sip of her steaming latte.

Christy waited, her expectant expression turning to an exasperated one when Katie didn't offer details.

"Oh, you want to know where it is? It's at the bookstore," Katie said at last. "I was talking to some people in line, and one of the guys said he was planning to work in the campus bookstore like he had last semester, but he just got a job today in town that pays more. The job for the bookstore isn't posted yet. He's going in at nine o'clock tomorrow morning to tell them he won't be keeping his position. If you get there at 9:05, I bet they would hire you right then and there."

"I don't know if I'll be done with the counselor by then."

"Okay, so you show up at nine-thirty. Better yet, I'll tell him he shouldn't go to the bookstore and resign until ten. That will give you plenty of time. He even said he would recommend you by name, if you wanted."

Christy hesitated. "Okay, I guess. Who is he?"

"I don't know. He's over there in the green shirt talking to Wesley. You know Wes, don't you? He's Sierra's older brother." Katie popped up before Christy could say anything and waltzed over to the guys with her plan. As Katie turned and pointed to Christy, Christy raised her hand and waved. She thought about going over and talking to them, but she was sure someone would take their booth.

Katie returned with an air of satisfaction. "That was easy. Ten o'clock. Or rather, five after ten. All you have to do is show up at the bookstore and talk to Donna. Act like you know what you're doing, and I'm sure you'll land the job."

"You know, you didn't have to do that, Katie." Christy wasn't sure why she felt resistant to this job. It sounded like an ideal situation, but Christy never had liked it when others felt she wasn't aggressive enough to make her own decisions or to take care of herself so they stepped in to make arrangements for her.

"I think it's a God-thing," Katie said brightly. "Do you know how few jobs are still available on campus?"

"I just don't want to work too many hours," Christy said. "I want to have some time for a social life this year."

"Tell that to Donna when she interviews you. She's really nice. I wouldn't mind working for her. Besides, everyone goes to the bookstore, so part of your social life will be mixed with your work. It's perfect."

Christy sipped her lemonade slowly. "Are you sure you don't want to show up at five after ten tomorrow and apply for the job yourself?"

Katie grinned. "I have enough in my savings to get me through until January. Then I'll be looking for a miracle job. Until then, I'm going to enjoy the rare freedom and pursue my social life to the fullest."

"You're making me feel sorry for myself, and I don't even have the job yet."

Katie didn't seem to hear Christy's comment. Instead, Katie had fixed her attention on something outside the window. Christy looked and saw about two dozen students gathered around the patio tables outside The Java Jungle. From her side of the booth she didn't see Pete or Matthew, and she was certain she didn't know any of the others. Christy guessed they all must be returning students because they were hugging and laughing and waving to others who were heading that way.

"Wait here," Katie said. "I think my number just came up."

"Your number?"

"Yeah, number fourteen," Katie called out, rushing to join the mob of returning students on the patio.

3 Christy, are you awake?" Katie asked much later that night as Christy lay in bed.

Rolling over, Christy forced her eyes open. The soft yellow light she had left on over Katie's desk several hours earlier seemed too bright.

"I'm so sorry, Chris. I started to talk to a bunch of people, and when I went back to the booth, you were gone. I know I left you there a long time. I'm sorry."

"It's okay. I could see you were having a good time catching up with everybody. I wanted to come back to the room to call Todd before it got too late. I should have told you I was leaving."

"The time just got away," Katie said.

"Don't worry about it. We can't apologize every time stuff like that happens." Christy propped herself up on her elbow and stretched her stiff neck. "You already have a lot of friends here. I don't expect you always to wait for me or to take me with you wherever you go."

"You're right." Slipping off her shoes, Katie turned on the overhead light.

Christy flinched at the brightness.

"I'm glad you said that." Katie reached for her bucket of bathroom necessities. She cleverly had arranged her shampoo, soap, and facial scrub in a bright plastic sand bucket and had poked holes in the bottom so she could take it in the shower. "Open policy between us. Always."

"Always," Christy said, feeling more awake. "Now tell me about Matt, number fourteen. Was he happy to see you?"

"It wasn't him. Or at least by the time I got outside he wasn't there. If he was even there to begin with." Katie pulled a pair of flannel shorts and a T-shirt from her dresser drawer. "I don't know for sure if he's coming back this year. I'm going to take a quick shower. Some of the guys were goofing off, and I got shaving cream down my back. See you in a bit."

Katie whooshed out the door just as Christy said, "Could you turn off the . . ."

Forcing her feet to hit the bare floor, Christy turned off the overhead light herself. "I have to buy a rug," she muttered before crawling back into bed. She knew if she and Katie started a conversation after Katie returned from her shower, they would end up talking for hours. Christy wanted to keep up on her sleep while she could, so she coaxed herself to fall asleep before Katie returned.

The next sound Christy heard was the irritating buzz of her alarm clock. It made an obnoxious sound, but Christy found she could fall back to sleep too easily with a softer alarm or music.

"What is that?" Katie bellowed from her side of the room.

"It's just me. Go back to sleep," Christy said softly. "I'm getting an early start for my appointment."

"Humph," Katie grunted, turning toward the wall.

Christy tiptoed over to the window and raised the curtain a few inches. Another clear, sunny day. The skirt and top she had laid out last night were still a good choice for the day. It was her nicest casual outfit and seemed right for the job interview that would most likely follow the meeting with her counselor.

Quietly pulling her desk chair to the window, Christy reached for her Bible and diary and settled in. The morning light fell across the open pages on her lap. After praying, she began to read where she had left off a few days ago. Her goal had been to read through the New Testament that summer. She had only made it through the first chapter of John.

Christy's eye caught on verse twelve, and she underlined it, reading it again in a whisper. " 'Yet to all who received him, to those who believed in his name, he gave the right to become children of God.' "

She made a note in her journal.

I have been given the right to become one of God's children because I have received Him into my heart and life and I have believed in His name. It's like God has adopted me into His family.

Christy chewed on the end of her pen and thought of all the orphans she had grown to care about in Basel. They were waiting for someone to give them the right to become an adopted child. Just the thought of those young hearts and eager faces was enough to bring tears to her eyes. Christy had intended to read to the end of the chapter, but instead she prayed for each of the orphans by name. The sun pouring through the window began to warm her arm, and she knew she needed to get going. She could spend the whole morning praying in a melancholy daze.

Slipping out of the room to take a shower, Christy left all

the orphans behind when she closed her Bible and told herself she had to move on.

The meeting with the counselor went well. All Christy's transcripts had arrived from Basel, and the extra courses she had taken provided her with more transferred credits than she had calculated. If she wanted a bachelor's degree in elementary education, the next step was to plan her student teaching. However, Christy told the counselor she had changed her mind and no longer wanted to go that route.

"I'm thinking of changing my major to humanities," Christy said. "Or maybe English literature."

"I see," the counselor said. He wrote something in pencil on the inside of her folder. Christy tried to see what he wrote without being obvious.

"I think I'm leaning more toward literature," she said.

"Either major would work," he said. "You have a good solid base for both of them. I was adding up the credits, and if you went with English literature, you could graduate in June. You would need to add another three units this semester and carry a full load of sixteen units next semester."

"That's okay," Christy said. Then she wished she hadn't spoken so quickly. After her intense year of study in Basel, she had hoped to take it easier this semester. Especially with a job, which she didn't exactly have yet. And a social life, which was still high on her priority list.

"Would it be okay if I looked over all this and came back the first of next week?" Christy asked.

"Sure. The sooner the better. I have an open slot at four this afternoon, if you know what you want to do by then. Take this catalog with you. I've marked the classes you still need." The counselor gave Christy a reassuring grin. "It's nice to be in the final stretch, isn't it?"

Christy nodded and left the administration building fighting the panicky feelings that taunted her. A few days ago Katie had made the same sort of comment about Christy and Todd being in the final stretch in their relationship as they readied themselves to head down the church aisle. The counselor's comment reminded Christy that she was in the final stretch to head down the graduation aisle. At this moment, she didn't feel ready to walk down any aisles.

Her visit to the bookstore at exactly ten minutes after ten was less stressful. That helped her to focus on the present.

When Christy entered the busy bookstore and asked for Donna, a beautiful woman in a buttery yellow blazer stepped out of the back room and said, "Are you Christy?"

"Yes."

"Great. Come on back here." Donna's skin had a warm, caramel tone. Her golden brown hair was pulled up in a twist and held in place with what looked like two chopsticks. On her desk sat a small blue teapot alongside a china teacup.

"Please, sit down." Donna pointed to several unopened boxes of books that were stacked beside her small desk. "It's a little crowded, I know. It will be this way until we clear out all these textbooks next week. Would you like some tea? I think this is still hot." She felt the side of the teapot.

"No, thanks. I'm fine." Christy tried to figure out a dainty way to perch on top of the highest box.

Donna sat down and smiled at Christy. They chatted a few minutes before Donna asked, "How many hours a week can you work?"

"About fifteen, I think. Or less. I just found out I have to take another class this term."

"I could use you about fifteen hours a week for the first two weeks of school. After that it would be about ten or twelve hours. Would that be okay?"

"Sure. That would be just right, I think."

"I'll need a copy of your class schedule, but I don't have any open hours on the weekends, so you would work only Monday through Friday. Is that okay?"

Christy had expected more of an interview than this. She smiled at the gentle yet direct businesswoman. "That's perfect. Thank you."

"No, thank *you*," Donna said. "Ten minutes ago I thought I'd have to spend the next week going through the hassle of job posting, but you came highly recommended."

Christy thought it funny that some guy she had never met had recommended her simply because Katie talked to him last night at The Java Jungle. That must be one of the advantages of attending a small, private Christian college; the trust factor was strong in this cozy community.

In less than twenty minutes, Christy had filled out all the paper work Donna handed her, and Christy did agree to a cup of tea when Donna offered it a second time. The peach tea was refreshing.

"I'll go over all the other details with you when you start on Monday," Donna said. "Do you have any questions?"

"I don't think so."

Donna smiled. "I'll see you Monday."

Christy left the bookstore and headed back to her dorm room amazed at how easy that had been. She had almost an hour before Aunt Marti would arrive for lunch, and Christy wanted to call her parents to let them know about her job.

As she imagined, her mom sounded relieved. "Your father will be glad to hear this, honey. He was asking me again last night, and I was wondering if anything had opened up for you."

"Did you know Aunt Marti is coming to take me to lunch?" Christy asked.

"Is she?" Mom paused. "That's nice of her."

"Do you think she's upset that I didn't call or go see them when I got back from Switzerland?"

"I don't know."

"I asked Katie to come with us just in case I need some moral support."

"How are you and Katie getting along?" Mom asked.

"We're getting along great, as always. Katie is the one who helped me get this job."

"Didn't she also help you find your job at the pet store?"

"That's right; she did. I'm glad you remembered that. I'll have to thank Katie doubly now. If it weren't for her, how would I ever find work?"

Mom chuckled. "You would manage. Any young woman who can chart her way through a year at school in Switzerland can manage just about anything."

Christy was going to tell her mom she still had to make a final decision about her major. But when her mom said all those nice things about Christy managing her own life, she decided to hold her thoughts. It would be much easier to call home again after she had the major figured out. Especially since Mom's comment made Christy feel competent and accomplished.

Katie arrived at the dorm room only a few minutes before Christy received a call from the lobby letting her know Marti had arrived.

"Are you ready, Katie?" Christy was about to suggest

Katie change from her shorts and T-shirt into something nicer. But then Christy knew she would be doing to Katie what Aunt Marti had done to Christy for years. She didn't want to direct other people in what they said, did, or wore, Christy decided.

Katie apparently thought she was dressed appropriately and accompanied Christy to the lobby. Christy silently inventoried the outfit she had put on that morning—the casual yet crisp skirt and the clean, unwrinkled top. Certainly Marti couldn't find fault with Christy's appearance.

The two friends stepped into the lobby, and Christy looked around, not seeing her aunt among the four people sitting in the lounge.

Then a short woman with long, flowing, dark hair and wearing a wrinkled gauze skirt, a silk tank top, and strings of tiny colored beads rose and came to Christy. The woman kissed Christy on each cheek with sublime elegance.

"Aunt Marti?" Christy choked on the words. She couldn't stop staring at her transformed aunt. This woman, who had always dressed in the most expensive, chic, and traditional outfits, this woman who always wore her hair short and perfectly styled, this woman who never even went downstairs in her own house without wearing makeup, now stood before Christy and Katie looking as if she had dressed as Mother Earth for a costume party.

"Aunt Marti?" Katie finally said, echoing Christy's surprise in face and voice.

"What do you think, girls?" Marti turned around. "It's the new me." She held out the ends of her long hair. "Extensions. Aren't they glorious?"

"Glorious," Christy repeated mechanically. It came out sounding more like a question than an affirmation.

"I surprised you both, didn't I?" Marti said. "This is the new me. Fresh. Renewed on all levels. I finally have come into harmony with my artistic aura."

Christy and Katie exchanged quick glances. If Christy hadn't known Marti to be a strict, controlling, no-nonsense person, Christy would have thought this some elaborate joke. The voice was Marti's. So were the bony fingers that grasped Christy's elbow and pushed for them to be on their way.

"I . . . um . . . I invited Katie to go with us." Christy wiggled her elbow free from Marti's grasp.

"How generous of you," Marti said sweetly. She turned to Katie and said, "Sorry, Katie dear. Not this time. This is just for Christy and me."

"No problem." Katie looked just a little too eager to pull back.

Christy gave Katie a desperate "thanks a lot" look and in complete bewilderment followed her aunt out into the afternoon heat to Marti's silver Lexus parked in front of the dormitory. Christy numbly opened the passenger door and slid onto the leather seat. She couldn't help but feel as if she were being kidnapped. Abducted by an alien. She turned to stare once more at her transformed aunt. Something inside Christy made her want to shake this woman and scream out, "I don't know who you are or what you've done with my aunt, but give her back this instant!"

Then Christy remembered what her aunt was like before she found her "artistic aura," and for half a minute Christy didn't know which version of Marti was worse.

This is absolutely bizarre! What am I doing? What is my aunt doing? I should have made an excuse and told her I couldn't go or at least insisted we eat on campus so I'd have witnesses if she tried to make me join her in a rain dance or something!

"Marti, where are we going?" Christy asked as they sped down the hill into town.

"I was going to take you to the Colony in Palm Desert, but it's not pottery day, and I'd much rather you come on pottery day. So today is simply our time to be together. I want to hear all about Switzerland, and I'm sure you want to hear all about the changes in my life."

Christy suggested Taco Bell. It was close, and lots of students stopped there. She felt safe going to Taco Bell.

Apparently Marti's aura wasn't in the mood for Mexican food, so they ended up at a quiet Japanese restaurant. They had to take off their shoes and sit on the floor at low tables. Marti ordered for both of them and then turned to Christy and said, "Now tell me all about Switzerland."

"It was a good year," Christy began.

Just then a fly buzzed past them, and Marti swatted at it with a fierceness that surprised Christy.

"Vile creature," Marti spat. "And in a restaurant, no less. You would think the proprietors would take appropriate measures against such filth."

For the first time, the old Marti sounded as if she was back in the room with Christy. But then Aunt Marti shifted her attention back to Christy and said, "You were saying?"

"Switzerland was wonderful," Christy said. "Thanks for all you did to work it out so I could go there."

"Of course. No need to thank me."

"It was a difficult year in some ways, but definitely worth it."

"Good," Marti stated firmly, sounding like a hammer driving a nail into a board. "Now, you're probably wondering about the changes in me."

That was a quick summary of my last year!

"Christina, I never would have imagined this, but it turns out I'm somewhat of an artist. It all began when I met Cheyenne at an art show in Laguna Beach. He invited me to one of his pottery classes, and no one was more surprised than I was to discover that I have substantial talent in that area. Cheyenne sponsored me into the Colony."

"Aunt Marti, it sounds like you've been pulled into a cult of some sort."

"A cult? Why, there's nothing religious at all about the Colony. We're a group of artists. Mutual spirits who find expression in the creation of beauty. Believe me, I don't want anything to do with religion. Ever since your uncle had his born-again experience last summer, the man has been impossible to live with. He has a mistress, you know. He left me for her."

Christy couldn't hide her shock. She knew Uncle Bob's conversion to Christianity had been a radical change since he had been such an outspoken agnostic before coming to Christ. But he wouldn't turn against the Lord so quickly and have an affair, would he? How could he?

"Don't look so stunned, dear. I'm referring to the church. Bob's mistress is the church. He goes to her every chance he gets and talks about her all the time. He and I have less and less in common. These past few months he's tried to get me to give up the Colony, and I've tried to get him to give up the church. It seems we've reached an impasse."

The petite waitress in a silk kimono arrived and knelt at their table. With a bow of her head, she served them soup in white ceramic bowls. They were instructed to drink it by holding the sides of the bowl with both hands instead of using a spoon.

Christy paused and prayed, wishing she were brave enough to pray aloud in front of her aunt like she used to do. Today her words felt as if they caught in her throat. The warm broth washed the words back down into someplace deep within Christy. If this wasn't all so disturbing, she would think her aunt's dramatic performance was humorous.

"When you come on pottery day to the Colony," Marti said, "I want you to bring Todd. You can bring Katie, if you wish. And bring your friend with the curly blond hair. What's her name? Sienna?"

"Sierra."

"Ah yes, Sierra. Bring her, too. I'll show all of you the pottery I've made. It has freed my inner self, Christina. Wait until you see my creations on display. You will be so proud of me."

"Marti, I . . ." Christy tried to find the words to say she didn't need to see pottery to feel proud of her aunt. And she didn't want her aunt to dictate when she would kidnap Christy again, especially since this second kidnapping involved her friends.

"You don't need to . . . I mean, I think . . ." Christy couldn't form her thoughts.

The waitress appeared with a tray to clear the soup and present each of them with a plate of sushi, raw fish, complete with tiny bowls of sauce. Christy lost her appetite altogether. It was all she could do not to lose her soup.

Marti continued to talk as if Christy hadn't even begun to say anything. "Now, before I tell you what I'm going to tell you next, I need you to promise me you won't tell anyone. Not a soul. Not Todd, not your mother. No one."

Christy felt they had played games long enough, but she

was so uncomfortable she guessed the only way to speed up this lunch would be to go along with whatever Marti said. With a slow nod, Christy acknowledged her aunt's wish.

"I need to hear you say it," Marti said. "Say you promise you won't tell anyone."

Christy hesitated. She took promises very seriously. That's why she had stayed on at the orphanage even when she knew it would be a huge strain on her. She had made a commitment to stay for a certain time, and so she had stayed. To her, a promise was a vow. And the Bible made it clear that God paid attention whenever a person made a vow. He held that person to complete whatever had been promised, whether it was a vow to God or a vow to another human.

Christy felt the soup sloshing around in her stomach. Just the smell of the sushi was enough to torture her into a quick release from this luncheon meeting. Pushing the sushi away, Christy nodded slowly. "I promise I won't tell anyone, Aunt Marti."

Satisfied with Christy's sincere response, Marti drew herself up, took a long breath through her nose, and said, "You promise, then, that you will tell no one. Especially not your uncle Bob, because he doesn't know yet."

Marti paused. It seemed to Christy that Marti was waiting for her to say, "Doesn't know what?" But Christy wouldn't give her aunt the satisfaction of seeing Christy beg that way.

"You are the first and only person I've told this to." Marti seemed to enjoy the moment as much as Christy hated it. "And that's why you must keep it a secret. You see, I've made a very important decision. Cheyenne is opening a second Colony in Santa Fe. The property becomes available in January."

Christy couldn't see why that was such big news.

Marti leaned closer. "I'm going with Cheyenne. I'm moving to Santa Fe."

4 Let me get this straight," Todd said later that night. He, Christy, and Katie were sitting at a small pizza parlor in town. Todd had arrived on campus about an hour after Marti had returned Christy to her dorm, and Katie and Christy had helped him to move his stuff into his room. Then he announced he wanted to treat them to pizza, so off they went in his VW van, Gus the Bus.

Todd leaned back in the booth and swished the ice around in his plastic cup. "You're telling me Marti showed up in a wig?"

"Hair extensions," Katie corrected him. "Long. Dark. Very strange looking on her."

"And she took you to lunch at a Japanese restaurant."

Christy nodded. "I wanted Katie to come but—"

"But my aura wasn't in harmony with the moon," Katie said. "Or something like that."

"What did you and Marti talk about?" Todd asked.

"Her life. How she's finding herself through creating art. Pottery. She makes pottery."

"I've seen some of her pottery at their house," Todd said. "It's very good."

"Is it really?" Christy asked.

Todd nodded. "Did she say anything about Bob?"

"Not exactly," Christy said. She wished with all her heart she hadn't promised to keep the big move to Santa Fe a secret. When Christy had asked Marti if that meant she was leaving Uncle Bob, all Marti said was "That remains to be seen."

"I wonder what your uncle thinks of her transformation," Katie said.

Christy wished she could spill the secret about Santa Fe so the three of them could discuss everything. Yet she knew that a promise was a promise. The only acceptable reason she knew for not keeping a secret or a promise would be if the person was going to be hurt and disclosing the secret would keep that from happening. Certainly Bob was going to be hurt if Marti ended up leaving him. But if Christy broke Marti's confidence, how would that prevent any hurt from happening? It might only prompt Marti to leave sooner.

Christy felt awful. Her conscience wouldn't allow her to share the information as a prayer request. All she could do was pray on her own, and she had been doing that for hours.

"What do you think is really going on with your aunt?" Katie prodded.

Christy didn't answer.

"I've never seen anyone flip out like that. I mean, she went from one end of the pendulum to the other, didn't she?" Katie shook her head and looked at Todd. "You should have seen her. With that fake hair and no makeup, you would have never known it was Marti."

"Did she say anything about Bob's being more active at church?" Todd asked.

Christy nodded. "She doesn't like the way he's so involved with church now that he's a Christian. She called church his 'mistress' since he prefers to be at church instead of with her."

"Oh, that is low." Katie picked at the pepperoni on the final piece of pizza. "How unfair. I mean, I know the church is referred to as the 'Bride of Christ' in the Bible, but how twisted to call it a mistress. How could Marti be so blind? Christianity is the best thing that ever happened to your uncle."

"I know," Christy agreed. "Uncle Bob has become a totally new person since he came to Christ."

Katie said, "Yeah, and it sounds like your aunt is trying to become her own new person. The only problem is that's impossible without the Lord."

Christy remembered the verse she had read that morning and paraphrased it for Todd and Katie. "Only those who receive Him and believe on His name have the right to become children of God."

Todd, who usually quoted Bible verses and came up with bits of wisdom at times like this, looked at Christy with an expression of pleasant surprise.

"I read that this morning. First chapter of John."

"How did you have time to read your Bible this morning?" Katie asked. "You had an early appointment. I don't know how you did it. I slept until eleven, and don't ask me about my quiet time. It didn't happen. I know that's a terrible thing to admit when you go to a Christian college."

"Just keep being honest about it, Katie," Todd advised.

"It's only bad when you fake it with God or with the rest of us."

"Did I ever tell you what my roommate did last semester?" Katie asked. "She was so funny. She made this fancy sign that said *word* and taped it to the foot of her bed. Then she went around telling everyone that she had spent six hours in the word that night."

Todd grinned. "That's not exactly what I meant by honesty."

"I don't get it," Christy said.

Katie rolled her eyes. "She was 'in the word' because she put the sign *word* on her bed."

"I know, but—"

"It's a Christian college lingo thing," Katie explained. "You'll start to hear it more and more. When people talk about their quiet time with God, they say they were 'in the Word.' You know, studying the Word of God."

"Oh."

"I guess those kinds of jokes weren't real big in Basel," Katie said.

"No," Christy said flatly. "I was amazed when I met a few other Christians, and we could actually attend church together. I can't tell you how much I looked forward to being here with you guys."

Suddenly Christy remembered the other "guy" she was supposed to meet for dinner at six. Matthew Kingsley.

"What time is it?" Christy asked.

Todd turned and read the clock on the far wall. "Seven-thirty. Do you need to get back?"

Christy sunk in her seat. "No." She decided it was too complicated to try to explain that she had made dinner plans with another guy on the same night Todd arrived on campus.

How could I have forgotten? Did I forget on purpose?

Christy didn't think she had ever mentioned Matthew to Todd. At the moment, she didn't have the energy to delve into all that now. She could call Matthew when she got back to the dorm. He would understand.

However, Matthew wasn't in his room when she called him a little after nine that night. She was too tired to stay up with Katie and some of the other girls on the floor who were watching a movie in their suite lounge in the middle of the hallway. It was a comfortable family room–den that was for the women in the upper classes and only open to visitors and guys on designated nights. That meant the girls could hang out there in their PJs most of the time.

Christy slept deeply and woke feeling refreshed, until she remembered Aunt Marti and that she needed to call Matthew to apologize for not meeting him for dinner.

She left Katie sleeping and slipped out of their dorm room. Christy's plan had been to go to the chapel at the edge of the campus for her morning quiet time. On the way, she stopped at the cafeteria, wondering if Matthew might be there for breakfast. Only a few dozen students were in the cafeteria as Christy moved her tray through the line and filled a plastic cup with foaming orange juice from the machine. Matthew Kingsley wasn't one of them. She realized that the only people who would be up at this early hour on a Saturday were probably students who had weekend jobs and were on their way to work.

Christy sat at a small corner table by herself and thought about the way she had felt warmed inside when she had seen Matthew walk into The Java Jungle.

Why did I feel that way? It's not possible that I still have a little bit of a crush on him after all these years, is it? This is college, not elementary school. How can firefly flutterings left over from the playground at George Washington Elementary School have any place in my life now?

Slowly eating her yogurt and muffin, Christy watched the door in case she saw anyone she knew. Todd probably would sleep in. The two of them hadn't made any plans for the morning. He had said last night that he wanted to go over to Riverview Heights in the afternoon and set up the classroom for Sunday. Christy had agreed to go with him. Until then, she had nowhere to go, no one to see, nothing to do. It felt strange. So opposite from the last year.

With a bittersweet sense of loss, Christy remembered all the Saturday mornings in Basel when she had made her early-morning trek to her favorite *Konditorei* for coffee and a fresh pastry. Those mornings were her thinking time.

"Is anyone sitting here?" a girl asked.

"No," Christy said, moving her tray and feeling grateful for the company.

Before the girl had placed her tray on the table, someone from across the room called to her. She looked relieved and hurried to join her friends without saying anything to Christy. Christy watched as the girl greeted her buddies with a hug, and the group of four girls talked and laughed. They looked like freshmen.

Christy wondered what it would have been like to go away to college her freshman year instead of staying home and taking classes at the community college. She didn't regret the past few years. The extra classes and summer school programs had paid off, and she had plenty of credits. But she hadn't had much of a social life.

An unexpected thought floated into Christy's mind. *What would it be like to go out with Matthew Kingsley?*

The thought surprised her. *Why would I think that? I'm with Todd. I love Todd. Why would I want to go out with Matthew?*

Christy suspected the thought was linked to her musings about rushing through college, accumulating units instead of dates. Todd had been in Spain when Christy started college, and aside from a bunch of fun dates she had had with Doug during her first semester as a freshman, Christy hadn't gone out with anyone. She and Doug were close buddies, and their friendship had stayed strong even after Doug and Tracy ended up getting married.

When Todd and Christy got back together in January of her freshman year of college, Christy felt certain she and Todd would be together from then on.

But what if my family hadn't moved to California when I was fifteen? What if we had stayed in Wisconsin? Would Matt and I have become a couple?

She knew her imagination was taking her into the land of if only, and she didn't trust what she was feeling. It was thrilling to speculate about dating Matthew, and for the moment those thoughts overpowered her deep, steady love for Todd. She felt dizzy, as if she couldn't trust her own instincts.

Why am I even thinking such things?

Christy pushed herself to her feet and carried her tray to the back of the large cafeteria, where she tossed her silverware in the appropriate bins.

I need to go to the chapel and have my quiet time. That will get my heart back on track.

The walk to the chapel was along a beautiful trail leading to the edge of the mesa. Rancho Corona formerly had been a working cattle ranch. When the owner donated the land to the college, he had asked that a chapel be built with a stained-glass window depicting the ranch's original insignia. The beautiful glass window, a gold crown with a cross lying in the crown's center at a slant, was above the altar. The Spanish name of the original ranch was "Rancho de la Cruz y la Corona," which meant "Ranch of the Cross and the Crown."

Christy entered the small, silent chapel and felt a welcoming hush come over her. She walked softly to the front and sat in one of the pews, where she bowed her head to pray. As she prayed, her mind began to wander.

Why am I having thoughts about Matthew? Is there something between us that would grow if it had the chance to be explored? Would it grow stronger than what Todd and I have between us?

Convinced she wasn't going to get any serious praying done, Christy opened her Bible and readied her pen and journal. She read two chapters and jotted a few notes. Then her gaze rose to the stained-glass window. She noticed how brightly the sunlight poured through the amber gold pieces of glass that made up the crown.

I should talk to Katie about all these confusing feelings. Katie always helps me get my mind out of the fog. Even if I don't always like what she says, she gives me fresh perspective, and that's what I need right now.

Christy left the chapel and took the path that led past the baseball field instead of across the open meadow. As she approached the baseball diamond, she noticed two guys standing on the pitcher's mound. One of them was Matthew.

Christy's heart did a funny little flutter. *This is it. Time to test my feelings. If there is anything between us to explore, now is the time.*

Matthew spotted Christy and jogged over to where she had stopped beside the bleachers. "Hey, I missed—" Matthew began.

"I'm so sorry—"

They both laughed at how their greetings overlapped each other.

"I'm sorry," Christy said. "I went into town with Todd and Katie, and I didn't get back in time for dinner last night."

"I thought I was the one who missed you," Matthew said. "I ended up being about twenty minutes late, and I thought you had given up and left."

"No, sorry." Christy took inventory of her feelings. She felt surprisingly calm. The initial burst of fireflies had all flown away.

"Would you be interested in joining us in a little game?" Matthew tossed the softball in the air and grinned at Christy from under his well-worn baseball cap.

The other guy approached, and Christy recognized him as Wes, Sierra's older brother.

"Sierra and her roommate, Vicki, were supposed to meet us here," Wes said. "Matt thinks they slept in. I think Sierra forgot."

When Wes called Matthew "Matt," Christy realized she still thought of him by his full name. He had become "Matthew" in grade school because two Matthews were in their class.

"What do you say?" Matt asked. "We'll even let you bat first."

"Okay." Christy was surprised to find herself agreeing to

anything athletic. "I can't guarantee my catching or pitching skills, but I can usually hit the ball if you pitch it nice and slow."

"Nice and slow," Matt echoed, returning to the pitcher's mound.

Christy gripped the bat and felt a wonderful, childhood kind of happiness come over her. This felt like a funny little dream come true. She was playing baseball with Matthew Kingsley! In fifth grade this never would have happened because she would have been too shy to enter into such a game.

The first pitch came slow and too low. Christy picked up the ball and heaved it back to the pitcher's mound. It fell about two feet short.

"Did I ever tell you that you throw like a girl, Christy Miller?"

Christy laughed. "I am a girl, Matthew Kingsley, in case you never noticed."

"Oh, I noticed," he said.

She couldn't see his face because of the shadow from his baseball cap, but from his stance, he appeared to enjoy the teasing as much as she did.

"Okay, here's my special pitch just for girls who like it nice and slow." He gave an exaggerated windup with his arm, making big, slow circles in the air.

"Very funny," Christy called out. "Now see if you can manage to get it over the plate this time!"

Wes moved in from the outfield. "Right here, Christy." He slugged his fist into his mitt. "Hit it to me. Right here."

Christy took her position. The bat made contact with the ball, and a delicious thrill coursed through her as she dropped the bat and dashed to first base. Wes caught the pop fly, tagged her leg, and offered some advice. "Next time put more muscle behind it, and you'll have a nice swing. Use your shoulders and not just your arms."

Christy didn't care about his advice. She was feeling euphoric over actually *hitting* the ball and playing with the guys.

"Hey!" Sierra's voice sounded at the edge of the field. "What's the big idea starting without us?"

Sierra wore a baseball jersey and had managed to collect her wild, curly blond hair into a ponytail and had looped it through the opening in the back of her baseball cap. She looked as if she was ready for a serious game as she strode onto the field with five other people. Christy was introduced to Vicki, Sierra's roommate, who was a gorgeous brunette with flawless skin. The others, all freshmen and friends of Sierra's, seemed to know Wes, but none of them knew Matt.

After the introductions, a serious game of softball ensued. Several other students joined in, and before the morning was over, Christy had batted four times, hitting the ball three times and striking out once. The rest of the time she spent in the outfield.

Christy smiled through the entire game. She loved everything about this morning: the feel of the warm breeze across her cheeks, the friendly banter among these friends, the way Matt smiled at her. This is what she had missed during her year in Switzerland. The European trains and the scrumptious pastries at the Konditorei had been wonderful. But this—this felt like home.

A little more than halfway through the game, Christy watched Matt on the pitcher's mound, and she inventoried her feelings again. No firefly flutterings or wishful wonderings rose to the surface.

Who knows why my mind took off for the land of if only at breakfast. Matthew Kingsley is just Matthew Kingsley. He'll always be my first crush—nothing more and nothing less.

The last play of the game, Vicki hit a ground ball. Christy ran to scoop it up and pitched it underhanded to Wes, who tagged Vicki out at second base. With a loud cheer, Christy joined the rest of her team in celebrating the win.

The thrill of victory was short lived. Sierra loudly challenged Matthew's team to make it the best two out of three games. Wes took the challenge and said they would meet Sierra and her "bunch of losers" on the field tomorrow afternoon at four.

They all headed for The Golden Calf, talking and laughing as if they had been friends for years. Matt walked beside Christy. "You know what I realized when I saw you there in the outfield?"

"Let me guess. You realized I was serious when I said I couldn't catch."

Matthew laughed. "No, you did great. You made the winning play with Wes."

"I guess I did, didn't I?" Christy beamed.

With a sincere expression Matt said, "What I realized, Christy, is that I wished you hadn't moved to California. I wish you and I had had the chance to finish growing up together. I wonder what would have happened."

Without thinking, she said, "I've been wondering some of those same things."

"You have?"

Caught off guard by her own honesty, Christy quickly added, "I mean, I think Brightwater was a great place to grow up. It would have been fun to go through high school with the same people I started school with."

"I agree," Matt said. "It would have been nice to have you around in high school."

Unsure of what to say, Christy offered only a timid smile and a nod.

They were entering The Golden Calf, and Christy spotted Todd seated at a nearby table. With a chin-up gesture he motioned for Christy and the others to join him. The instant Christy saw him she felt a familiar certainty settle over her.

Now, that's the man I'm in love with.

As if to test her response, Christy turned and watched Matthew as he went through the food line ahead of her. There was no comparison between Todd and Matt. All the "what if" questions she had entertained earlier about Matt seemed to evaporate. She didn't know why. But at the moment, it didn't matter.

She looked across the room at Todd. He was watching her with "that look" again. Even though they were at least thirty feet away from each other in the noisy cafeteria, the moment their eyes met, Christy felt as if the rest of the world had rushed away. An invisible bubble had taken just the two of them to a magical place where her heart didn't flitter and flutter, but rather beat steadily and sure.

It's a marathon for us, isn't it, Todd? Not a quick, flittery sprint. You love me with all your heart. I can see it on your face. And I love you. I know I do.

Christy followed Matthew through the sandwich line, content that her feelings had settled themselves. If she had stayed in Wisconsin, she and Matthew might have ended up testing their relationship on a deeper level.

But I didn't stay in Wisconsin. I moved here, I met Todd, and this is the relationship I want to stay committed to. I don't think God jerks us around the way my thoughts about Matthew jerked around this morning. I don't need to waste my time daydreaming about "what if." All I need to do is keep asking God, "What next?"

Just as Christy and Matthew left the sandwich line and headed toward Todd's table, Katie bounced in front of them. With all the energy she had gained from sleeping until noon, she greeted them with an enthusiastic, "Hi! I thought that was you. Hi!"

At first Christy assumed Katie was talking to her, but Katie's focus was on Matthew. Christy began to make the introduction. "Katie, this is—"

"Matt. Yes, I know. Hi! How are you?"

Then Christy made the connection and nearly dropped her tray. "Is he Matt number fourteen?"

"Yes, Matt number fourteen!" Katie beamed. "I'm so embarrassed, Matt. I don't know your last name!"

"Kingsley," Christy and Matt answered in unison.

"I guess I'm embarrassed, too." Matt looked at Christy and then back at Katie. "Have we met before? Do I know you?"

Christy watched as her best friend's heart crashed to the floor.

"Matthew," Christy said with a hint of scold in her voice, "this is my roommate, Katie Weldon. You two met last year after a baseball game."

"Oh," Matt said slowly. An awkward pause followed, and then Matt said, "You want to sit with us, Kathy?"

Katie's green eyes turned to ice. "It's Katie, not Kathy. Katie Weldon."

Christy quickly pulled her friend to the side and said over her shoulder, "We'll join you guys in a minute."

Matt headed for the table, and Christy winced when she saw Katie's pained expression.

"Katie, I am so sorry!" Christy whispered. "I never in a million years imagined that your Matt number fourteen was the same as my Matthew Kingsley."

"*Your* Matthew Kingsley?" Katie sputtered.

"We grew up together in Wisconsin. I had a huge crush on him in elementary school."

Katie stared without saying a word.

"I told you about him. I know I did," Christy said.

"No, you didn't. I would have remembered if you told me about Matt." Katie's face turned red. "Did you see the way he looked at me? I can't believe it! I committed to memory every word from the conversation we had last June. And then I wasted my entire summer dreaming about him. What a loser!"

Christy wanted to put her arm around her friend, but Christy was still holding her cafeteria tray. "You're not a loser, Katie."

"I didn't mean me, I meant *him*! Matt number fourteen Kingsley is . . ." Katie paused. She lowered her voice and said, "He's the loser. He could have gone out with the cutest, most adorable, most fun-loving redhead on campus, but he just lost his chance." With a swish of her hair, Katie turned and marched off.

Christy stood still, watching as Katie went to the frozen yogurt machine. Apparently, she planned to drown her sorrows in an extra-large chocolate mocha swirl.

CHRISTY AND TODD THE COLLEGE YEARS

5 Christy felt awful as she carried her tray to the table and sat beside Todd in the noisy cafeteria. Matt had taken the empty seat on the other side of Todd, and the two guys had introduced themselves and were talking as if they were close friends. Katie had left the cafeteria with her frozen yogurt in a plastic foam cup.

Determined to remedy what had just happened, Christy tried to think of ways to smooth things over with Matt and Katie. She thought of setting up a double date with them or taking Matt aside and explaining how much Katie liked him. None of her ideas seemed like a good one.

It wouldn't have been so bad if he hadn't called her "Kathy." He could have at least pretended he remembered her when he saw how excited she was to see him. Why are guys so clueless?

"Hey, Christy," Matt said, "do you want to go to Riverview Heights with Todd this afternoon?"

She nodded since her mouth was full. *Why is Matt asking me? I already told Todd I would go.*

Apparently Todd had invited Matt along. The three of them left the cafeteria and drove to the church in Todd's van. From the conversation that was still going at a lively pace between Matt and Todd, Christy discovered that Riverview was the church Matt had attended the last school year. He was giving Todd all kinds of information, since Matt had helped out with the youth group on a couple of outings.

"The adult couple who organized everything moved in June," Matt explained. "That's when the church leaders decided to hire someone. Not many teenagers come, but a lot of them could."

"Why don't they attend?" Christy asked.

"They haven't had anything consistent except for Sunday school, and the couple who taught didn't seem to care about the students. They lectured the whole time. There wasn't any music or any chance for relationships to develop."

Christy could tell Todd appreciated all the inside information.

"You are going to start out with music tomorrow morning, aren't you?" Christy asked.

"I was planning on it." Todd parked in the church lot, and Matt led the way to the room where the group would meet.

"Do you have anyone helping you with music?" Matt asked.

"I don't have any volunteers yet," Todd said, giving Christy a grin. "Unless either of you wants to sing with me."

Christy liked to sing, but she had never been in the front, leading a group. Her voice blended well if the person next to her sang loudly. She wasn't a soloist.

"I could help," Christy said hesitantly.

Todd's clear-eyed, grinning expression told Christy she

had just won her boyfriend's undying admiration. "Thanks. I know you're still thinking about teaching, and I want you to take as long as you need to decide."

Christy didn't feel pressured to say yes to teaching, but she did feel more open to the possibility. She liked being part of the start-up process in this new season in Todd's life.

"I'd be glad to help with whatever else you need," Matt said.

"Thanks, man," Todd said. "You can see I'm at ground zero on all this."

They spent a half hour setting up the room for the next morning and taking inventory of the available resources.

"You know what?" Christy said as they were about to leave. "We should pray before we go."

"Great idea," Todd said. "What's that verse? 'Unless the Lord builds the house, its builders labor in vain.' I want this to be God's youth group."

Christy smiled. "Then we should pray about it."

Todd reached for Christy's hand, and to her surprise, Matt reached for her other hand. The three of them stood in a tight circle, and the guys stretched their arms across each other's shoulders.

Todd prayed for God's blessing on the future of the group and for God's guidance over all the planning, teaching, worshiping, and fellowshiping that would happen in that room. Christy tried to concentrate. She knew they were holding hands as a gesture of being united in what they were praying, but Christy found herself comparing the two guys. Her hand felt at home in Todd's hand. It felt familiar and safe. Matt's hand was rough with the permanent calluses of someone who had shoveled snow and pitched hay. Christy thought of how her dad's hands felt the same way.

She tried to focus back on Todd's prayer as he boldly claimed this territory and these hearts for God's kingdom. "Whatever it takes," Todd prayed, "let them see how real you are, Father."

Matt prayed, then Christy prayed. Todd closed off their time with his own version of "Amen," which was, "Let it be so."

They all looked up and released their hands as Matt said, "This is going to be good, Todd. These kids are going to be so glad to have you here."

"Why didn't you apply for the position?" Todd asked Matt.

He lowered his head slightly and with a bashful expression said, "I did. But I withdrew my application a couple of weeks ago because I wanted to stick with the full class schedule I have this fall and I wanted to play baseball in the spring. I knew I couldn't give the time that would be needed. I'm better off volunteering than being responsible for the whole program."

Todd threw his arm around Matt's shoulder, hugged him from the side, and said, "I appreciate your heart, Matt."

Christy smiled warmly at Matt. She was trying to come up with something appropriate to say when the pager on Matt's belt beeped.

He jumped slightly and said, "My roommate gave me this crazy thing so he can always get ahold of me." He pulled it off and checked the number. "I'll be right back."

Christy and Todd stood alone in the youth room, and she said, "You know what? This is where you belong. You were created for this."

Todd ran his hand across his smooth, square jaw. "You think so?"

Christy nodded. "Remember when we were at that Christian youth hostel in Amsterdam? You were in your element when you led the music and taught a Bible study."

"That was only for a few nights," Todd said.

"I know. But you were at home doing that. Didn't you think so?"

Todd seemed to ponder his answer as he and Christy walked to the door. He remained silent all the way to the car, where they stood waiting for Matt.

When Matt joined them a few minutes later, he said, "Would you mind dropping me off at Stereo World on Mesa Verde? Pete wants me to check out some speakers before he buys them."

The three of them climbed into Gus the Bus, and Todd dropped Matt off in front of Stereo World. Before he got out, Matt put his hand on Christy's shoulder and said, "Don't forget, you still owe me a dinner. We need to finish the conversation we started before lunch."

As Todd drove back to Rancho Corona, Christy remained quiet, trying to process what Matt had said and what he had meant. Todd seemed to be processing Matt's comments, as well. He pulled into the parking lot of a city park and turned off the engine. Giving Christy a confused look, he asked, "Did you meet Matt before today?"

At first Christy thought Todd was kidding. "We grew up together. In Wisconsin."

Todd's expression told her he most certainly didn't know that. "I thought he was friends with Wes and Sierra and that you just met him today in the lunch line."

Christy laughed. "No, our families have been friends since before either of us was born."

Todd looked out the window and then at Christy. "Did I know that?"

"I thought you did. Didn't I tell you that I saw him the other night when Katie and I were in The Java Jungle?"

Todd shook his head.

Christy filled Todd in on Matt being the same Matt number fourteen Katie had told them about on the train in Europe.

Now Todd looked even more surprised. "And neither you nor Katie knew that until today?"

"No, and the worst part was that Matt didn't remember Katie."

"Ouch," Todd said.

"Yeah, ouch. That's why Katie didn't join us for lunch."

"He's a great guy," Todd said. "I appreciate his servant's heart."

"He is a great guy," Christy agreed. *But not the guy for me, that's for sure.*

Todd shifted in the driver's seat and turned toward Christy. "What did he mean about you having dinner with him?"

Christy wondered if she should explain to Todd her crazy little jaunt to the land of if only that morning and how she had let herself wonder what would have happened if she had gone out with Matt. But it all seemed like nothing to her now, so she decided not to mention it.

"Matt and I were going to meet at the cafeteria last night, but I forgot all about it. That's why I asked you what time it was when we were having pizza with Katie."

It occurred to Christy that, although her fleeting thoughts about Matt had left her, she didn't know if their long-ago, unexplored interest in each other was a closed subject for Matt. Perhaps the reason he wanted to finish their conversation was because he also had taken a jaunt to the land of if only and was possibly still there.

Did I say or do anything to make Matt think I would be interested in going out with him? I didn't mean to. He knows Todd and I are together, doesn't he?

Christy realized that she and Todd hadn't done or said anything while they were around Matt to lead him to believe they were a couple. If Todd had thought that Matt was one of Sierra's friends whom Christy had just met at lunch, perhaps Matt thought the same about Todd.

Christy realized the parked van was becoming uncomfortably hot. Todd opened his door and asked, in what sounded more like a statement, "Do you want to walk?"

"Sure." Christy was glad to climb out of the hot van and off the uncomfortable seat. She had complained a week ago that the passenger seat was "decomposing" since the springs were poking through. Todd had fixed it by covering the seat with a piece of cardboard and then placing a folded beach towel on top of the cardboard. The whole contraption slid as she got out.

Todd reached for her hand, and they walked along a cement pathway around the park's perimeter. The playground to the left was filled with noisy children who were busy swinging, climbing, and sifting sand in the sandbox.

Christy and Todd headed away from the noise.

"I wanted to talk about something you said at the church," Todd said. "You said I was 'at home' there. I think you're right. And you know why that's so hard for me to comprehend? I don't know that I've ever been 'at home' before. Not completely. Except with you, Kilikina."

Whenever Todd called Christy by her Hawaiian name,

she melted. This afternoon was no exception.

"I feel at home with you, too," Christy said. "Completely at home."

"Do you?" Todd asked.

"Yes, I really do." Christy put aside her unsettled thoughts about Matt and concentrated on Todd. If she had miscommunicated anything to Matt, she could talk to him later and clear it up. Right now, this is where she wanted to be, and Todd was the one she wanted to be with.

"The thing is, I don't know what a normal family is supposed to act like," Todd continued. "I have an idea of what I want for my future family and what I consider to be normal, but I've never had that. I have few role models. When I came to the Lord, church became really important to me. I wonder if that's why it seems I'm at home, as you said, in a youth ministry situation. Church, and particularly youth groups, are the most stable, positive model I've ever had for anything."

"Was your childhood pretty awful?" Christy asked.

"Why do you ask?"

"I've wanted to ask you lots of times before, but it didn't seem as if you liked to talk about that part of your life. I want to hear more," Christy said. "Especially about your childhood."

"You knew my parents were both on drugs when they met," Todd said.

Christy wasn't sure if that was supposed to be a joke. She waited for Todd to explain. He led her off the trail to the shade of two old trees. Todd sat with his back against a broad tree trunk and Christy to his side, facing him.

"They really were on drugs. I never told you this, but my mom was pregnant with me when they got married."

"She was?" Christy wished she didn't sound so surprised.

"She was only seventeen."

Christy realized for the first time why Todd had cared so much about Alissa, a teenage friend of theirs who had become pregnant a number of years ago. Alissa had decided to have the baby and give it up for adoption. At the time, Christy thought it strange Todd was so involved and enthusiastic about Alissa's decision. Now it made sense. Todd had been an unplanned baby of a teenage mother.

A shiver ran up Christy's spine. *What if Todd's mother had decided he was an inconvenience to her life? What if she had believed twenty-three years ago that what she carried in her body was only a mass of tissue? What if . . .*

Christy stopped. She found herself breathing deeply and almost in tears. But she didn't want to tell Todd what she had been thinking. That morning, her thoughts of Matthew had taught her it didn't do any good to take a trip to the land of if only and spend a lot of time there.

The reality is that Todd's mom didn't choose to end her son's life. She gave birth to him. One day I'll thank her for that. And if I never thanked you, Father God, for giving Todd life, I thank you now.

"My parents got married because I think both my mom and dad wanted to do the right thing," Todd said. "I know they both tried to straighten out their lives after I was born. My mom told me once that the day she found out she was pregnant with me, she vowed never to do drugs again, and she didn't. It took my dad a little longer to sober up. When I was little . . . I don't know, maybe three . . . my parents had a fight over something, and my dad was stoned, and he hurt my mom."

"Todd, that's awful." Christy reached for Todd's hand and gave it a squeeze. The tears she had been trying to hold back were about to trickle down her cheeks.

He looked at her cautiously. "Are you sure you want me to tell you all this?"

"Yes, of course." Christy gave him an encouraging look and blinked back her tears. "I just didn't know how bad it had been for you. I was thinking of that night when we were talking out on the jetty at Newport Beach, and you and Shawn got in that big fight because he was so stoned. Now I can see why that upset you so much."

Todd looked down at their hands and said, "I still miss Shawn, if you can believe that." He stroked Christy's Forever ID bracelet with his thumb.

"That's because you really care about your friends. Forever."

Overhead a jet streaked into the west, leaving a mark like a white chalk line across the deep blue sky.

"Are you sure you want to keep talking about all this?" Todd asked.

"Yes."

"What else would you like to know?" Todd asked.

"What happened when your dad hurt your mom?" Christy asked in a soft voice.

"That was the day she left him. I don't know if he hit her or what. She never told me. I never asked my dad. He never hit me. He's never been violent or anything. I don't know. Maybe they just had a fight. Words can hurt for a lifetime, too, you know. For whatever reason, my mom left. She took me with her, and we lived on the road for a while, sort of hiding from my dad."

"I wonder if that's where you get your interest in traveling so much," Christy said. She was trying hard to be positive.

"I don't know. Maybe. After that, I'm not sure how everything fell into place. My dad sobered up. My parents got back together for a while, but it didn't work out. They tried to patch up things, but there were so many cracks it all came crashing in. When they finally divorced, they were just taking the legal steps to put on paper what was already true in their lives. Their marriage never had much of a chance. It was all a bunch of broken pieces from the start."

"Is that when you and your dad moved to Maui?" Christy asked. "Weren't you in third grade then?"

Todd nodded. "That was an important time in my life. My dad was trying to figure out who he was, and I was doing the same. We were more like brothers with eighteen years between us than father and son."

"Your dad was only eighteen when you were born?" Christy asked. "I never knew that."

"There's a lot you never knew because it didn't seem important," Todd said. "But I think it might help you to know so you can make good decisions."

Christy felt herself prickle slightly when Todd brought up her decision-making skills. But he was saying it in such a gentle way that she asked him, "Do you mean decisions about our future together?"

"Yes. And decisions about me. I realized I was beginning to assume a lot about us and about our future when I just figured you would want to teach Sunday school. What you said about getting more information and having a chance to think and pray about teaching also applies to us. You should have more information about me and my family so you can think things through carefully."

Christy felt her heart softening even more toward this man who sat before her. And he was a man. Todd was no longer a teenager, hanging around the beach, waiting for the perfect wave, taking each day as it came. She had been there through that season of Todd's life. The man who sat a few inches away was thinking about the future. He was making it clear that he wanted her to consider the whole package before agreeing to sign on for the next phase in their relationship.

"For instance," Todd continued, "I don't really know how to do stuff like birthdays and Christmas. If you and I end up together," Todd hesitated, as if trying to decide if he should go on. "I'm not trying to assume anything here, I'm just saying you should know that all the holiday kind of stuff would be up to you, or whoever I end up with. I mean, I'd help and everything, but since I didn't grow up with any traditions, I'd be learning it all for the first time."

"There's not much to learn." Christy felt compassion welling up inside. "You've been around my family for birthdays and holidays. Those times are whatever you want them to be. Whatever you make them."

"That's exactly what I mean." Todd let go of her hand and swatted away a bug from his face. "I want so much. I want birthdays to be an event. They never were for me. And if, you know, when I end up having kids someday, I'd want them to think they were the coolest kids on the planet every year on their birthdays."

"I think that's important, too."

Todd plucked a blade of grass, twirled it between his fingers, then let it fall to the ground. His voice softened. "One year when I was living with my mom, she forgot my birthday. It was the year I turned five. I remember because I was in kindergarten, and we were living in an apartment in Phoenix, I think. Or maybe that was when we were in Flagstaff. Anyway, I remember this guy from her work asked her out to dinner on my birthday."

"And she went out with him?"

Todd nodded. "My mom is a wonderful person, really. It's just that she was excited about the attention, you know. She forgot it was my birthday. She left me a peanut butter sandwich and told me to put myself to bed by eight-thirty."

"What did you do?"

Todd shrugged his shoulders nonchalantly. "I ate my sandwich and went to bed with my BB gun under the covers in case a burglar broke in while my mom was gone. I don't remember if I went to bed by eight-thirty or not."

"Todd, I can't imagine what that must have been like for you." Tears blurred Christy's vision.

Todd shifted his position uncomfortably. "It's not like I was some abused, neglected child locked in a closet and forced to eat dirt." He laughed nervously at his attempt at a joke.

"In a way you were," Christy said.

"I don't want to look at it that way," Todd said. "I knew both my parents loved me. They wanted me, you know? They could have easily gotten rid of me either before I was born or after, but they didn't. They provided everything I needed. I think they just didn't know how to love on a very deep level. They didn't know how to love each other. Or maybe they did love each other, but only as much as they could at eighteen years old. I mean, when I think about it, my mom was only twenty-three when I had my fifth birthday. I'm going to be twenty-three in a couple months,

Christy. I can't imagine what it would be like to have a son in kindergarten right now."

Christy felt funny. The warm feelings that had made her so compassionate toward Todd a few minutes ago were beginning to disappear. In their place, she sensed the same sort of tired, sad feelings that had drained her so much at the orphanage during the past year. She felt sad for Todd; yet she knew she couldn't do anything to change his childhood. It seemed as if she was being introduced to a different person from the blue-eyed surfer boy she had fallen in love with. This new man-version of Todd was more complex than she had expected him to be.

"I'm freaking you out, aren't I?" Todd asked.

"No. Well, maybe. A little. But I think it's good. I want to know this stuff about you, Todd. I want you to feel that you can talk openly with me about anything. I guess I'm a little surprised that we've known each other so long and been so close—or at least, I've thought of us as being close—yet I didn't know any of this."

Todd moved closer to Christy and put his arm around her, drawing her to his side. "We are close, Kilikina. I'm closer to you than any other person I know. And maybe that's why I never told you a lot of this. I didn't want to say anything that would cause you to pull away from me. You're such a merciful person. I didn't want to hurt you."

"You're not hurting me by telling me these things," Christy said. "I'm glad you're telling me. I want to know all this."

"But you want to fix me, and you can't go back and fix my childhood, can you?"

Christy pulled her head away from Todd's shoulder and

looked up at him. "How did you know that's what I was thinking?"

Todd brushed her cheek with the back of his fingers. "I know your heart, Kilikina. That's how I knew what you were thinking. I know your heart."

"I believe you do." Then pressing her head against his chest, Christy said, "And I want to know your heart, Todd."

She came very close to adding the words, "Because I love you." But she still couldn't say it. Not yet.

That night Christy lay awake in bed. The room was dark except for the soft yellow glow from the desk light she had left on again for Katie. Squinting her eyes to read the numbers on her alarm clock, Christy wondered when she should start to worry. It was three minutes after midnight. She had slipped into bed at ten, hoping for a good sleep before going to Riverview with Todd at eight the next morning.

Instead of good sleep, for the past two hours all Christy had experienced was an endless replay of Todd's words. He had opened himself up to her, and in every way she had expressed to him it was okay, she cared, and she was glad he had told her about his childhood. But since they had parted after dinner, Christy had been bombarded with worries and fears.

She was worried about Katie, too. Christy hadn't seen her since lunch and didn't know if Katie had drowned herself in chocolate mocha frozen yogurt or had bounced back and was out romping with some of her friends.

Christy turned on her side and tried to convince herself to go to sleep and to forget everything and everybody else.

It would all work out, somehow. Then a wild thought popped into her foggy brain. *What if Todd hurts me the way his dad hurt his mom?*

Christy angrily tossed to the other side. *Where did that thought come from? Todd would never hurt me.*

A moment later she thought, *What if he left me and took our kids the way his mom left his dad and took him?*

Christy tumbled out of bed. That's ridiculous! Why am I even thinking this?

She reached for the water bottle she had left sitting on her desk. Next to the water bottle was the bouquet of wilting white carnations Todd had given her a week ago when she had returned from Switzerland. On the shelf above her desk sat an old, beat-up Folgers coffee can. Inside were the dried brown remains of the first dozen white carnations Todd had given her on her fifteenth birthday.

Why did he wait so long to tell me what his life was really like? If we do end up getting married, will he always wait five years before telling me something? "Oh, by the way, honey, we're bankrupt and we have to move out of the house by tomorrow."

Christy plunged back into bed, more distraught than ever. Her wildly emotional thoughts turned to Uncle Bob. How would he respond when Marti told him, "By the way, honey, I'm leaving in the morning to go to Santa Fe with Cheyenne."

I have to talk to someone about Marti. I can't hold her secret. Not when I have all this other stuff to deal with. Why did I ever promise her I'd keep her secret? That was such a stupid thing to do.

Christy's thoughts beat her up until she fell into a deep, exhausted sleep in which nightmares came one right after the other. Crazy, tormenting laughter circled her, taunting her for being so naive as to love Todd Spencer and so foolish as to promise her aunt anything.

At close to four in the morning, Christy woke with a start and sat up in bed. The laughter from her brutal nightmares instantly ceased. The soft desk light was turned off, and she could hear Katie's rhythmic breathing in the bed across the room.

At least Katie is okay. And the rest of that stuff wasn't real. It was a nightmare. She tried to slow down her pounding heart. *It's okay. Pray, Christy. Pray and sleep. You need to sleep.*

Slowly lowering her head to the pillow, Christy prayed silently, moving her lips and whispering a word here and there. She prayed about everything. Her heart calmed. Her mind cleared. She slept a dreamless sleep for the next two and a half hours.

When Christy's alarm went off at six-thirty, Katie rolled over and gave one of her grumpy groans. "What's going on?"

"I'm going to church with Todd," Christy said. "Are you okay?"

"Yeah, I'm fine."

"Do you want to come to church with us?" Christy didn't know if her invitation was such a good idea since Matt would be there, but she offered it anyway.

"No, I'm taking Sierra down to San Diego to Paul's church. Will you wake me at eight o'clock?"

"I'll be gone before then," Christy said. "I'll reset my alarm for eight."

With a "humph-okay," Katie went back to sleep, and Christy got ready for church.

She met Todd at seven-thirty in the cafeteria for a quick breakfast, as they had planned the night before. Matt was eating with Todd when she arrived. The guys were almost through, so Christy had to gulp down her breakfast. She thought she should do something obvious to show that she and Todd were together, but the opportunity didn't present itself.

"How did you guys sleep last night?" Todd asked as the three of them drove down the hill in Gus the Bus.

"Awful," Christy said.

"Me too," Todd said. "I felt like I was being attacked. I couldn't figure out what was going on, and then I realized I needed to pray. We're stepping out to the front lines for the Lord this morning, but the enemy doesn't want us to do this."

"It was the same for me," Christy said. "Once I prayed, I finally could sleep." She felt hushed inside at the thought of evil forces trying to keep her from serving God this morning with Todd.

"Sounds like we better pray this morning, too," Matt said.

Matt had just said the word "pray" when Gus the Bus sputtered, lurched, and came to a stop in the middle of the road.

"Do you have your emergency lights on?" Matt asked as he slid the side door open and hopped out to motion to the car behind them to go around.

"They aren't working." Todd opened his door and climbed out. "Everything shut down. Christy, slide over here to the driver's seat and steer us to that parking lot, will you?"

"You mean over there in front of the dental offices?"

Todd didn't hear her. He was already around the back of the van, yelling for Christy to put it in neutral and make sure the brake was off. Christy had only driven ol' Gus a few times before and didn't feel comfortable behind the wheel at a time like this.

She followed Todd's instructions, and the car moved forward, thanks to the brawn of Todd and Matt. Biting her lower lip the entire journey of a block and a half into the parking lot, she steered as carefully as she could right into a space. It was marked *Compact Only*, but she was certain on a Sunday morning, with no one else in the lot, it wouldn't matter that Gus wasn't exactly compact.

"Put her in first," Todd called out, coming around to the open window on the driver's side. "And set the emergency brake."

Christy followed his instructions. That's when she realized her lip was throbbing from biting it. It was beginning to swell.

"What should we do now?" Christy asked. "Should we find a phone and call a repair service or something?"

"I don't think we have time for that," Matt said.

Todd had gone around to the side of Gus and opened the door. He was pulling out his guitar and his Bible.

"We better walk," Todd said. "It's at least a mile to the church from here."

Christy grabbed her Bible and strung her purse over her shoulder. Her mind flipped through half a dozen impractical solutions like calling a cab or hitchhiking. She didn't offer any of her suggestions as the three of them silently took off at a fast pace down the street.

"Probably the alternator," Matt said as they walked.

Christy knew it could be anything, since Gus was so old and subject to random seizures.

"I'll come back with my truck after church and look at it if you want me to," Matt offered.

"Sure." Todd was walking faster than Matt and Christy. His mind seemed not on his car but on what lay ahead.

Christy had gotten used to walking in Basel, and she found it easy to pick up her pace so she could keep up with Todd. "You know what? We never did pray," she said. "Matt was about to pray, and then Gus stopped."

"You're right," Todd said, as if Christy's words had snapped him out of a daydream. Then without slowing the pace, Todd spoke aloud. "Okay, Father, look at us here. I know you hold every detail of our lives in your hands. This didn't come as a surprise to you the way it did to us. You have a plan. I trust you for whatever you're going to do. We need you to make it clear because, to be honest, I'm not getting it right now."

They came to one of the town's main intersections and had to wait for the light to turn green before they could cross. Todd shifted his heavy guitar case to his other hand, and Christy wiped the perspiration off her forehead. The day's heat was already rising. The steady desert winds that had blown the past few days were absent, and the air felt close around them.

"And, Lord," Christy added to Todd's prayer, "we stand together on your Word against the enemy's plans. I think he's trying to put roadblocks in our way today. But this is your day, and we are your children. Please make our path straight."

The light turned green. They began to hoof it across the street when one of the cars at the crosswalk honked at them.

Christy thought the driver was honking to make fun of the three strolling minstrels who obviously were on their way to church wearing their nice clothes and carrying Bibles.

"Need a ride?" the driver called from the open car window.

"It's Donna," Christy said. "My new boss at the bookstore."

Within minutes, the three of them had jammed into the backseat of Donna's van, met her husband, and arrived in the church parking lot several minutes before the service started. Donna's husband, they found out, was a professor at Rancho Corona and involved in leadership at the church. He had been out of town last week when Todd was hired and asked if he could meet with Todd after the second service. With a round of thanks, Todd, Christy, and Matt dashed to the high school room.

Matt stopped to chat with two guys who were hanging out by the door. They both looked as if this was the last place they wanted to be, but they perked up when they saw Matt. Three girls arrived together. Christy followed Matt's lead and pretended she wasn't a shy person. She introduced herself to the girls and started a conversation with them.

Todd set up his equipment. The sophisticated computer on the stand in the back of the room projected the words to the first song off a disc Todd had inserted. He invited everyone to come in.

For the next fifteen minutes, Christy, Matt, and the five students sang the worship songs as Todd played his guitar. Since so few people were there, Christy didn't stand in front with Todd, but she did sing louder and more convincingly than any of the others.

Two more girls arrived halfway through and sat in the back whispering as the others sang. That bugged Christy.

She knew how wonderful a time of worship could be with friends since she had experienced that as a teenager. How could she tell those girls that this time was holy and meaningful and they should enter in?

When the singing ended, Todd asked the students to pull their chairs into a circle. None of them were too eager, but they did it anyway. He then introduced himself and asked that each person do the same and tell something about him or herself.

It didn't go so well, from Christy's opinion. She and Matt talked the most, but they ended up telling that they grew up together. The way Matt talked, it almost sounded as if he and Christy were boyfriend and girlfriend, and the two of them were there to support their buddy, Todd.

I definitely need to have a talk with Matt. The sooner the better.

Todd opened his Bible and taught a simple, straightforward lesson from John. He used the verse Christy had mentioned to him the other day about how those who believe and receive Christ are given the right to become God's children.

When the group dispersed, Christy carefully watched Todd's face. He was holding his easygoing grin steady, but she could read his eyes. His heart was breaking. This wasn't what he had hoped for, and she knew it.

"It went well," she told him quietly, giving his arm a squeeze. "It's the first week. They're trying to decide if they like you and feel safe enough to come back next week."

Todd nodded, but Christy could tell he was still heavyhearted. All during the church service she sensed he was battling with himself over how the class time went. She knew he was thinking through every angle, evaluating, restructuring, and planning.

She liked the service and the pastor and the way he presented the sermon. She told Matt afterward, "This church
reminds me of our old church in Brightwater."

"That's why I got involved last year."

Two older women came up to greet Matt, and he introduced them to Christy. Todd got in on the end of the introductions, and the women made a fuss over how delighted
they were that he would be working with their young people. Matt was at ease with these women, but Todd looked
nervous, as if he didn't know what to do or say around el-
derly people.

"I'm supposed to go to lunch now with the pastor and
some of the leaders," Todd said to Christy. "Do you want to
go with us?"

Christy looked over his shoulder at the pastor and two
other men who appeared to be waiting for Todd. "Why
don't you just go this time. I'll come with you the next
time."

"Okay," Todd said. "Can you guys find a ride back to
school?"

"Sure, we'll be fine," Christy said.

"You sure?"

"I'm sure."

"Okay, then I'll see you later."

"Yeah, later," Christy said with a grin. She wasn't used to
seeing Todd so nervous. No one else would realize his actions were expressing nervousness, but she knew. It was
kind of funny.

Donna gave Christy and Matt a ride to Rancho and
dropped them off in the parking lot behind the cafeteria.

"If you guys ever need a ride on Sunday, just call me,"
Donna said. "Anytime. And I mean that."

As soon as Christy and Matt sat down with their lunch trays, Christy plunged in. "I have to tell you something."

"Sure," Matt said. "What is it?"

"I don't know if you knew this, but Todd and I are together."

"Together together?"

"What does together together mean?" Christy asked.

"Are you two serious about each other?"

"Yes. We have been for a long time."

Matt stared at his plate of spaghetti a moment before saying, "By any chance is he the guy Paula told me about?"

"Probably," Christy said. Paula, her best friend from childhood, had been crazy about Todd the summer she had come out to California to visit Christy.

"Is Todd the guy who taught Paula how to surf?"

"Yes." Christy smiled at the memory. Paula and Christy hadn't kept their friendship going much after that summer when Christy turned sixteen. But when they were close, they had had some good times together. Paula had married while Christy was in Switzerland, but Christy didn't hear about it until a few weeks after the wedding. When they were young, Paula and Christy had promised they would be bridesmaids in each other's weddings. Christy still felt a little sad that that was one promise she hadn't been able to keep.

"If you can believe this," Christy said, "Paula and I had an agreement before we were in high school. We agreed that whoever went out on a real date first would get five dollars from the other person."

"Who won?" Matt asked.

"Me," Christy said. "And guess who my first date was with?"

Matt looked at his spaghetti again. "Must have been Todd."

"It was."

"When I met him at lunch yesterday, I didn't remember that he was the guy Paula told me about," Matt said. "I knew you had had a boyfriend for a long time, but I thought he was gone. Gone, as in spending the rest of his life in Fiji or something."

"The last time I saw you, Todd was gone. He was in Spain, actually."

"But now he's back," Matt said.

"Yes, Todd's back. And I'm back from Switzerland, and we're together. Together together."

"Well, you made a good choice, Christy," Matt said. He had such a straightforward look to him. He reminded her of her dad.

Christy remembered something her grandpa had said when she had asked her grandparents how they knew they were right for each other. He had told her, *"The real way you know he's the right person is to evaluate his background. Do you come from the same place? Then you have a much better chance of making it through the hard times."*

Her grandmother had disagreed. She had told Christy it was a choice and then repeated that annoying line, *"When it's right, you'll know."*

Christy glanced at Matt. *I don't know for sure that Todd is the right one, but I do know for sure that Matt isn't.*

Just knowing one thing for sure in her life felt really good.

"You know what?" Matt pushed his tray to the side and continued to look at Christy in a straightforward way. "I'm going to put myself out there and say something. I hope you don't mind my saying it."

Christy felt so buoyed up by the insight she had just come up with about Matt that she welcomed anything he had to say.

"I think very highly of you, Christy."

"And I think very highly of you."

"I hope you'll keep me in mind if things don't work out with Todd, but I have a feeling things will work out pretty well for you two."

"I have a feeling they will, too," Christy said.

"And you and I can still be friends?"

"Of course," Christy said. "I know Todd really appreciates all your encouragement with the youth group."

"I told him I'd help any way he wanted me to."

Christy debated whether she should say anything about Katie. She was about to suggest that the four of them go out on a double date. Then she decided it would be better not to say anything until she had a chance to talk to Katie.

Matt and Christy spent the next half hour comfortably talking. Matt filled her in on news of family and friends in Brightwater, and Christy told him about her time in Switzerland. When they left the cafeteria and were about to go their separate ways, Matt gave Christy a boyish grin and tagged her arm the way he used to on the playground at recess.

"Eenie-meenie boo-boo!" Matt called out, then took off running.

Christy laughed. She wasn't about to chase him and tag him back. Those days were long gone. She strolled to her room smiling.

That felt like a phone book lifting off me. Next phone book is for me to decide on a major. And to make sure Katie is okay. And to figure out what to do about my aunt. And . . .

She stopped herself before adding any more phone books to her stack.

One thing at a time.

When she arrived at the dorm room, Katie wasn't there. The only evidence that she had been was her khaki skirt, which she apparently had worn when she went to church that morning. The skirt was wadded up in a big ball in the room's corner.

Christy changed her clothes and wondered if she should go to the rematch softball game that was scheduled for four o'clock. She didn't feel like playing softball. They had enough players yesterday, and she didn't think she would be missed.

If Katie comes back in time, I'll send her in my place. Matt will be there, and it will give the two of them an opportunity to start over.

Christy opened the window, letting in some fresh air. She thought how convenient it would have been if Matt and Katie had discovered each other at the same time. That didn't mean it was too late for Matt to find out how terrific she was.

Staring at the clear, periwinkle sky, she wondered aloud, "Is Todd the right man for me? Is he the one I'm supposed to marry? Why can't I be certain enough to tell him I love him?"

She wished God would send her the answer in writing. He could just lower it on a long string and dangle the message in front of her window. No one else would need to notice it. Only Christy. All it had to say was *Marry Todd.* She wouldn't tell a soul. Not even Todd. He would have to propose to her and everything, but at least in her heart she would know he was the right one, and she would have no doubts.

Christy blinked. The silent sky hadn't opened up. No message on the end of a long string had come her way. She would have to figure this out the hard way. The normal way. Step by tentative step with lots of prayer.

Stretching out on her bed, Christy considered writing her thoughts in her diary. It always helped her to write from her heart and then look at the words later.

Not this time, though. She didn't want anyone coming across her diary and reading those thoughts.

Christy looked at the poster she had hung on the wall. It was a picture of a bridge near Hana, Maui. Todd had jumped off that bridge into the deep pool below. Christy had driven over that bridge in a Jeep right after she turned sixteen. It was "their" bridge. Now they were at another bridge. She knew Todd was ready to "jump." He was ready to move forward in their relationship and make a lasting commitment. She had been "driving" through this decision, which took a lot more time than getting there by jumping. Todd was being patient. But Christy was stuck.

"There are no guarantees, are there?" she said aloud to God. "There weren't any guarantees for Todd's parents. It doesn't look like there are any for Bob and Marti. So how can I possibly be certain that a marriage started at such a young age will last for the rest of our lives?"

Just then the dorm room opened. Christy stared at the red-haired woman who entered. She barely looked like the Katie Christy knew by heart. Her roommate's medium-length, swishy red hair had been cut short. It feathered across her forehead and to the nape of her neck in wispy, uneven layers. Katie looked completely different. This was a new look. A softer, more sophisticated look.

"You cut your hair!" Christy examined it from all angles. "I really like it! When did you decide to cut it?"

"This afternoon." Katie tossed a few shopping bags on her unmade bed and kicked off her shoes.

"You look completely different."

"That was the idea," Katie muttered.

"Are you okay?"

Katie flopped on her crumpled bed next to the shopping bags. She held her pillow across her middle as if she had a stomachache.

Christy moved the bags and made room for herself at the foot of the bed. "Katie, what is it? What's going on?"

Katie looked away. "I'm tired of myself."

Christy had no idea how to respond.

"I've been thinking a lot about what happened with Matt yesterday. I realized I presume too much and I assume too much. I want to change, Christy. I really do."

"Change in what way?"

"I don't know. That's why I started with my hair. I bought some new clothes, too." Katie pulled a blouse from one of the bags and held it up. "What do you think of this?"

"It's pretty."

"Good. I'm glad that's the first thing you thought when you saw it because I need something pretty. My wardrobe is all jeans and T-shirts. Do you realize I only have one skirt, but when I wore it this morning, I decided I didn't like it. I don't like khaki anymore."

Katie pulled a long, flowing skirt from the next bag, and Christy said, "Okay, now you're frightening me. That skirt is too similar to the one my aunt had on the other day."

"Don't worry. I'm not going to start checking my aura. I

wanted something casual yet soft. Not khaki. You should see Sierra's wardrobe. I was in her room last night, and between Sierra and Vicki, the two of them have the best outfits of anyone I've ever seen on this campus."

Christy liked the way Sierra dressed, too. She was an individualist and wore things no one else did, and she didn't seem to care if she was in style or not. Sierra made her own style. The first time Christy had met her, Sierra was wearing a pair of her father's old cowboy boots.

"Sierra shops at thrift stores, doesn't she?" Christy asked.

Katie nodded. "She was telling me about some of the vintage clothing stores in Portland, where she lives. It made me want to go there just to shop."

"Did you buy these clothes at a thrift store?"

"No, and I spent way too much money on them. But I needed to do something. Tomorrow is the first day of class, and I need this year to be better than any other year of my whole school career. I need a fresh start."

Christy folded the new skirt and placed it on the end of the bed. "Katie, may I bring up a topic that you probably don't want to talk about?"

"Do I have a choice?"

"Not really."

"Go ahead. Let me have it. You always let me shower you with my biased opinions. I guess it's only fair for you to have a turn."

"You know how you told me the thing about carrying too many phone books and ending up dropping them all? Well, I think that over the years you haven't exactly gotten over the hurt of some of your relationships with guys. You're carrying all the hurt like a stack of phone books.

That's why it hurts so deeply when a disappointment comes along like Matt's memory lapse yesterday." Christy had no idea she was going to say all this to Katie. She hadn't thought it through; it all just tumbled out.

"I think you were hurt yesterday by Matt," Christy continued, "but it reminded you of the hurt and disappointment you felt with Rick, Michael, Lance, and every other guy who has let you down."

Katie's face looked stubborn, set like a stone.

Christy cautiously proceeded. "So you don't just feel the hurt from one disappointment but also the hurt of half a dozen guys at the same time."

The room fell silent as Christy wondered why she was saying all this to her best friend.

A few minutes passed before Katie straightened herself and said with an edge to her voice, "So what do you recommend I do about it?"

Christy wanted to tell Katie that she hadn't planned to present this problem and so she certainly hadn't planned a solution, either. Instead, Christy said the only thing that came to mind. "You don't need to change anything on the outside. You need to change the inside. I think you have to forgive, Katie. You have to choose to forgive and start all over."

For a moment Katie looked as if she might throw something or yell. Instead, she muttered, "I hate it when you're right."

Katie adjusted her position on the bed and said with a challenge in her voice, "Just what makes you so sure I
haven't forgiven the guys who have hurt me?"

"Well—" Christy began.

"I'll tell you something. It would be nice if just
one of those jerks would acknowledge he was rude, insensitive, or mean, or all of the above." Katie rose and kicked at
her wadded-up khaki skirt. "I know that's a lot to ask, but
it sure would make forgiving easier."

"But what if none of them ever apologizes?" Christy
asked. "Are you going to go through your life carrying all
these phone books of pain with you?"

"No." Katie paced the floor. "I'll get over the hurt once I
meet Prince Charming."

"Katie!"

"What?"

Christy hesitated to say what she was thinking, but she
knew she couldn't hold it in. "What will happen the first
time Prince Charming lets you down? I mean, even if you
marry Prince Charming, he's not going to be perfect. Somewhere along the way he'll be insensitive, mean, or rude, and

then what? Instead of just carrying the hurt from that isolated incident, will you pick up all those phone books and carry them again?"

"I don't know. I don't want to talk about this, Christy. I need to get some air."

Christy glanced at the clock. It was almost four o'clock. "Do you want to play softball?"

Katie looked at Christy. "Why? Do you?"

"No. I was wondering if you would take my place on Wes's team. They're playing against Sierra's team at four o'clock."

Rummaging in a drawer, Katie pulled out a baseball cap and found her mitt in the closet. She laced up her tennis shoes and left with only a quick, "I'm outta here."

Christy sat in the empty room. *Why did I say all those things to Katie? She didn't need to hear all that today. And she certainly didn't need to hear it from me.*

Deciding she would skip dinner, Christy took a long shower, washed her hair, shaved her legs, and then called Todd. No one answered in his room, so Christy left a voice message suggesting they meet for breakfast in The Golden Calf at seven-thirty the next morning.

She took her laundry to the end of the hall, and while waiting for an open machine, she joined some other girls from her floor who had gathered in the den to watch *The Princess Bride*. The last time Christy had watched that movie was before she went to Switzerland. Katie had rented it and brought it over for their final girls' night. After watching it, Katie had declared she would never trust a guy who said "As you wish" to her every whim. She wanted a guy with gusto who would say, "Get it yourself," otherwise she knew she would sit around and get fat while he catered to her.

Christy knew when Katie had made those comments a year ago that she was just being her comical self. Now Christy wished Katie was watching the movie with her, making wisecracks, being the kind of roommate Christy had looked forward to. The other girls watching the movie were all nice, but something inside Christy made her feel as if she wasn't ready to make new friends. She was much more interested in maintaining her current friendships.

After the movie two of the girls said they were going down the hill for ice cream. They invited Christy to go with them, but she declined, saying she needed to get back to her room because she and her roommate needed to talk.

Christy returned to her room with a folded stack of clean clothes and found a note from Katie. She had written it on a 3×5 card and taped it to the corner of Christy's desk.

I'm staying with Sierra tonight. K.

Christy read the note twice, not believing it the first time. She imagined the worst.

Katie is so upset by what I said that she can't stand to be in the same room with me.

The note didn't say, "Come join us" or "Meet me for breakfast" or give any hint that Katie wasn't mad at Christy.

Katie is giving herself a makeover with her new hair and clothes. Is she trying to tell me she's doing a makeover with her best friends, too?

Tears came, and with them an aching loneliness she hadn't expected to feel at Rancho. She had felt alone many times in Switzerland since she was so far from home and close friends. But she never expected to be assaulted by these feelings when she was "home" with her closest friends.

Christy debated for a long time if she should call Sierra's

room or go there to try to settle things with Katie. The decision-making process, on top of her already thin emotions, exhausted her so much that Christy finally concluded she shouldn't try anything heroic tonight. She would sleep on her dilemma, pray about it, and see if she and Katie could talk in the morning.

———

The next morning Christy was glad to see Todd waiting for her in front of the cafeteria at seven-thirty. He greeted her with a kiss on the temple and said, "I tried to call you back last night, but no one answered."

"I didn't check my voice mail," Christy said. "You probably called while I was doing my laundry and watching a movie."

They moved through the line, and Christy forced herself to put some food on her tray, even though she wasn't hungry. She knew, after skipping dinner last night, that she needed some protein.

Todd led Christy to a window table with two chairs. He turned the chairs so they could look out the window and keep their backs to the rest of the students.

"We got Gus running," Todd said after they had prayed.

"That's good."

"Yeah, thanks to Matt. He has a real talent for fixing cars. And he agreed to help me put together the mission trip to Mexico."

"What mission trip to Mexico?"

"I didn't tell you yet, did I? When I had lunch with some of the church leaders yesterday, I mentioned I'd like to take the group to Mexico, and they were all for it. I'm thinking we'll go over Thanksgiving. Do you want to come?" Todd sunk his teeth into a blueberry bagel.

"Sure."

Todd stopped chewing. With a swallow he looked at Christy and said, "That was a quick decision."

"It was, wasn't it?" Christy knew her decisiveness was prompted by her feelings of loneliness. Any invitation to go anywhere or do anything with her friends appealed to her this morning.

"I think I alienated Katie yesterday," she muttered before taking a bite of her scrambled eggs.

"What happened?"

With a dozen concise sentences, Christy explained to Todd that she had given Katie unwanted advice, and as a result, Katie had stayed in Sierra's room last night.

"We only lasted a week together in the same room. I wish I had kept my mouth shut."

Todd's expression suggested he wasn't taking her doom and gloom assessment too seriously. "Don't be so hard on yourself. It sounds as if you were speaking the truth in love. It might take a while for all that truth to sink in, but I think what you said was honest and helpful. It'll work out. You'll see."

Christy shook her head. "I don't know. At least I didn't try to set up a double date for Katie with Matt like I was thinking of doing yesterday. Katie wouldn't have appreciated that at all. I sent her to the softball game in my place so she could be around Matt, but now I don't know what happened."

"Matt didn't go to the game," Todd said. "He was with me, working on Gus."

"That's not good. That means Matt and Katie haven't

connected yet. I was hoping they would make a fresh start yesterday."

Todd's grin was too obvious to ignore.

"What?" Christy asked. "What's so funny?"

"You. You're in one of your save-the-world moods."

Christy put down her fork. "What is that supposed to mean?"

Todd covered her hand with his. "Don't get upset." He was still grinning. "You're cute when you get like this."

"Cute!" Christy felt the blood rushing to her face.

Todd's expression remained jovial. "Yeah, cute. It's like you don't have enough challenges of your own to figure out so you take on the world's burdens. I always know when you're feeling responsible for the deterioration of the ozone layer. You get this squiggly wrinkle across your forehead right here." He traced his finger across her forehead and laughed.

To her surprise, Christy broke into a smile. "Am I really that bad?"

"You are really that caring," Todd said. "That's not bad, as long as you don't take it to an extreme, of course. It's one of the many qualities I admire in you."

Todd's calm words and loving attention soothed Christy. She felt her appetite returning and ate three sausages off Todd's plate before he complained.

"You can go back for seconds, you know," he said.

"No thanks," she said with an impish grin. "I'm full now."

Todd and Christy left the cafeteria holding hands. After he walked her to her first class, they stopped by the door. As the other students rushed past them, Todd ran his hand over her long tresses and said in a low voice,

"Na ka Makua-O-Kalani, e malama mai ia makou."

Christy looked at him, waiting for an explanation. His words sounded Hawaiian, but she had never heard Todd say them before.

He seemed just as surprised at his words as Christy because all he added was, "I can't believe I remembered that."

"What did you say?"

"It's a prayer that Lani used to say every morning before I left for school." Todd seemed lost in a memory.

"I'll be at the bookstore until three," Christy said. She was uncomfortably aware that all the seats were filling fast in the classroom. "Meet me there if you can." She wanted to hear who Lani was and what the prayer meant when they had more time.

Only a few seats near the center of the large auditorium were still open when Christy entered her Old Testament introduction class. Old Testament and New Testament introduction were required for all graduates of Rancho Corona, so Christy suspected lots of freshmen were in this class.

She took a seat and noticed Sierra along with several of her friends sitting near the front. Next to Vicki was an empty seat. The instructor had already begun, so Christy didn't feel comfortable moving to join Sierra's group. Even though Todd's encouragement over breakfast had helped Christy believe everything was going to turn out okay with Katie, she didn't want to face Sierra yet—just in case Katie had spent the night telling Sierra and her friends what an insensitive roommate Christy was.

When class was over, Christy slipped out and hurried to the administration building to make an appointment with her counselor. The first opening he had was the next morning at ten. She took the appointment, determined to decide on her major and settle her class schedule before the end of the week.

Christy arrived at the bookstore just as her new boss, Donna, was about to enter the store with a box in her arms. Christy reached to open the door for her.

"Good, you're a little early, Christy. Did I show you how to log in on the computer when you start work?" Donna asked.

"No."

"I didn't think I did. Come with me, and I'll help you set up."

Christy followed Donna to the back of the bookstore, where she showed Christy how to access her time card on the computer and how it automatically logged her in when she typed in her code. Beside the computer, stacks of boxes stood open with a label gun resting on the top box. It brought back memories of her first job at the pet store in Escondido. Only, there she spent hours labeling fish food and rubber cat toys that smelled like old tires. She liked the ink and paper smell of these boxes of books much more.

"The same textbooks are in these first three boxes," Donna said. "I need you to label them on the back like this and then change the label gun and mark the books in these other four boxes at $15.95. Have you used one of these before?"

Christy nodded and told her about the pet store.

"Okay. Well, let me know when you've finished, and I'll start you on the register."

Christy was glad for the chance to begin with something simple. She liked feeling productive and able to measure her accomplishments.

"You can't be done already," Donna said when Christy joined her at the register a short time later. A long line of students was waiting to pay for textbooks.

"I think I finished all the boxes you pointed out."

"Lovely," Donna said. "You are the answer to my prayers, believe me. Why don't you watch me go through a few transactions, and then you can jump in."

The computer and credit card system were similar to what Christy had worked with at the pet store. She stepped in to try the machine after watching Donna on three transactions and went through the motions as if she had been doing it for years.

"You've got it," Donna said. "I'm going to shelve some of those books, and then I'll open this other register. Let me know if you get stuck on anything."

Christy didn't know why, but the act of serving like this, of using her hands to accomplish things, gave her a sense of well-being. The world was somehow a brighter place when she could get things done. She knew she was going to like working in the bookstore.

I wonder if having a degree in literature would be useful if I ended up working full time in a bookstore?

In the back of her mind she began to imagine in the most romantic way possible how dreamy her life would be if she and Todd married and lived in a cozy little house somewhere. They would have a vegetable garden in the backyard and a woodburning fireplace. She would bake cookies for the teens in the youth group, who would hang out at their house every Friday night. Every morning Christy would hop on a bike, like the one she had borrowed all the time in Switzerland, and she would pedal off to a charming little bookstore where, at ten o'clock, she would host a story time for toddlers. Customers would come from all over to browse in Christy's bookstore. She would serve them cookies and tea—Katie's Indian summer herbal tea, once Katie perfected the recipe.

But by two o'clock, Christy's imagination was having a difficult time glamorizing a bookstore owner's life. She hadn't eaten lunch, and her stomach was complaining loudly. The line of students hadn't diminished. The computer went down for almost half an hour, and all the credit card charges had to be done manually. As more students flocked into the store with lists of required textbooks, Christy wished she had a stool to sit on or at least a thicker rug beneath her feet.

She realized she had been daydreaming about being married to Todd. It had been a natural assumption, a logical, comfortable foundation in her daydream. Christy felt a wonderful thrill of hope.

I must love Todd enough to commit myself to him for the rest of my life if I include him in my daydreams so easily. I have to tell Katie about this.

As soon as she thought of Katie, her spirits swooped down a couple of notches.

That is, if Katie is still speaking to me.

Christy finished a transaction for a girl who wore a hearing aid. She seemed to be immensely relieved when Christy presented her with the total for all her books and it was less than she had expected. That's when Christy realized that the majority of the textbooks she was selling were the ones off the used bookshelves in the back.

Christy wished she had been more organized and had shopped for her textbooks sooner, before all the used ones were gone. That was one check she wasn't looking forward to writing because she knew it would drain her savings.

At three o'clock, Christy signed off the computer, and another student took her place. Christy went to the back of the store and scanned the used textbook shelves. She found three of the books she knew she needed. The others would have to wait until she received an updated list after she made a final decision on her major and her classes.

Christy left the bookstore with her heavy textbooks and went to the guys' dorm to see if Todd was there. She entered West Hall and asked one of the guys on the couch how to call the rooms. He pointed to the phones on the wall, and she tried to call Todd. No answer.

That was one of the things that bugged her about being at a conservative Christian college. In Switzerland she had been in a co-ed dorm, and the guys and girls were both free to come and go as they wished. That meant she didn't always have her room to herself, if one of her two roommates was already there with a boyfriend. But that had only happened once. Christy was the one who stayed in the dorm room the most; so her roommates were the ones who went to visit the guys' rooms.

And there I was again last night, alone, while my roommate went off to be with someone else.

Christy left a simple voice message for Todd, saying that she would be in her room until five, when she planned to eat an early dinner. Then she had a class from seven o'clock until nine.

Trudging across campus, she silently moaned about how far the guys' dorms were from the girls' dorms. The books she had bought felt heavier with each step. *It was much easier in Basel with all the housing in one area. It's so ridiculous for them to separate us across campus like this and put all these restrictions on us.*

Christy was hoofing it past The Java Jungle when someone came running up behind her and said, "Hey, cutie, where have you been?"

With a playful smirk, Christy turned and said, "Where have *you* been?"

Todd had a stack of books under his arm and looked red in the face, as if he had been working out. "I was hung up with the counselor. When I got to the bookstore, your manager said I just missed you."

"It looks like you're all set with your books," Christy said.

"I only need two more," Todd said. He reached for Christy's arm and pulled her toward the door of The Java Jungle. "Do you have any money on you?"

"Yes, about five dollars."

"Good. I'm broke. How about buying me something to drink?"

The booths inside the air-conditioned café were packed. Only one table remained open. They dropped their books on it and spent all but three cents of Christy's five-dollar bill on drinks and snacks.

"Did you figure out your schedule?" Christy asked.

He grinned.

"I take it that means yes."

"I can graduate in December," Todd said.

"Really?"

Todd nodded proudly. "You were so right about taking those two summer school classes after I got back from Europe. That's what made the difference."

"I don't remember telling you to take summer school classes."

"That's right, that was Katie's idea. She convinced me on the plane on the way home. Of course, she didn't take any classes like she said she was going to."

"She worked all summer," Christy said. "That's why she has time for a social life this fall and why I'm working every spare minute I have."

"How did it go your first day on the job?" Todd asked.

This time Christy was the one who answered with only a grin.

"I take it that means you liked it."

"I like it so much that I was daydreaming about owning my own bookstore someday." She decided to leave out the part about being married to Todd and snuggling with him in front of the woodburning fireplace. "And having a vegetable garden," she added.

"Now, would the vegetable garden be part of the bookstore?" Todd asked. "Were you thinking the garden would be in front of the store? Out back? Inside?"

"Sure," Christy answered in an effort to avoid giving specifics. "Any of the aforementioned is possible. Don't you think a vegetable garden sounds charming?"

Todd gave her a skeptical look.

"What about a woodburning fireplace?" Christy ventured further into her imaginary world and hoped Todd would find part of her dream appealing. "Do you like fireplaces?"

He leaned back in his chair and asked, "Now, would this fireplace be in the garden or in the bookstore?"

"Never mind." Christy felt as if she was getting nowhere. "Some daydreams are best left undiscussed, I guess."

Todd gave her hand a squeeze. "I like fireplaces. And I like you. I like hearing about your daydreams. The vegetable garden, though . . . I don't know. But I know I like you."

Christy smiled.

Go ahead. Say it. Say, "I love you, Todd." Right here in the middle of The Java Jungle with all these people. Stand up and shout it!

Christy opened her mouth, but what came out was "I like you, too."

Todd grinned. "I like you a lot."

"I like you a lot, too."

"I like you more," Todd said.

"No, I like you more."

Todd leaned forward and, with the warmest glow ever in his clear blue eyes, said, "I love you, Kilikina."

Christy froze. She couldn't make her lips part. She couldn't push out the words. A single tear was all that escaped her heart and raced down her cheek.

Todd moved his chair over so that he was right next to Christy. He kept his hand in hers. With patient, gentle words he said, "You don't have to respond, Christy. I don't want you to feel pressured. Ever. In any way. Just let me love you, okay?" He leaned over and kissed the tear where it clung to the edge of her jaw. "Just let me love you."

CHRISTY AND TODD
THE COLLEGE YEARS

8 Todd and Christy spent most of the rest of the day together. They dropped off their heavy books in their dorm rooms, sat together in the cafeteria, and then Todd walked Christy to her evening class. At nine, he was there to pick her up after class. As he agreed to do earlier, Todd went to the library with Christy to review her schedule with her.

Sitting close on a couch in the library's lobby, they read the classes from the catalog and Christy began her list on a note pad. She felt good as she listed everything so she could see the schedule and figure out what worked.

"That's it," Todd said after reading through the list of required classes for an English literature major. "Do you want to go through the classes for the humanities major now?"

Christy did some math on the side of the page. "No, more and more I like the idea of being a lit major. It's more focused than humanities, and literature fits me better. Like you said this morning at breakfast, I already have a save-the-world complex; a humanities major would only move me further in that direction. It would be like going back to the orphanage in Basel."

Once Christy had everything written out, she stared at the paper and realized the list of classes was all that lay between her and a BA in English literature. It was bite-size, a clear road map.

"I think literature is a good major for you, especially if you want to open that bookstore someday." Todd looked at Christy's calculations. "Is that total right? You could finish in two semesters?"

Christy nodded. "That's what the counselor told me, too. I had to see it for myself, but I could graduate next spring."

Todd looked as if he had taken a deep breath and then dove, headfirst, someplace deep. She was certain that when he surfaced, he would hold sunken treasure in his fist.

Todd emerged after two full minutes from his underwater daydream. With a deep breath he said, "Okay."

Okay? That's all you're going to tell me? Okay? Where did you just go? What did you see there, deep inside?

Christy knew that Todd wouldn't tell. And why should he? She hadn't yet given him the password that would allow him to open her heart's safe so he could store his fistful of treasures there. But she already knew what he was thinking because she was thinking the same thing.

We can get married, then, can't we, Todd? Katie wasn't pushing it as much as I first thought she was, was she? We are in the final stretch. The only thing missing is my commitment. I have to decide. I have to know for sure, and you understand that, don't you?

"Do you feel ready for your meeting with your counselor in the morning?" Todd asked.

"Yes."

"Good."

You're going to wait for me, aren't you, Todd? It doesn't matter

how long I take to make up my mind, your love for me is estab-
lished.

"I better get back to my room." Christy felt overwhelmed by her intense thoughts. "If Katie's there, I need to talk things through with her."

Todd walked Christy to her dorm and gave her a warm hug.

"Sweet dreams," she whispered in his ear.

"Sweet dreams to you, too."

She watched him walk away and felt as if an invisible string were attached to her heart. With each step Todd took, that string unraveled another loop. If anything or anyone ever threatened to sever that invisible string, Christy knew she would fight with every ounce of her being to keep that thread intact. She and Todd were connected. Strongly, deeply, wonderfully connected.

Opening the door to her room, Christy found Katie plopped in the beanbag chair, tears streaming down her face.

"Katie, are you okay?"

"Read this," Katie said, holding up a letter.

Christy took the handwritten, one-page letter from her roommate and immediately checked the signature.

"Rick? You got a letter from Rick Doyle?"

Katie nodded and wiped the tears from her cheeks. "He says he's sorry," Katie said before Christy had a chance to read the first line. "He got his life back together with God this summer, and he's apologizing for not . . . how does he say it? For not treating me with respect."

Christy scanned the opening paragraph. "It says, 'I ran into Doug, and he told me you and Christy were going to Rancho this year.' "

"Keep going," Katie said.

Christy read the second paragraph to herself and said, "He's asking you to forgive him for being a jerk and not treating you with the dignity and respect you deserve."

"Can you believe that?" Katie said. "I never expected anything like that to happen. Remember how just yesterday I said it would help if one of the guys who hurt me would apologize?"

Christy nodded and lowered herself to the edge of Katie's unmade bed.

"This has to be the creepiest God-thing I've ever experienced," Katie said. "I make that big declaration, and the very next day I pick up my mail and find this letter from Rick. At first I thought it might be a joke, but read that last part."

" 'This summer I finally surrendered my life completely to Christ, and He's real to me now. Very real. I just want to make things right with you, Katie. You don't have to write me back. I know God has forgiven me. I hope you can, too.' "

Christy looked up. "He sounds like he really means it."

Katie nodded. "Christy, I have to apologize to you, too. And I really mean it. I shouldn't have left in such a huff yesterday. What you were telling me was all true. I just didn't want to hear it."

Christy rushed to her friend and gave her a hug. "I'm the one who needs to apologize. I was so insensitive, Katie. I'm sorry. I should have come to Sierra's room last night so we could clear things up."

"No, I needed time to think everything through. It took me a while to realize you were right. I need to start forgiving completely. I had decided this afternoon I was going to start by forgiving Rick because I think he hurt me the most. I went to the chapel after dinner and prayed, and then this." Katie pointed to the letter Christy still held in her hand. "This blew me away. I mean, Rick Doyle is asking for my forgiveness. So what am I doing avoiding you? You and I are a team, Christy. We've waited for years to be roommates, and within the first week, I go and mess things up."

"You didn't mess anything up, Katie. We got off track, that's all. We need to talk things through whenever we get upset with each other. For whatever reason."

"You're right," Katie said. She rose and tucked the folded letter into the back flap of her Bible. "Did you check your mail today?"

"No, why?"

"Don't you wonder if Rick wrote you, too?"

"Me?"

"Yes, you. Rick didn't exactly treat you with the utmost dignity while you were dating him."

"But he and I settled it all back then," Christy said. "I don't think he has anything to apologize for. I didn't exactly handle the relationship with a lot of sensitivity to him. I tend to get pretty intense about things and only see them from my point of view."

Katie's sly grin returned. "We all are basically self-centered, when you think about it. That's why we need a Savior. Has Dr. Mitchell said that yet in Old Testament Survey? He said it all the time last year. Whenever we were studying about how all those heroes of faith had messed up so badly in the Old Testament, he would say, 'And once again we see this is why we all need a Savior.' "

Christy smiled. She was thinking of Rick and the verse from John about how those who believe and receive Christ have the right to become God's adopted children.

Rick is really, truly one of God's kids now.

"You're thinking about Rick, aren't you?" Katie asked.

"How did you know?"

"I was thinking the same thing. The original 'poser' got saved for real."

"Where did that word come from? What is a 'poser'? I heard Todd use it a couple of times with the group in Sunday school."

"You've been in the Alps too long," Katie said. "I first heard it as a surfer term. A 'poser' is someone who acts like he can surf, but he never actually gets up on a board. You know the kind—they put surfing stickers on their cars, wear shirts with surf logos, and talk about how great the waves were last week, but they don't surf. They just make you think they do."

"Do you think that was the situation with Rick? He was just a 'poser' Christian when we were in high school?"

"Who knows? It's for God to judge, not us. I'm just amazed he's got it together now and he wrote me."

"Are you going to write him back?" Christy asked.

"He didn't include a return address." Katie tilted her head. The gesture was especially charming now that her hair was short and wispy. It made her look playful rather than slightly frenzied, which is what that same gesture suggested when her hair was longer and swishy. "But Doug might know where he is. Or I could send a letter to his parents' home in Escondido."

As Christy got ready for bed, Katie cranked up her stereo and went to work composing a letter to Rick. By the time Christy had washed her face, brushed her teeth, and was snuggled under her covers, Katie the night owl was ready to talk.

"How does this sound: 'Dear Rick, I got your letter, and it made me cry. Of course I forgive you, you big baboon. Now it's my turn to ask you to forgive me. I don't think I was exactly at my best as a Christian or as a friend while we were hanging out together. I'm so excited to hear about what God has been doing in your life. Let's keep in touch, okay? Friends forever, Katie.' What do you think?"

"Big baboon?"

"I had to say something like that, or he wouldn't think it was from me."

"Then it sounds good," Christy said with a yawn. "It sounds like you, and it sounds sincere."

"You're not going to sleep now, are you?"

"Katie, it's almost midnight."

"But I'm going to write letters to all my lost loves. I want you to tell me if they sound okay."

"I'll read them in the morning."

––––––––––

Christy never did read Katie's letters. She thought of them on Friday, the end of their first week of classes. While they were checking their mailboxes before dinner, Christy remembered and asked Katie if she had ever mailed her letters.

"I only mailed the one to Rick." Katie and Christy stepped out of the student center and strolled toward The Golden Calf. "My mom gave me his parents' address, and I sent it there. The other letters didn't need to be mailed because they ended up turning into one long letter I wrote to God asking Him to forgive me for not forgiving those guys. I put the letter in my Bible. On the back of it I wrote out some verses that really helped me. One of them was the part where Jesus is hanging on the cross and He says, 'Father, forgive them. They don't know what they're doing.' That verse helped me the most because it made me realize that most people don't know what they're doing when they hurt us."

Christy was about to respond to Katie's insight, when Matt came running across campus toward them.

Christy smiled at him and said, "Hey, Matt, where have you been all week? This is the first I've seen you."

"Hi, Christy," Matt said quickly. His gaze was fixed on Katie. "Wes just told me you're Katie. Are you?"

A cute, flirty sort of grin lit up Katie's face. The expression wasn't typical for Katie, but it fit her new, softer, more sophisticated image. "That depends," she said. "There's probably more than one Katie on this campus. Which one are you looking for?"

Matt glanced at Christy and then at Katie and said, "I don't know her last name."

"Oh, really?" Katie played this moment for all it was worth. "What do you know about the Katie you're looking for?"

"I'm trying to find the Katie who played in the softball game last Sunday afternoon against Wes Jensen's team."

"That would be me."

"Oh, good. Well, here's the deal. Wes said you were supposed to take Christy's place at their last game, but you sided with Sierra's team and single-handedly beat our team."

Christy hadn't heard all this before.

"We're trying to set up a rematch sometime this weekend," Matt said. "Best two out of three. Sierra said you were going to stay with her team. I'm playing in the rematch, and if we could get you on our team, we'd win for sure. What can I do to convince you to join with Wes and me?"

Katie glanced at Christy. Then, with her dancing green eyes locked on Matt, Katie said, "That depends. How much money do you have?"

Christy wanted to burst out laughing when she saw the look on Matt's face.

"How much were you thinking about?" Matt asked cautiously.

Katie started to laugh. Christy knew that laugh. It was Katie's happiest laugh, the one she used when the two of them had gone searching for the statue of the *Little Mermaid* in Copenhagen last June. It was the laugh she used in Christy's car her first day on the job as a Santa's helper elf, when they tried to hide from Rick, and Katie's pointed ear kept falling off.

"I'm only kidding," Katie said to Matt. "But Todd tells me you know your way around a Volkswagen engine. If you can tell me why the dashboard lights won't turn on in Baby Hummer, I might be persuaded to join you and Wes."

"And what is a Baby Hummer?" Matt asked.

"My car. It's a VW Thing."

"The yellow one?" Matt asked. "That's yours? Hey, I'll check that Baby Hummer out any day. Where did you get it?"

"One of my brothers works at an auto body repair shop."

"Do you know how rare those cars are in Wisconsin?

My friend found one on the Internet that he wanted to buy, but he would have had to go to Mexico to get it."

"She's parked out in the side lot. Do you want to meet her after dinner?"

Christy rolled her eyes and pressed her lips together to keep the laughter from bubbling over as she watched her coy friend and bumbling Matthew Kingsley. It appeared the two of them had discovered each other at last.

"I'm going on into The Golden Calf," Christy said. "The line looks like it's growing."

"We might as well wait, then," Matt said to Katie. "Wait to eat, I mean. Why don't you show me your car now?"

Katie took off with Matt. She turned her head just enough for Christy to see the gleeful expression on her face.

Christy shook her head at her wacky friend. Matt hadn't given any indication that he remembered Christy introducing him to Katie a week ago and telling him that Katie was her roommate. Of course, Katie looked different with her new haircut. She was even wearing her "soft" skirt and "pretty" blouse for the second time that week. Apparently, as far as Matt was concerned, this was the first time he had ever seen Katie.

A fresh start for my dearest friend! I love it! And no phone books of unforgiveness for her to lug around.

Christy headed for the salad bar, where she proceeded to make a huge creation out of lettuce, broccoli, cheese, shredded carrots, and raisins all drizzled with ranch dressing. She had missed the variety of fresh California vegetables in Basel.

Spotting Todd at what had become their private table

by the window, she walked over to join him. The first thing she said even before she sat down was "It happened!"

"What?"

"Matt discovered Katie, and I had nothing to do with it." She gave Todd the full rundown. He appeared as humored by the story as Christy had been. Digging into his salad of lettuce and peas, he added a forkful of mashed potatoes to the mix. His next bite was one of his chicken strips smothered in honey mustard dip.

"You sure enjoy variety, don't you?" Christy asked.

"Why do you say that?"

"I've been watching you eat this week. You eat a little of everything until it's gone."

"So?"

"I never noticed that about you before." Christy smiled at him. "I'm learning new things about you. I like it. We've never been able to see each other so consistently for so long."

Todd scooped up some more mashed potatoes and dipped them in his puddle of honey mustard.

Christy contentedly ate a few more bites of salad. She wondered if Todd had been noticing this week that she tended to eat just one thing at a time before moving on to the next item.

"Does it bother you that I hopscotch all over my plate?" Todd asked.

"No, not at all. I just mentioned it because I'd never noticed that about you before."

"And it honestly doesn't bother you?"

"No." Christy couldn't read the expression on his face.

"Does it bother you that I usually eat everything in order?"

Todd shook his head. Then, with a half grin, he added, "Except that one time when you insisted on eating everything in alphabetical order."

Christy swatted him with her napkin. "I've never done that."

They ate quietly for a minute before Todd said, "I have to confess something to you. I've been nervous ever since our talk in the park last Saturday."

"You? Nervous? Why?"

"I felt like, after you heard about how I grew up, you had enough reasons to turn away and run for your life."

"Todd, I didn't feel that way. I was a little surprised at some of the things you told me, but you can't do anything to change who your parents were or the decisions they made. You're not responsible for their choices."

"I know." Todd's eyes fixed on Christy. He reached over and stroked the side of her face, gazing at her like a boy who had just been told the boogeyman wasn't real. "It doesn't change anything, then? I mean, now that you know what you do, you still want to move forward in our relationship?"

"None of what you told me changes anything. Todd, you are who you are because of what God has done in your life. And you are incredible in so many ways. I love you just as you are."

Everything around Christy seemed to come to a sudden stop. *Did I just say I loved him?*

Todd's steady gaze rested on Christy, waiting for her to continue. He looked neither surprised nor relieved at her slipped-out declaration. He seemed to be waiting.

I said I loved him just as he is. That's different than saying I love him. Isn't it?

Christy felt flustered. She knew her cheeks were turning red. Looking away, she said, "You're wonderful, Todd, just the way you are." Then she took another bite of her salad and chewed the lettuce to a pulp.

The day I tell Todd I love him, it will not be in a noisy cafeteria over chicken strips and salad!

Todd didn't seem at all tortured the way Christy was. He calmly finished his dinner and waited for Christy to finish hers.

In an effort to change subjects, Christy said, "Do you have any plans to go home soon?"

"Home? Do you mean to my dad's in Newport Beach?"

His answer reminded Christy of Todd saying he felt at home with her. He had lived at his dad's beach house for several years, off and on, but that apparently didn't seem like home to him.

"I was thinking I should visit my aunt and uncle one of these weekends," Christy explained. "Let me know if you have any plans to go, and I'll go with you."

"We can go tomorrow, if you want."

Christy didn't really want to; she felt she should. If Todd came with her, Aunt Marti might tell Todd of her plans, and then Christy wouldn't be the only one concerned about her aunt.

"What time would be good for you?" Todd asked.

"I should call my aunt first to make sure they're going to be home."

Todd suggested they use the phone in the cafeteria's

lobby. On their way out, they saw Matt and Katie coming in to dinner.

"Guess what?" Katie said. "Matt fixed the lights on Baby Hummer."

"Does that mean you're going to play on his team?" Christy asked.

"I guess it does," Katie said.

"When's the game?" Todd asked.

"Sunday afternoon at three," Matt said. "You want to play?"

Christy noticed that Matt seemed to direct the question to Todd and not to her. That was okay. She had had her moment on the field at the first game. Now that they were recruiting all the "professionals," Christy didn't think she would enjoy playing as much as she had before.

"No," Todd said. "I was wondering if both of you wanted to go to Newport Beach with us tomorrow."

"Sure!" Katie said.

"I've been wanting to go to the beach," Matt said. "I only went twice last spring when I was here. Both times I went by myself, so I didn't know where I was going."

Christy said, "You can't be this close to the beach and not go every chance you get. Todd, you have to take Matt surfing."

Matt's expression lit up. "You have a surfboard?"

"Yep," Todd said. "You want to go surfing tomorrow?"

————

By eight o'clock the next morning, the group was on their way to the closest beach, which was San Clemente. Christy didn't mind that they weren't going to Newport, the beach where her aunt and uncle and Todd's dad lived.

She could confront her aunt another time. Today was a perfect autumn day, and she was on her way to the beach with Todd and the gang.

Five cars formed their group. Sierra, her roommate, Vicki, and two other friends rode with Katie in Baby Hummer. Matt followed Todd's van in his truck and took his roommate, Pete, and another guy with him. Todd had Christy and four guys in Gus the Bus with three surfboards strapped to the roof. Wes drove by himself because he had to leave early, and Paul, Sierra's "just good friend," as she called him, was driving up from San Diego.

Todd led the way as they drove over the Ortega Highway with all the windows open and the radio blasting out Christian music from a station Todd had told Christy he now listened to all the time. Christy was using her beach towel for extra padding on the decomposing front passenger seat. That helped to make the hour-long drive more comfortable.

They parked close together and found Paul already there, waiting for them. Christy watched carefully to see how Sierra and Paul greeted each other. She was surprised to see how casual it was, as if he was just one of the guys. But then Christy remembered how casual she had been around Todd the first few years. It was better that way. Their friendship had plenty of time to grow through the ups and downs that would come along.

The group headed to the beach with their arms full of gear. Christy marched beside Todd. "We have a few memories at this beach, don't we?"

Todd nodded. "We broke up on this beach at sunset. How many years ago was that? Three? Or was it only two? That was one of the worst days of my life."

"Mine too," Christy said. "The worst part for me was that we didn't talk to each other the entire drive back to my parents' house."

"The worst part for me was that it forced me to follow through with all my big talk. I kept saying I was going to live in some faraway country, and you made me actually do it."

Christy stopped walking. "You're saying I made you go to Spain?"

"Yes and no. I always thought I wanted to go to Papua New Guinea. I ended up in Spain. But you made me live up to all my big talk. What I really wanted was to stay right here and be with you."

Christy could hardly believe Todd. She dropped her towel and bag in the sand and put her hands on her hips. "You're telling me, after all these years, that you wouldn't have left if I hadn't told you that day we should break up?"

Todd thought a moment before saying, "Probably not. Maybe. It's hard to say."

"Todd, how could we have been so bad at communicating with each other?"

"I'm not saying it should have been any different than it was." He lowered his orange surfboard, which he affectionately had nicknamed "Naranja," into the sand.

"You're saying it's my fault you left because I said we should break up."

"Not at all!" Todd protested. "I'm glad we broke up that day."

"You're glad?"

Katie approached them cautiously. "Sorry to interrupt

you guys. But if you're going to fight for a while, could I borrow your board, Todd?"

"Here," he said, practically shoving it at her.

"Sorry, but one more thing. Chris, did you bring any sunscreen?"

Christy thrust her whole beach bag at Katie.

"Thanks. I'll go ahead and take your towel, too," Katie said. "I'll put it over there by mine, and whenever you want to come on over, it'll be waiting for you."

With that, Katie slinked away, leaving Todd and Christy alone by the lifeguard stand, both of them with their hands on their hips.

CHRISTY AND TODD
THE COLLEGE YEARS

9 Christy," Todd said with an edge to his voice, "you're missing the point of what I'm trying to say. I believe God directed you to break up with me, which prompted me to move forward with my dreams. I don't regret any of it. The time I spent in Spain was life-changing. Then, when God brought you all the way to Spain, and you didn't even know I was there, well, it was the confirmation I needed."

Christy still was fuming. All she could think about were the buckets of tears she had cried over Todd, the months of missing him, never knowing where he was or why he didn't write. She couldn't remember any wonderful changes for her as a result of Todd stepping out of her life.

"What confirmation?" she finally asked.

Todd looked at the waves and let out a deep breath. Then he directed his gaze at Christy. "It confirmed I wasn't supposed to be a full-time missionary to some tropical isle, like I had always thought I should be."

Christy calmed down a notch. She and Todd had talked about this once before. Todd had said then that he had learned a need didn't constitute a call. Just because an opportunity existed on the foreign mission field, that didn't mean God was calling Todd there.

"While I was in Spain I found out I was pretty good at leading a group of younger teens, leading worship, and teaching. I don't know if I would have figured that out if I had stayed here. That's what prompted me to change my major to Bible and to consider going into youth ministry."

Christy folded her arms across her stomach and looked down at her feet. The sand had filled her tennis shoes, and she wished she had taken them off or had worn a pair of sandals. During the short summers in Basel, she had kicked around in a beat-up pair of sandals but hadn't brought the shoes back with her.

"I guess I wouldn't have gone to Switzerland," Christy said slowly. "Since you went to Spain, I started to think beyond what I had expected for my life. I didn't even know if I'd go to college; yet here I am, within view of a Bachelor of Arts degree."

"You know," Todd said, relaxing his stance and moving closer to Christy. "If it were only up to you or me to determine what should happen in our lives, we would have reason to be upset about decisions we made in the past. But God is very much involved. Both you and I have surrendered our lives to Christ and given Him the controls."

"Not that I don't try to take those controls back every now and then." Christy brushed her hair off her face and looked up at Todd. His expression was tender.

"We can only go on from here. We can't change the past."

"I know," Christy agreed. "Instead of saying, 'What if,' we need to say, 'What next?' "

Todd nodded. "And let's be completely honest here. I'm the one who seems to have a pretty clear view of what I think should happen next. You still have doubts or hesitations or something."

Christy was about to protest, but Todd held up his hand as a request for her to wait and let him finish what he was saying. "I want you to know that's okay. You don't have to decide about me or our future or anything until God makes it all clear to you. I'm not going anywhere. I'm right here. And I'm staying here. I'm trusting God that He will make our paths straight. He'll show us the next step to take at the right time."

Christy felt a wonderful peace as Todd spoke. Her anxiety about having to decide if her love for Todd was the kind that could last a lifetime began to float away. Ultimately, the decision wasn't hers to make on her own. God was in control. All she had to do was trust Him and wait. Hadn't Todd said the other day that trust was the most important foundation for any relationship?

"You're right." Christy offered Todd a weak smile. "God was working in our relationship the day we stood on this beach and broke up. And He's working in our relationship now."

"He is," Todd said. "All we have to do is trust Him."

"Thanks for reminding me of that."

A slow grin warmed Todd's previously set face. He was looking at her "that way." Without hesitation he said, "I love you, Kilikina. I will always love you."

Christy leaned forward and stood on her tiptoes to kiss the lips that had showered those beautiful, giving words over her. The kiss was sweet and tender and lasted only a moment.

From their friends who had planted themselves closer to

the water, there arose a chorus of cheering and applause as Todd and Christy's kiss ended.

Todd waved casually, then grinned and waved some more. "Our first big argument in public, and we practically get a standing ovation."

Christy grinned at the audience and then looked back at Todd. "I think the applause is over our decision to kiss and make up rather than break up."

"I couldn't agree more," Todd said, then looked toward heaven. "Nice going, Lord," he said. "I can't say I always understand your plan or agree with your methods, but I sure like it when you surprise us with good things."

Christy was used to Todd breaking into prayer at unusual moments. They looked at each other and smiled.

"How about it?" Todd asked. "Are you ready to go in the water?"

"Sure," Christy said.

With that, Todd scooped her up and dashed to the water.

Christy squealed, "Wait! I'll go in by myself. I don't want to get this T-shirt all wet!"

Her cries had no effect on him. Before she could squirm free, both she and Todd were in the water. That seemed to be the cue for the rest of the gang, and within a blink they were all in the salty water, splashing each other and laughing like crazy.

Christy noticed that Matt was particularly enjoying the romp and that Katie was his target for splashing. A glob of seaweed floated near Christy, and she picked it up and heaved it toward the shore. She hated slimy seaweed with its rubberlike tentacles.

"Hey, Christy Miller!" Matt yelled over the roar of the breaking wave. "You still throw like a girl."

Her only response was a big smile. At that moment she felt like a girl. The happiest girl on the face of the Earth.

Surely there will be beach days in heaven. And everything will be exactly as it is right here, right now. Except maybe the water will be a little warmer!

The rest of their day was filled with sunshine, laughter, teasing, and soothing ocean breezes. All they needed, in Christy's estimation, was a bonfire at sunset and some marshmallows to roast while they sang. However, Christy and Todd were the only two who had thought to bring warm clothes to change into. They knew how cold it could get on the beach at night. Especially in the fall.

Since everyone else was cold, tired, and hungry, the group packed up and drove to Rancho Corona just in time to make it to the cafeteria for what was left of dinner.

A spirit of camaraderie continued among the beach bunch through the rest of the weekend and into their second week of classes. Todd had more volunteers for helpers with the youth group than he had teens in the group. Many of their beach buddies stopped by the bookstore to see Christy early in the week.

The only negative result of their sandy adventure was that several of them got sunburned and convinced the others that it would be unfair to hold the softball rematch under such conditions. The game was postponed until the following weekend.

Katie zipped about as energetically as ever that week. Christy smiled each time Katie flew into their room and announced she was off to another practice session with Matt at the baseball field.

When Todd walked Christy to class on Wednesday morning, he again quoted the Hawaiian prayer of blessing at the door.

"You were going to tell me what that means," Christy said.

"Meet me at the fountain before you go to work," Todd said. "I'll tell you the whole story."

When they met, so many people were gathered in the plaza that Todd and Christy had to find another place to sit. They ended up on a couch inside the lobby of Dischner Hall, the music building. From down the long corridor came the sounds of someone playing his heart out on one of the pianos in the practice room.

"I never have told you much about when we lived in Maui," Todd began.

Christy gave Todd her full attention. She had the feeling this was going to be one of those important conversations like the one they had at the park before school started.

"Did you know that we lived with my dad's girlfriend, Kapiolani?"

Christy shook her head.

"She was from the islands, and my dad was really in love with her. I called her Lani. She was an amazing woman. I was closer to her than I've ever been to my own mom. She used to make Spam and rice with teriyaki sauce for my friend Kimo and me whenever he came over. That was his favorite."

Christy made a face. "Spam and rice?"

"You should try it. The first time I had it was when Kimo and I put up a tent in the backyard and slept out there." Todd smiled at the memory. "We told each other scary stories about centipedes and the *menehunes*."

"The men of what?"

"The menehunes. They're the imaginary little people of the islands."

"Oh. Like leprechauns?"

Todd nodded and went on with his memory. "Four huge plumeria trees stood in the backyard, and Lani always wore plumerias in her long hair."

Christy smiled. Todd had given her several plumeria leis over the years. She knew he loved the sweetly fragrant white flowers. Now she knew why. She wondered why he had never talked about his dad's girlfriend before.

"You said she used to say a prayer over you before school."

"Oh yeah. Na ka Makua-O-Kalani, e malama mai ia makou.

"That sounds so beautiful," Christy said. "What does it mean?"

"I'm pretty sure it means, 'Let our heavenly Father take care of us all.' It's a sort of blessing or benediction."

"I'd like to learn it," Christy said. "Keep saying it to me every day, and I'll try to repeat it."

They practiced saying it twice before Christy asked, "What happened to Lani? She sounds like a wonderful person. Why didn't your dad marry her?"

Todd grew quiet and smoothed Christy's hair by running his hand from the crown of her head all the way down her back. He did that twice before asking, "You know my surfboard?"

Christy had no idea what his beat-up orange surfboard had to do with this conversation. "Yes, I know your surfboard."

"Lani gave it to me on my tenth birthday."

Christy now understood why it was so thrashed. Before

she could add up how old Naranja was, Todd finished his thought.

"She died two months later. Ovarian cancer. We only stayed on the islands a short while after that. My dad couldn't handle it. That's when we moved to Newport Beach. He never fell in love again, at least as far as I know. And he hasn't been back to the islands since then, either."

"But you have," Christy said.

Todd gave Christy a tender smile. "Yes." He leaned closer and whispered in her ear, "I have fallen in love."

Christy felt her face warming. "I meant, you've been back to Hawaii."

"That too." Todd leaned back and rested his elbows on the back of the couch and stretched out his legs in front of him, crossing them at the ankles. "I think the way I've healed up from stuff in the past is by going back and remembering. My dad seems to deal with it by going on. That's why I never talk about any of this, I guess. It's not an open topic with my dad. And of course, I'd never talk about any of this with my mom because she doesn't know any more than that we lived on Maui for a while."

Christy slipped her hand in Todd's. "I like hearing about all this, Todd. I like knowing more about you. You can talk with me about any of this, any time you want. Especially if you want to talk about Lani." Cautiously she added, "Or any other girl."

"She's the only one," Todd said in a calm breath.

Christy smiled. She was realizing that Todd hadn't thoroughly processed his life's journey yet. She suspected that, as he told each part of his story, he could process it because he knew he was safe and at home with the listener. Christy felt honored to be that listener.

Little by little, as the next few weeks unfolded, Todd gave Christy more details of his childhood, telling her aspects of his life he had never told anyone. None of his revelations was as stunning as the first two sessions were, but each bit of information drew Todd and Christy closer together.

Every Monday, Wednesday, and Friday morning they met for breakfast, and Todd walked her to class. He repeated his Hawaiian blessing over her at the door of her classroom. By the end of the second week, Christy had it memorized.

She felt that their heavenly Father was taking care of them. Life was on a straight track now. This was the way it was supposed to be. No surprises.

Each morning Christy tried to wake up early enough to read her Bible and have some quiet time with the Lord. Most mornings she managed. Not all. Every day she diligently made it to class on time, worked her full schedule, ate well, and kept up with her homework.

Those simple, routine acts helped Christy immensely. She felt settled. And that turned out to be more important to her than she had realized it would be.

Katie turned out to be the star of the well-attended Sunday afternoon softball game. She and Matt secured a nine-to-five victory for their team over Sierra's team, and the cheering could be heard halfway across campus.

Matt and Katie seemed to be spending more time together, but Katie refused to comment on how she felt about him. All she would say when Christy asked was, "What's the big rush? Can't people be friends for a while before everyone wants to know if they're dating? Give me a break!" Christy thought the new, improved, low-key approach suited Katie. More than once Christy spotted her roommate gallivanting around campus with other guys and appearing to be enjoying every minute of it.

Todd was full of ideas about what to do with the youth group. On his third Sunday at Riverview Heights, Katie, Matt, and Christy had all accompanied him. Five more students were there than the first week. Todd decided to keep all the students together for the next few weeks instead of breaking them up into classes, since there were so few of them. That meant the pressure was off Christy to decide about teaching Sunday school. She scolded herself for making such an issue of it earlier.

Everything always works out. Why can't I remember that?

At the end of their third week of classes, Todd and Christy strolled hand in hand across campus and headed for the gym, where weekly chapel was held each Friday morning.

Their conversation centered on the youth group camping trip to the desert that Todd had been talking about since Sunday. He had decided it should be the next weekend.

"A week from today?" Christy questioned. "Are you sure you can pull it off in that short time?"

"Sure," Todd said. "What's to pull off?"

"Everything. Do you have tents? Who's going to do the food? What about permission slips? Don't the kids have to have medical release forms signed or something?"

"I'm working on all that."

They entered the gym and went to the same area in which they had sat the last two Fridays with Sierra and some of her friends. Katie was already there.

Christy sat down, thinking about last summer when she had taken off on a camping trip with Todd, Katie, and their friend Antonio in Italy. None of them had done much planning ahead of time, and although the trip wasn't a disaster, it wasn't Christy's favorite experience.

"Todd, this isn't going to be like our camping trip to Italy, is it?"

"That was an awesome trip," Katie said, jumping into the conversation. "What are we talking about? The camping trip with the youth group? Did you decide on a date?"

"Next weekend," Christy said. "And you're right, Italy was an awesome trip. All I'm saying is that it would have been a *really* awesome trip if we had thought to bring a few things with us ahead of time."

"Like what?" Todd asked.

Christy gave him an exasperated look. "Oh, I don't know," she teased. "Like maybe food and sleeping bags."

Katie laughed. "It did get pretty cold, didn't it? Remember when the rain came through the tents, and we all ended up in the van?"

"But you both liked the fresh fish, didn't you?" Todd asked.

Both girls answered him with their piercing stares.

"Okay, okay." Todd held up his hands in surrender. "By any chance, would either of you be interested in helping me work on those minor details?"

"What have you figured out so far?" Christy asked.

"Well," Todd said with a boyish glimmer in his eye, "I have the weekend selected. Next weekend. How's that for a start?"

More people started to join them. Christy knew this conversation needed to be finished later. Her mind began to sort through ideas of what kinds of food would be easy to cook on a camping trip in the desert. When they had camped in Italy, all they had to eat was the fish they caught.

Christy wanted to make sure they wouldn't be dependent on the local desert game for their food. Lizard stew didn't sound appealing.

Sierra joined them and sat behind Christy. She leaned over and said, "Did you hear that Randy is going to play for chapel this morning? He started up a new band with some guys in the dorm. Isn't that great?"

Sierra reached over and gently tugged on the ends of Christy's long, straight hair. "How do you get your hair so silky? You have such gorgeous hair, Christy. Trade you."

Christy laughed. "Any day. I love your hair, Sierra. Do you know how impossible it is to get mine to curl? The longer it grows, the straighter it becomes."

"What do you use on it?" Sierra asked. "Shampoo, I mean."

"Whatever is on sale."

Sierra nodded her understanding. "I know exactly what you're saying. Believe me, I am so broke. I didn't want to have to work this first semester, but I think I have to find something. Do you know if they're hiring at the book-store?"

"I don't think there are any openings, but I'll ask."

"Thanks," Sierra said. Leaning closer and lowering her voice she added, "By the way, I was meaning to tell you, I'm glad things worked out between Katie and you. I was worried that first week of school when she came to our room because she was so upset. She never told me what was wrong, but I guessed it was something between the two of you. I used to get that way with my older sister because we always had to share a room."

Christy was surprised. To Katie's credit, she had kept her

conflict with Christy private. Christy admired her friend for that.

"You and Katie are my supreme role models," Sierra went on. "I'm sure you know that. You both are such great examples to me of WOGs."

"Wogs?" Christy asked.

"Women of God," Sierra said. "WOGS. You really care for other people. I don't know if I ever thanked you for being so nice to me when we met in England. You both treated me as an equal, even though I was younger. You made me feel like part of your group, and I've never forgotten that."

Christy smiled at Sierra. She had such an innocent, clear-hearted face. Sierra's blue-gray eyes smiled back at Christy.

Randy and his band started chapel by asking everyone to stand. They played three songs in a row as the students' voices filled the gymnasium. Christy loved it. She closed her eyes and let the voices all around her move from her ears into her heart. She loved hearing Todd's strong, deep voice blend with hers as she sang and worshiped God.

When the third song ended, the silence jolted Christy to open her eyes and sit back down. She wanted to sing some more.

"Makes you eager for heaven, doesn't it?" Todd whispered in her ear. "Can you just imagine what it's going to be like to sing with the multitudes in the courts of heaven? Man!"

Christy slid her hand into Todd's and whispered, "I know!" She looked past Todd and noticed Matt had just come in and was slipping into the open space on the other side of Katie. He looked over at Christy, smiled, and waved.

Christy smiled back.

Glancing at Katie, Christy examined her friend's profile. Katie's face was more complex than Sierra's. Her expression was open and energetic like Sierra's, but Katie had an outdoorsy sort of beauty to her. She was solid, like an oak tree, yet rounded and defined in all the right places. The new haircut framed her face like the curling petals of a rose.

Katie is a woman.

Christy's thought surprised her. This tomboy buddy of hers had blossomed. Had Matt noticed that, as well?

Katie is a WOG. She's a woman, and she's a Woman of God.

Turning her attention to the chapel speaker who now stood at the microphone, Christy thought about how much she loved being at Rancho Corona. She loved sitting beside Todd, singing together, and being surrounded by their friends. It made her think that this camping trip could be close and wonderful, as well.

That evening, in the cafeteria, Todd presented Christy with a list of what he had worked on so far for the camping trip. Two items were written down:

1. Vehicles
2. Tents

"Have you arranged for these things, or is this your list of things to do?" Christy asked.

"To do," Todd said. He showered two scoops of peas over his mound of lettuce and then pressed in the center with the bottom of the salad dressing ladle. After filling the hollow center with blue cheese dressing, he stuck a celery stick in the middle.

"You make the most bizarre salads I've ever seen," Christy said, creating her usual lettuce, broccoli, and carrot salad laced with ranch dressing and dotted with raisins.

"Beauty is in the eye of the beholder," Todd said.

"Like that beautiful tostada you created yesterday at lunch?" Christy teased. "I've never seen anyone put a layer of pickles on his refried beans and then pour peas over the whole thing."

"It was pretty good," Todd said. "I like peas."

"So I've noticed."

They made their way to a table where some of their friends were seated. "Does this mean we should put peas on this to-do list for the camping trip next weekend?" Christy asked.

"Great idea. We could buy one of those ten-pound cans. Write that down on the list. Peas and what else?"

Christy gave Todd a tucked-chin, raised-eyebrow look. "Is this your way of asking me to make up the menu and the shopping list?"

"Hey, I'll help you. We already have peas on the list. Peas go with everything. What else do you think we should put on there?"

If Todd weren't so absolutely adorable, Christy would have slugged him.

10 By the time Todd and Christy had eaten their fill of Friday-night cafeteria pizza and salad, they had a complete camping menu figured out. Sierra joined them and was able to help calculate amounts because she came from a family of six children. Twelve students and volunteers would go on the trip, Todd estimated.

The equipment list took a little longer to prepare. Christy wished Matt could have been in on this conversation because he had done a lot of camping with his family and would make sure they didn't forget anything. Matt wasn't at dinner, and neither was Katie. Christy thought Katie would have told her if she had plans with Matt, but then the decision to eat together could have been spontaneous, which happened often with Katie.

After dinner, Christy and Todd drove into town to check out the prices on camping equipment at a sporting goods store.

"We could buy some of the stuff we need, like the camp stove," Todd suggested on their way. "Then it would be ours."

"Ours?" Christy asked.

"Yeah, yours, mine, ours. We could use it whenever we go camping."

"I don't have much money right now." Christy wondered, *If Todd's savings are as limited as mine, why would we buy camping gear?* A fleeting vision paraded through her imagination of her and Todd living in a lean-to shelter made of palm fronds on some deserted beach. Their framed college degrees served as a welcome mat. Christy was shooing the sea gulls away from their breakfast while she cooked scrambled eggs on the only material possession she and Todd owned—a gleaming, brand-new camp stove.

"I have some money saved up," Todd said. "We could use it."

That surprised her. "Did you get your first paycheck from the church?"

"No, I've been saving and making a few investments."

Christy waited until after they left the sporting goods store and had stopped for ice cream before she asked the questions that were rolling around in her head. They were seated at a cement patio table outside the small ice cream shop near the movie theater. The evening had cooled after an especially hot afternoon, so Christy had grabbed Todd's navy blue, hooded sweat shirt from the floor of Gus and put it on before they went into the ice cream store. She felt that if she could help herself to her boyfriend's clothes and help him shop for camping stoves, she had a right to know about his savings and investments.

Todd took a bite of his top scoop of pineapple coconut.

"I never understood how you could chew ice cream," Christy said. She had picked one scoop of caramel fudge swirl and was slowly eating it from a cup with a spoon.

"That would give me a headache and a toothache at the same time."

"You still seem to find my eating habits fascinating, don't you? First the salad and now the ice cream." He didn't sound upset. He actually sounded flattered that Christy would notice all these things about him.

"No, but as long as we're talking about some of the more specific, little-known details of your life, you said you have some money saved and that you've been making some investments."

"I've been trying to keep the balance in my checking account low and put everything I can into savings."

Christy wasn't sure what Todd's answer meant. She had been thinking a few days earlier that part of her hesitancy to verbalize her commitment to Todd was because, if he knew she was ready to take the next step, that would launch them into specific conversations about their future. And if they decided to get married right after college, what would they use for money?

If Todd was planning for their future the same way he was planning for the camping trip, they were in big trouble. She could see why she subliminally had avoided taking the next step. If she opened up her heart to getting married only to discover that, to be practical, they would have to wait another five years before Todd could afford to even buy her an engagement ring, she would be frustrated to pieces.

Carefully, Christy asked, "How do you have money left over to put in savings after school bills?"

"My dad's paying for college."

Christy put down her spoon. "I didn't know that. Then why have you been working two jobs like a crazy man for the past year?"

"I've been preparing for the future."

Christy's hopes began to soar. "You have?"

"Of course."

As she let the ice cream melt on her tongue, Christy wondered if this might be one of those areas in which Todd would blow her away with his careful attention to detail. He had shocked her more than once with his perception of life's realities.

"What do you think? Should we go back to buy the camp stove?" Todd asked.

"I guess so," Christy said. "Unless the church has any equipment you could borrow."

"They don't have a camp stove. I checked around. We can use all the pots and pans from the church kitchen, as well as dishes and silverware, if we wash and return everything in perfect condition. But they don't have a camp stove."

Christy noticed a bunch of people coming their way. Apparently the movie had just ended. She expected to see some students from school in the crowd, and she guessed right. Katie and Matt were headed toward them.

"Hey, how's it going?" Todd greeted them.

"That was the worst movie I've ever seen," Katie blurted out.

Matt chuckled.

"What did you see?" Christy asked.

"Something about baseball," Matt said.

"See? We can't even remember the name of it," Katie said. "It sounded like a great idea when Wes suggested it this afternoon, but then he ditched us, and the movie turned out to be a loser."

"Want to go with us to buy a camp stove?" Todd asked.

Christy held back a smile. Todd was so excited about this big purchase. It would be their first purchase together, unless she counted the bookshelf she bought years ago at a garage sale while Todd circled the block in Gus because no parking was available.

"Are you going to Bargain Barn?" Matt asked.

"Bargain Barn?" Todd said. "Where's that?"

"It's a warehouse of all kinds of surplus stuff. They have everything from patio furniture to piñatas. You'll get a good price there, if they have any stoves."

Todd's expression lit up. "Let's go."

"I don't think they're open this late. We could go tomorrow."

"Cool," Todd said. "I wonder if we could buy some of this other stuff on our list for the camping trip." He proceeded to tell Katie and Matt about his big plans for the youth group outing.

"Hey, if you need more help, I'm available," Matt said.

"You counted me in, too, didn't you?" Katie asked. "Baby Hummer loves the desert. I take it you're going to announce all this to the group on Sunday morning."

Todd nodded.

"Kind of short notice," Katie said. "How many do you think will actually go?"

"I'm not sure."

"We planned food for twelve," Christy said.

"Better make it fourteen," Todd said. "I don't think we had Matt and Katie on the list yet."

"What list?" Christy asked.

"The list we need to start with the names of all the people who are going."

Christy looked at Katie and, with a playful oh, brother

look, said, "Right now the four of us are the only names on this so-called list."

"That's okay," Todd said. "If we plan it, they will come."

Katie burst out laughing. "I'll be nice and not comment on that one, Todd. But boy, could I."

"What did I say?" Todd asked Christy.

She smiled at her charming, take-the-next-wave-as-it-comes boyfriend and calmly said, "What time should we go to Bargain Barn in the morning?"

———

By eight-thirty the next morning, the chummy four-some was on its way to Bargain Barn in Todd's van. Christy had pulled back her long hair into a braid and wore a blue bandanna she had bought in Switzerland. She took a notebook with her, ready for the role of safari assistant.

Within the first ten minutes at Bargain Barn, they found a perfectly good camp stove still in the box for half the price of the one they had looked at the night before. Christy checked it off the list, and they moved on to tarps, folding camp chairs, and ropes. Everything they needed they found, and everything was a better price than they could get anywhere else. Christy thought Todd would be ready to go after she checked the last needed item off the list.

But Todd was still shopping. He seemed to be on a treasure hunt, going through bins of closeouts and ex-amining shelves of broken and mismatched merchan-dise. He could think up a use for just about anything they saw. He didn't buy any of it, but he seemed to take great delight in imagining what he would do with the stuff if he did buy it.

Christy wandered off and found a rug for her room. She picked up two and showed Katie. "Do you want one of these?"

"No, I think I've reached my limit with this stuff." Katie showed Christy her three sets of pillowcases still in plastic bags.

"Do you know how old those must be?" Christy asked.

"I know. Aren't they cool? Collectors' items. Look, Winnie the Pooh, Minnie Mouse, and my favorite, the Little Mermaid!"

Christy laughed. "She looks nothing like the statue in Copenhagen."

"She's about the same size," Katie said. "Now I can lay me down to sleep and have sweet dreams of the *Lille Havfrue* anytime I want."

"As long as you wash them first," Christy said.

"Yes, Miss Tidiness. And I'm also getting this." Katie motioned toward a goldfish bowl that Matt was holding for her. "It's only a quarter."

"What are you going to use it for?" Christy asked.

"A fish, of course. We need a pet."

Christy was about to protest, when she saw Todd starting down the plumbing aisle. "Why don't you guys wait in line? I'll grab Todd so we can get out of here." Fortunately, very few of the faucets and sink stoppers prompted creativity in Todd's imagination, and the plumbing aisle was a quick trip.

"You're really enjoying this, aren't you?" Christy asked as they stood in the checkout line.

"I haven't had so much fun in a place like this since I was a kid. When we lived on Maui, an old Salvation Army Thrift Store was between my house and Kam III, the elementary school. Almost every day Kimo and I would stop in there after school and go through all the stuff. It was the best entertainment a kid could have. We read comic books and played with a huge boxful of action figures. The guys there taught me how to fix the stereos and TVs that came in. That's where I bought my first guitar."

Christy liked the way Todd had been opening up and talking more about childhood memories, especially Maui memories.

The cashier announced their total, and Christy pulled her folded-up cash from her pocket and handed it to Todd.

"What's this for?"

"That's my contribution toward the camp stove."

Todd took the money and gave Christy a big bear hug. "We must be serious about each other if we're buying appliances."

Christy enjoyed all the planning for the camping trip that week. Her only regret was that, when it came time to shop for the food on Thursday afternoon, she had to work at the bookstore.

Katie came into the store with something behind her back and pranced up to the register, where Christy was running the afternoon totals.

"Meet Chester," Katie said, holding out a plastic bag with a nervous-looking goldfish darting about in the three inches of water.

"What happened to Rudy?" Christy asked. Katie had insisted they buy a goldfish on their way home from Bargain Barn last Saturday. She had situated the fish in his new, twenty-five-cent fishbowl and had named him Rudy. She talked to him every day and fed him way too much.

"Rudy went to fish heaven this morning," Katie said sadly. "Chester wants to live with us now."

"You better get him in the bowl pretty soon," Christy said. "He looks like he's drowning in that bag."

"Drowning, ha-ha. Very funny."

"Okay, then, he's suffocating."

"I'm on my way back to the room now. I just wanted to find out when you're going shopping for all the food. I'll drive you, if you want."

"Todd has the list," Christy said. "He's at the store right now."

"You let Todd go shopping alone?" Katie asked.

"It's a grocery store, Katie, not a thrift store. He'll do just fine without me."

Katie gave Christy a wary look. "You think so?"

"Yes."

"Love sure messes with a person's logic," Katie said, turning to go. "I'll be leaving now with Chester, and you would do well to consider your boyfriend's shopping skills before it's too late."

Christy soon found out what Katie was warning her about. Friday night the group arrived at the camping area in the Joshua Tree desert, and as they tumbled out of the cars, the entourage consisted of fifteen students; six tents; one brand-new, co-owned camp stove; boxes and boxes of food; and miscellaneous paraphernalia Christy hadn't had a chance to identify. That's when she discovered that Todd had improvised on the menu she had made up.

The air was cold, and a wind snapped at the tents as the group tried to set them up by the light of Coleman lanterns. Christy asked one of the high school girls to help her organize the food. That's when they discovered enough day-old bread and gigantic cans of peanut butter to feed an army for a week. They had eaten at a drive-through hamburger place on the way to the campground, so dinner was taken care of. But Christy had planned for s'mores around the campfire when they arrived.

After quickly surveying the boxes by flashlight, Christy went to find Todd. He was telling two young guys to stay out of the girls' tents. Matt had started a fire, and most of the teens were gathering around it. As soon as Todd sent the two guys to the fire, he gave Christy his full attention.

She tried to be as nice as possible. "Todd, I can't seem to find the marshmallows, chocolate bars, or graham crackers. Do you know where they might be?"

"I forgot to tell you. I had to adjust the menu a little because of my budget. I eliminated the chocolate, graham crackers, and marshmallows because they were too expensive. I got a great deal on turkey hot dogs instead. I thought if they wanted to roast something over the fire, they could roast the hot dogs."

Christy stared at Todd. "You're kidding, right?"

"No, the hot dogs are in the ice chest. They're probably better for these guys than all that sugar anyhow."

"Todd, I saw the hot dogs. They're still frozen."

"So they'll just take a little longer to cook, right?"

"Todd, how are these guys going to cook frozen hot dogs?"

"We have some sticks around here, don't we?"

"Todd, we're in the desert. That's why I put wire coat hangers on the shopping list."

"Oh!" Todd's expression lit up. "*That's* why you put hangers on the list. I couldn't figure out why you wanted hangers. I thought it was to hang up dish towels or something. I bought six plastic hangers. They're in a bag somewhere."

If the situation hadn't been so funny, Christy might have cried. Instead, she laughed.

"What?" Todd said.

"Katie was right. I shouldn't have let you go shopping by yourself."

"I don't think these guys are hungry anyhow. We can just skip the snack and go right to the campfire time. That's the real reason for the trip anyway, isn't it?" Todd brushed Christy's forehead with a kiss and took off with long strides toward the campfire, which was whipping about dangerously in the shrill desert wind. All the students were standing back at least five feet from the fire.

"Watch out for the sparks!" Matt motioned for the teens to step back even farther. "It's too windy to keep this going. We're going to have to put it out."

Even dousing the fire proved to be a challenge. The only water they had brought was in bottles sealed in plastic and shrink-wrapped in cardboard flats. The first three water bottles did little to calm the flames. Matt found a shovel and managed to put it out with scoops of desert dirt.

With the fire out, the night turned very dark, except for the Coleman lanterns near the tents.

"Look at the stars," one of the girls said.

Christy stood shivering, her chin tilted toward the heavens in silent awe of the thousands and thousands of glittering diamonds suspended in space.

"Hey, there's a shooting star!" someone called out.

Everyone joined in with his or her discoveries.

"Isn't that Orion's belt?"

"Can anyone see the Big Dipper?"

"What is that bright, blinking star over.there?"

"That's an airplane."

"No, it's not. It's a satellite."

"Where's the moon?"

Todd quoted several verses that Christy recognized from Psalm 8. " 'When I look up into the night skies and see the work of your fingers—the moon and the stars you have made—I cannot understand how you can bother with mere puny man, to pay any attention to him! And yet you have made him only a littler lower than the angels and placed a crown of glory and honor upon his head.' "

Christy was so absorbed in the canopy of wonder that she didn't notice Matt when he slid over next to her. "What was it you told me when we were watching the fireworks back in Wisconsin that summer?" he asked her. "Something about the one who rides across the ancient heavens. Your friend was writing a song about it, wasn't he?"

"I'm surprised you remembered that," Christy said.

"Did he ever finish the song?"

"Yes, it's from Psalm 68." Christy began to sing Doug's song softly.

" 'Sing to the One

Who rides across the ancient heavens
His mighty voice thundering from the sky
For God is awesome in His sanctuary.' "

Katie joined her and so did Todd. When they finished singing, one of the girls said, "Sing it again." This time, as they sang, several of the teens joined them. It seemed like a wonderful, holy moment until Christy noticed several of the guys slipping away from the rest of the group. She tapped Matt's shoulder and pointed. He took off after them.

It turned out to be that kind of night. The group ended their impromptu song time when several of the girls declared they were too cold and made a dash for their tent. Then the girls tried to sabotage the inside of the guys' tent. Matt caught them, and Todd gave the group stern instructions about how he expected them to act. Stern for Todd, at least. It didn't turn out to be stern enough for two of the younger guys, who tried to sneak out again after everyone was supposed to be zipped up in the tents.

Todd was helping Christy cover the boxes of food with a tarp to keep out sand and desert critters, when the guys tried to escape. Todd turned his flashlight on them, and they slipped back into their tent.

Christy had a hard time falling asleep. She was warm enough because she had made sure she wore sufficient layers of clothes, and she had a decent air mattress under her sleeping bag. But she kept listening for the sound of a tent zipper and wondered if Todd was going to have to sit up all night on guard duty.

The morning sun rousted all of them as soon as it appeared because the penetrating heat immediately warmed the tents. Christy hadn't spent much time in the desert and was surprised at how far she could see when she looked out across the sand. Aside from an occasional cactus lifting its two arms, as if frozen in time like an Old West bank teller in a holdup, she could see nothing for miles in any direction.

The air warmed quickly, and Christy felt her skin drying and tightening. The wind was gone this morning. Her extra layers of clothes quickly became too hot, and she peeled down to a T-shirt and shorts.

"I'm impressed," Katie told Christy after they had fed the group and were putting away what was left of the cereal and milk.

"Impressed with what?" Christy asked.

"You. Look how happy and organized you are. This is a big improvement over our camping trip last summer."

"You said the key word," Todd said, reaching into the back of Matt's truck for his guitar. "Organized. Christy likes being prepared."

"Yeah, well, she could teach you a thing or two," Katie said. "What about that shade you promised?"

"Matt is working on it with the tarps over behind the biggest tent. We're going to sing and have our morning devotions, and then we're going to take the dune buggies out for a spin."

Christy finished cleaning up and joined the others. Her favorite part of any camping trip was the chance to sing with the group. It turned out to be a short string of songs because it was getting so hot, and only a few of the kids were singing.

As Todd taught, holding his Bible open and standing

before the group, Christy glanced at the teens. A few of them really were listening. Mostly the girls.

These guys don't know what a gift Todd is to them. He really cares about them. He'll be their friend for the rest of their lives, if they'll let him. And what he's telling them right now is the truth. They do need to trust God in every area of their lives. Why aren't they soaking up his words? It could mean the difference between life and death for some of these guys!

Christy decided to pray. She had been doing that a lot lately. Ever since that first Sunday morning when Gus broke down on the way to church, she realized they were fighting a battle with invisible enemies for these teens' souls. As she felt the sun pouring over her right shoulder and burning her forearm, Christy adjusted her position so the sun was to her back and kept on praying for Todd.

"Let me leave you with this thought," Todd said in conclusion. "None of us knows when his life will come to an end, and he will stand before Almighty God. The Bible says that to be absent from the body is to be present with the Lord. Each of us will stand before God one day. Not Saint Peter at a golden gate. Not in front of a clerk at a desk like you see on TV. We will stand before the Lord."

Christy began to look around the circle and prayed for each student, even though she didn't remember all their names.

"The Lord Jesus Christ will hold out His hands to you, and you will see the scars that are still there two thousand years after He died in your place. He will say to you, 'Come on in. I've been waiting for you, my friend. The relationship we started when you were on earth can now be made complete here in my home.' Or He will say, 'I invited you to come to me, but your whole life you pushed me away. Now it's too late. You didn't want me so now you will spend eternity separated from me.' "

Christy noticed how quiet the group had become. All eyes were on Todd.

"What's it going to take for you to come to Him? Don't wait. Nobody knows when he will die. And once it's over, it's just begun. Either you'll spend eternity with Christ in heaven or eternity without Him in the place He made for the demons, those fallen angels who turned from Him."

Todd paused a moment, then added, "What's it going to be for you? Heaven is a very real place. And so is hell."

The two troublemaking guys snickered, but everyone else sat still. Todd closed the time in prayer. Instead of saying "Let it be so" at the end, he concluded the prayer in a way Christy had never heard before. "As you wish," Todd said. The group wasn't sure the prayer was over yet.

Once they figured out that they were done, the teens took off for the recreation vehicles and spent the rest of the day doing what Katie called "frolicking." They took turns going out into the desert flatness in the various vehicles Todd had arranged for the trip.

Christy stayed at the camp, and close to noon, she talked two of the girls who were there into helping her to make peanut butter sandwiches so the food would be ready for whoever wanted them after the runs in the sand.

The dry heat dried the sandwiches so quickly that all the bread was as stiff as toast within minutes after the peanut butter and grape jelly were spread on them. Christy tried stuffing the sandwiches back into the plastic bags as soon as they were made, and that seemed to help. The good thing was that Todd had bought so much bread and so much peanut butter that even if they had to toss out the entire first batch of sandwiches, Christy knew no one in the group would go hungry this day.

Around four o'clock, when the wind was returning and the blazing heat had subsided, Todd drove into camp in one of the vehicles, saying he needed to take the can of gas out to Katie, who was stranded in Baby Hummer. "Do you want to go with me?"

"Sure," Christy said. For a moment, she was reminded of when she and Todd had taken Aunt Marti for a boat ride, and they had run out of gas. A darling girl on a Jet Ski had come to their rescue. Christy had always wished she were the girl on the Jet Ski instead of being the one who was stuck in the stalled boat with her aggravated aunt.

Christy wondered what was happening with Bob and Marti. She had mentally pushed away their situation, but as soon as she thought about it again, she felt a sickening heaviness. If she couldn't talk to anyone else about Marti's decision, then Christy needed to talk to her aunt, and the sooner the better. She decided she would call her aunt right after the camping trip. What Christy would say was another matter, but at least she would open up the subject again.

Todd fastened the gas can with bungee cords to the back of the two-seater dune buggy and told Christy to buckle up. Then with a jerk and a roar, they took off across the sand. Christy held on tight to the side of the roll bar and clenched her teeth to keep from biting her tongue. Every bone in her body felt as if it was being jolted and jarred beyond anything any of them had experienced before. She turned to Todd and smiled, her teeth still clenched.

He shifted gears and roared on.

Talking to him was impossible. It was far too noisy. Understanding him might be another impossibility.

What does he see in this? It's kind of fun, but it's mostly uncomfortable.

They arrived at the spot where Katie was waiting with two of the girls in Baby Hummer. They were laughing about something when Todd cut the engine and it became quiet enough to hear.

Katie came over and gave Christy a friendly punch in the arm. "Isn't this fun? I love it." Katie's face was red from sunburn or windburn or both. Her long-sleeved T-shirt was streaked with dirt. Only a few flyaway wisps of her short hair had dared to peek out from under her baseball cap.

"Have you driven this thing yet?" Katie asked.

Christy shook her head.

"You want to drive Baby Hummer?"

"No, that's okay."

"You're good to go," Todd said, strapping the empty can to the back of the dune buggy.

"Great," Katie said. "Thanks for bringing the gas to us." She turned to settle back into Baby Hummer's front seat but then turned to Todd and said, "Make sure Christy drives that buggy."

"You want to drive?" Todd asked Christy.

"No, that's okay."

"You sure?" His expression was classic Todd as he stood there, eyebrows slightly raised, dimple showing on the right side of his cheek. Christy was flooded with memories of other times he had given her that look, and she always had tried whatever he was willing to teach her, from surfing on a body board to water-skiing. The only time he had given her that look and she had turned him down was when he had asked her to go "to the ends of the earth" last summer to the Arctic Circle. Todd had gone on the train alone while Christy and Katie traveled to Copenhagen. More than once she had regretted missing the experience of seeing a polar bear with Todd.

"You know what?" Christy said. "Why not? Tell me what to do." She didn't know why her heart was beating so fast. She trusted Todd enough to take this chance with him, and she felt as if she was ready for anything.

CHRISTY AND TODD
THE COLLEGE YEARS

Todd hustled around to the passenger side of the dune
buggy and belted himself in while Christy
settled into the driver's seat. He gave her a
quick run-through of the gears and the way
the clutch tended to stick. Katie had taken
off in Baby Hummer, so the desert was silent when Christy
turned the key to start the deep, rumbling engine. She
stalled it three times. Todd patiently explained what to do,
and on the fourth try, they took off, jostling their way back
toward camp.

"Okay, now!" Todd yelled. "Next gear."

Christy shifted, gave it gas, and shifted again. A bubbling
sense of delight started in her gut as she pressed her foot to
the gas. The delight surfaced in a burst of laughter as they
bounced over the ruts in the sand and plowed across the
Mojave Desert. She hadn't driven with Todd beside her since
the bridge in Hana.

"This is fun!" she yelled, giving the vehicle more gas and
becoming braver with her steering. She glanced at Todd. His
smile spread from one side of his face to the other. It looked
like he was laughing, but she couldn't hear him.

With a variety of twists and turns, Christy invented her own trail back to camp. A guy from their group roared past them in a one-person vehicle, with Matt following him in another one-seater. Christy tried to wave. When she took her hand off the steering wheel, she hit a rut and stalled the engine. Suddenly silence prevailed. Christy turned to Todd, who was still grinning, and then she burst out laughing, throwing her head back and bumping it on the roll bar.

"Ouch!" she hollered, rubbing her head and trying to blink back the tears that sprang to her eyes.

"You okay?" Todd asked. He sounded so compassionate.

"I bumped my head." Christy laughed at her klutziness.

Todd reached over and rubbed the tender spot.

"Ow!"

"Do you want to keep driving?" he asked.

"Maybe you better in case I have a delayed concussion," Christy said.

Todd looked at her skeptically.

She laughed again and said, "I'm only kidding!" She grinned at him, and when she did, she met his screaming, silver-blue-eyed gaze. He was looking at her "that way" again.

In one lightning-bolt second, a life-changing thought seared into Christy's thoughts. *He's the one!*

Christy could barely breathe. *Todd, you are the one for me.*

She felt as if the whole world had stopped twirling, and she and Todd were the only two people on the face of the earth. *You are the one for me. And I'm the one for you, aren't I? This is it! My grandma was right. I know! I really, truly know!*

Todd climbed out of the vehicle to change places with her. Christy felt as if everything was in slow motion as she got out. They met at the back of the dune buggy, where

Todd grabbed her by the shoulders and brushed her cheek with a kiss before dashing around to take his place in the driver's seat.

Christy stood still. She knew something strange and wonderful had happened in her heart. She never would have expected it to happen now, in a place like this. But she knew this was the mysterious "it" she had waited for. She had to tell Todd she was in love with him.

No, she needed to tell Todd that she was more than in love with him. She had to tell him that she loved him. Truly loved him. And she gladly would commit to loving him for the rest of her life. No matter where they lived, or what they did, or how their lives turned out, Christy knew—absolutely knew, without a shadow of a doubt—that she wanted to be Todd's companion, friend, wife, and the mother of his children for as long as they both shall live.

Christy felt her heart pounding up to her throat as she watched him fasten his seat belt. His back was to her, but Christy knew she couldn't wait another minute to make her declaration, her commitment known. "Todd!" she called out.

He had just turned the key in the ignition, and the rumbling engine's noise drowned out Christy's voice.

"I love you!" she yelled.

Todd couldn't hear her.

Christy smiled to herself. *This is so ironic.* She went around to the passenger's seat, settled in, and buckled her seat belt. Todd punched the engine into gear.

It's enough that I know for sure right now. I'll wait until a more romantic time and place to tell him. And when I tell him, he will hear me all the way to the very core of his heart.

With a lion-sized roar, they took off across the desert.

Christy watched for a second opportunity to make her declaration known to Todd. As she was fixing the evening meal, she let her giddy imagination examine every possible way she could communicate with him. One crazy idea was to write the words on paper towels with the mustard bottle and hang the message inside Gus from the plastic hangers. But someone else might see it, and this was just between her and Todd.

More important, Christy decided as she lay awake in her tent that night, when she told Todd she loved him, she needed to tell him with her voice. He needed to hear the words, not just to read them.

Sunday morning was cooler than Saturday because a thin layer of clouds had drawn themselves over the sky like a sheer mosquito netting gathered over a bed in the tropics. And like a weary safari assistant tucked safely under that mosquito netting, Christy didn't want to get up. She ached, was tired, and dearly wished she could stand under a warm shower to revive herself slowly.

A shower came, but it wasn't warm. Great drops of rain splashed on the group gathered for morning worship. The sprinkling lasted only a moment. Then the sun shone through and instantly dried everything. Christy looked at her arm. It was as if the rain's objective was to turn the dirt on her skin into mud and then to send the sun to bake the mud on permanently.

None of them had to be coaxed to tear down the tents and clean up. Matt joined Christy as she tried to yank two tent poles apart.

"Let me try," he said. With a twist, he had them separated.

"Thanks," Christy said. "It's as if the dirt turned to glue

when the rain hit it. Can you give that pole over there a try?"

Matt succeeded to divide that pole, as well. He came back over to Christy, looking as if he was checking to see if anyone was close enough to hear them. "Can I talk to you a minute?"

"Sure." Christy kept working on tearing down the tent.

"Over here." Matt motioned for her to follow him to the back of his truck. "I know this may sound like we're back in elementary school, but I have to ask you something." He kept his voice low. "Do you think Katie is, you know, interested in me?"

Christy felt funny talking to Matt about this. "I think you should talk to her about that," Christy answered. "I mean, I thought you and Katie were getting pretty close. You two have been together a lot." The truth was, she didn't know. But she didn't want to tell Matt that.

Matt looked hard at Christy. As he did, his eyebrows pushed inward. "Does it look like we're together? Because I didn't mean to give that impression to her or anyone else."

Christy felt sorry for her best friend. Had Matt been leading Katie on? Was Katie expecting the relationship to be more than it was?

"You and Katie just need to find a time and place to talk privately about all this." Christy lightly touched Matt's arm.

Just then one of the high school girls stepped over toward them, oblivious to the privacy of their conversation. She asked Matt if he could come help her with the tent.

Christy looked over her shoulder toward the main camping area and saw that Katie was watching them.

"Thanks for the advice." Matt placed his hand on

Christy's shoulder and gave her a big smile. "I appreciate you, Christy."

That evening, after the group returned to the church and began to unpack the gear, Katie asked Christy, "So what were you and Matt talking about this afternoon?"

Christy knew anyone could easily overhear their conversation, so she said, "I'll tell you later."

———————

They didn't reach their dorm room until almost eleven-thirty, and Christy was exhausted. She gathered her shampoo and soap to indulge in the long-awaited shower. But before she could leave the room, Katie said, "Oh, Chester, you poor little thing. Look, Christy, Chester went belly up, too."

"Did you feed him too much?"

"I don't think I fed him enough. Or maybe the bowl got too much direct sun from the window. The water feels pretty warm." Katie scooped up the lifeless creature and followed Christy to the rest room to conduct what she called "burial at sea."

"I'll buy two goldfish tomorrow," Katie said. "I think Chester died of loneliness since we were gone all weekend."

"Katie, you're going to end up spending so much money on goldfish. If you're buying more than two, you're better off with an aquarium instead of that small bowl."

"*Now* you tell me all this." Katie placed her hand over her heart and had a personal moment of silence before sending Chester to the "Great Goldfish Pond Beyond the Sewer."

Christy shook her head and entered the shower, where the warm water felt heavenly.

Katie stood outside the shower stall and said, "So are you going to tell me what Matt said to you this afternoon? Or do I have to figure it out for myself by trial and error, as well?

Christy had hoped for five minutes of privacy and silence under the shower. She had dreams of Todd to tend to. However, she knew Katie wouldn't leave her in peace until Christy answered her every question.

"I think I'll take a shower while I'm here, too." Katie's voice was now coming from the shower stall next to Christy's. Katie raised her voice over the rush of water from both showers. "Let me borrow your shampoo. And do you have any soap over there?"

Christy handed Katie her soap and shampoo and finished her shower in much shorter time than she had planned. "I'm going back to the room," she said.

"Don't fall asleep," Katie warned. "I'll be right there."

Changing into her favorite pajamas, Christy brushed and dried her hair. Katie returned and got ready for bed, as well, but the dryer's noise made it impossible for them to talk. So Christy was tucked in her bed before she divulged her information to Katie.

"Matt and I talked about you," Christy said.

"Me? What did he say?"

"I told him he needed to talk to you."

"And what did he say to that?"

Christy paused. "Katie, do you like Matt a lot?"

Katie's expression became pinched. "No," she said slowly. "I know you probably can't believe this, after the way I made such a dramatic scene out of seeing him again this year. But now that I've had a chance to get to know him, I don't think there's anything between us."

"You don't?" Christy hadn't expected that response.

"I know, I know. I was so flipped out about him, but I was never so wrong about anything in my life. I think Matt is a great guy and a good friend. I just don't feel anything more for him." Katie roughed up her short hair with a bath towel and let the feathery ends fall where they may.

"I think the image of him was what I had the crush on, you know?" Katie said. "The safe, friendly boy next door who loves baseball and apple pie and eventually would decide he loved me." Katie came over and settled herself on the end of Christy's bed. "Tell me he doesn't have a big crush on me."

The words popped out of Christy's mouth. "Matthew Kingsley does not have a big crush on you."

Katie snapped to an upright position and looked hurt. "He doesn't?"

Christy wished she had been less direct. Slowly shaking her head, Christy said, "He told me he's only interested in you as a friend. I'm sorry."

"Why do you keep apologizing for stuff that isn't your fault? This is good, actually," Katie said. "I was afraid he was going to ask me to spend more time with him, and I was trying to figure out how to turn him down nicely."

"Then I guess it's a good thing," Christy said. "You two can keep being friends, and the three of us can keep helping Todd with the youth group. You and Matt can skip that whole 'Are we a couple?' phase of your friendship." Feeling as if the matter was sufficiently settled, Christy dove under her covers.

Katie wasn't about to let the subject end there. "What about you?"

"What about me?"

"What's happening with you and Todd?"

"We're in love," Christy said brightly. "My heart is completely settled. I love him. And I told him."

"You did?" Katie's eyes grew wide.

"But Todd couldn't hear me because the noise from the dune buggy was so loud." Christy chuckled at herself. "Typical, huh?"

"So Todd doesn't know," Katie surmised.

"Not yet."

"Christy, how can you do that to the poor guy? Go call him right now and let him hear you say you love him. He's been waiting long enough."

"It's the middle of the night!" Christy protested. "I don't want to tell him over the phone. I want to say it to his face so he can see I mean it."

"Hey! That's like that line from the John Donne poem." Katie sprang over to her desk and lifted the literature textbook she had been reading before they left for the camping trip. "Have you read this section yet on John Donne?"

"Yes." Christy and Katie were taking the lit class together.

"Did you read this one? Listen. This is from the poem called 'The Good Morrow.' "

"My face in thine eye, thine in mine appears,
And true plain hearts do in the faces rest;
Where can we find two better hemispheres,
Without sharp North, without declining West?"

Katie looked up from the book with a glow on her face. "Isn't that romantic?"

Christy loved poetry and usually was the one to present Katie with lyrical gems. She wasn't sure what this one meant.

"That's you and Todd," Katie said. "You are two true plain hearts. You balance each other perfectly with your differences. You round each other out."

Christy smiled. Her heart felt full. She knew all over again that she was in love. Forever-after kind of love.

"Do me a personal favor," Katie said. "If you won't call Todd tonight, call him first thing in the morning, okay?"

"I'll see him at breakfast."

"Then you better tell him at breakfast. I don't think the actual setting is going to matter to Todd when his 'face in thine eye and thine in his appears.' You don't need to wait for the perfect romantic setting with the sun shining and the birds singing and all that. You just need to tell Todd that you love him." Katie pointed to the title of the John Donne poem and with a twinkle in her eye said, "Tell him on the 'Good Morrow.'"

———————

Monday morning Christy waited for Todd at their usual table in the cafeteria. When he didn't show, she guessed he had slept in after the exhausting weekend. She wished she didn't have an early class so she could have done the same.

Hurrying so she wouldn't be late to class, Christy settled into her seat just as Dr. Mitchell was discussing blessings. He read Deuteronomy 28:2, which Christy turned to and underlined in her Bible. "And all these blessings shall come upon you and overtake you, if you will obey the voice of the Lord your God."

I want always to obey you, Christy silently prayed. *Let me hear your voice clearly. I want to always do what you direct me to do.*

Very softly, very clearly, as soon as she finished her prayer, Christy felt compelled to find Todd and to give him her words, her heart, her blessing. But she stayed in her seat, logically evaluating that she should wait. She was paying for this class. She was here. She shouldn't leave.

I mean, really, God. It doesn't make sense that you would want me to ditch class to find Todd and tell him I love him.

Christy ignored the promptings she was feeling and stayed in her seat. The longer she sat still, the more her heart pounded. It seemed to be pounding so fiercely that Christy thought for sure the people around her could hear it. She thought of how Sierra had said a few weeks ago that love isn't always planned and logical.

Compelled by something stronger than her logic, Christy finally clutched her backpack and exited as quietly as she could. As soon as she was outside the air-conditioned building, she felt she could breathe again.

Now what? What next, Father?

Christy suddenly felt foolish. Her declaration to Todd could wait at least until that afternoon. She was missing important information in class. Besides, she had no idea where Todd was. If he wasn't asleep in his room, she could search the campus all morning and still not find him.

This is crazy!

Christy hiked all the way to West Hall, the guys' dorm,

and called Todd's room. His voice mail answered, just as she had expected. He might still be asleep. Or he could be in The Golden Calf. Or in the library or a dozen other places on campus.

Trudging back toward class, Christy realized she only had twenty minutes before her next class started. Todd knew she worked in the bookstore that afternoon; he would probably come see her there. She could stand with him at the end of the row of used theology books because that part of the store smelled more "bookish" than any other spot. There she would look into his eyes and make her heart's declaration known in hushed whispers that would sink all the way to the bottom of his heart. All the way down to that place where he dove for treasure. A smile played across her lips, just imagining the romance of that moment.

Christy passed The Java Jungle and went inside, just in case Todd was there. She didn't see him, but she saw another couple sitting close and studying together in one of the booths.

Something continued to push Christy to find her beloved, but she fought against it. The reasonable thing to do would be to check her mailbox and then go to her next class.

But her heart wouldn't stop pounding. Picking up her pace, Christy dashed through the student center. She slipped into the cafeteria. He wasn't there.

She checked out all the places they usually went to talk: the couch in the music building, the library, the chapel. She now was late for her second class, but she didn't care.

As fast as she could trot, she hurried to West Hall and

called his room again on the phone in the lobby. Once again she got his voice mail, but this time she left a message. "Todd, I have to see you right away. Where are you?"

Hurrying back to the student center, Christy walked through the building twice, scanning each face, begging Todd to be there. He wasn't. She finally went to the central plaza and sat on the edge of the fountain.

Where is he? Where could he be?

Kicking off her shoes and dipping her toes into the water, Christy remembered, for some reason, a portion of the Song of Solomon she had read last summer after Todd had gone back to California and she was still in Basel. Three or four times in that short book, located in the very heart of the Bible, Christy had underlined the repeated phrase, "Do not arouse or awaken love until it so desires."

That phrase had become her counsel to herself whenever she thought of Todd. They were so far apart that she knew it was useless to stir up or awaken those deep feelings within her or to dwell on them because she couldn't do anything about them. She had taken everything in stride, sending Todd e-mails and praying for him regularly. During this past month they had been together, Christy felt she still had done a good job of controlling her feelings and letting everything between her and Todd unfold calmly and naturally. But now it seemed love had indeed been stirred up and awakened inside her. She could barely think straight.

Did God literally have to knock me over the head to get me to release my true feelings for Todd?

Christy splashed her toes in the cool water. She felt like the woman in the Song of Solomon who ran around the town seeking her beloved but couldn't find him. She remembered something about the woman crying out to her friends, the Daughters of Jerusalem, and telling them that she was "sick with love."

I don't know if I'm sick yet, but I'm feeling something. I don't know what this feeling is.

Christy held her stomach and pulled her wet toes from the water, letting them air dry. Inside she ached. *Todd, where are you?*

Matt and several other guys she knew called out to her as they passed through the plaza.

"Matt," Christy cried out, "have you seen Todd?"

He left the others and came over to the fountain. "I haven't seen him since yesterday. I think he was going to return the tents this morning to whoever let us borrow them."

"Oh," Christy said, feeling herself calm down. "That makes sense. Thanks, Matt."

"Are you okay?" He sat beside her. "You look a little spooked."

"I've been trying to find Todd. I need to talk to him."

"Seems to be a lot of that going around," Matt said. "I thought about what you said at the camping trip yesterday, and you're right. I do need to talk to Katie before any misunderstandings start up between us."

Christy was about to say something general to Matt about how he didn't have to worry, but she noticed Katie pulling into a no-parking area in the lot and jumping out of Baby Hummer.

"It looks like you may have your chance soon enough." Christy waved to get Katie's attention.

Katie broke into a run as she came toward Matt and Christy.

"Is it my imagination," Matt said, "or does she look like she's about to strangle someone?"

Christy jumped to her feet. She had never seen Katie look like that before. "What's wrong?" Christy called out.

Katie rushed to Christy and grabbed her by the shoulders. Katie's skin was gray and perspiration poured from her face.

"What's wrong?" Matt was beside her now, too.

Katie gulped air. "Gus!" she spouted. "There's been an accident! Come on!" Katie grabbed Christy's arm, and the two of them ran to the parking lot. Matt was right behind them as they jumped into Baby Hummer.

"Katie," Matt said firmly, "what kind of accident? What did you see?"

"I saw them putting Todd in an ambulance."

CHRISTY AND TODD
THE COLLEGE YEARS

Christy and Matt pelted Katie with questions and yelled at
her to slow down as they zoomed through
town to the first freeway on-ramp. Katie
said she didn't know much more than the
half dozen words she had already offered
them. She had been driving back to school from the nursery
where she had gone to buy some fertilizer for her herbs.
When she had moved into the slow lane to take the off-
ramp to Rancho, she saw a vehicle that looked like Gus the
Bus smashed up. As she drove by, she saw the paramedics
wheeling someone into the ambulance.

"Was he moving?" Christy's fingers gouged into the passenger's seat.

"I couldn't tell. I just saw someone with blond hair being
rolled on the gurney into the ambulance." Katie started to
cry. "I'm going right to the hospital."

Christy's heart pounded fiercely as they entered the freeway. She heard herself say, "Calm down, Katie. Maybe it
wasn't Todd. Maybe it was a VW bus that just looked like
Gus. Maybe . . ."

But then she saw the tow truck on the other side of the

freeway and the smashed wreckage. Christy knew it was Gus. "Katie!" She covered her mouth in terror. "Katie, look!"

"Try to stay calm," Matt said firmly as Katie kept the steering wheel steady. "The hospital is about five more exits down."

"That stupid, stupid, stupid van!" Christy yelled. "Why didn't Todd trash that piece of junk years ago?" She closed her eyes and tried to swallow gulps of air.

"Pray!" Katie commanded. "Pray, you guys!"

Christy grabbed the seat cushion with both hands and squeezed with all her might as Matt began to pray aloud. Some of the terror siphoned from her shaking body. By the time Katie peeled into a parking space by the hospital's emergency entrance, Christy was trembling all over. She jumped out of the car and ran with Katie and Matt to the emergency room's desk.

Katie spoke first, articulating fairly well that they were checking to see if Todd Spencer had just been admitted after an auto accident.

The attendant went to check and left Christy and Katie holding each other and trembling.

"Yes," the attendant said as she came back around to the counter. "Todd Spencer is here."

"Is he . . ." Christy couldn't finish her sentence. She felt as if she might black out.

"How is he?" Katie kept a strong-armed grip around Christy's shoulders.

"I can't say." The clerk sat down and handed Christy a clipboard. "If you'd like to sign in, I'll have a doctor speak with you as soon as possible. You'll have to wait over there."

Christy had watched emergency-room shows on television, and somehow in her frantic state, she thought she should be allowed to go in, the way the television camera went behind the closed doors and did a close-up of the patient's face. She wanted to hear the assessment immediately. She wanted to help them save his life.

"Come on," Matt said. "We'll wait over here." He directed Christy and Katie to the waiting area. The three of them sat on an empty couch in the corner. None of them spoke.

Christy felt her head throbbing as she closed her eyes and saw the sight of Gus all over again. The roof had been smashed down, the sides bashed in, and glass was everywhere.

Don't take him to heaven, God! Please, not yet! Let me at least tell him I love him. He hasn't heard me say it yet. Let me at least tell him. She dissolved into a puddle of choking tears.

Katie braced Christy with her arm and kept murmuring, "Hold on. Keep praying. Keep praying."

Both of them managed to calm down. Christy realized for the first time that other people were in the waiting room, and she felt self-conscious about them watching her. Matt had gone to the edge of the waiting room and nervously paced, watching for the doctor. Christy turned to stare out the window at the parking lot, not saying anything. Her silent prayers became more coherent. God was with her. She knew that. She could feel His peace calming her.

"We should call his dad," Christy said. She knew Todd's phone number in Newport Beach by heart. She rose to find a phone. No one followed her, and she was glad because, for some reason, she thought she would be stronger if she was by herself. As she took each step toward the phone, she felt as if Jesus was walking right beside her.

The answering machine picked up the call, and Christy tried to calmly leave the appropriate information for Todd's dad. Her hand was shaking, and her voice quivered so much that she didn't know if she said everything correctly. If nothing else, his dad knew where they were.

Christy then called her parents. Her mom answered, and as soon as Christy heard her mom's voice, she cried again.

Matt had come over to the phone area. He placed his hand on Christy's shoulder and softly said, "Would you like me to talk to her?"

Christy nodded. The tears had drowned out her voice. Matt explained to Christy's mom that they were at the hospital waiting to hear from the doctor.

Christy could hear her mom's stunned voice through the receiver when she asked Matt, "Is Todd still alive?" For the first time Christy allowed the thought of his being dead to fully enter her mind. She backed up to the wall and pressed herself flat against it.

"We don't know yet," Christy heard Matt tell her mom. Then he said, "Yes, I think it would be good if you could come." He gave the name of the hospital and then hung up the phone.

"Is there anyone else we should call?" Matt asked.

"Uncle Bob," Christy said in a small voice. "Uncle Bob would want to be here." She dialed the number for Matt and let him relay all the information.

"Do you want to go back to the waiting room?" Matt asked.

Christy didn't answer him because she saw a doctor in a white coat heading in that direction. She hurried to catch up with him and asked if he had been taking care of Todd.

The doctor asked if they were friends or relatives.

"Friends," Christy and Matt said in unison.

"We called his dad," Christy said. "He wasn't there, but we left a message for him to come to the hospital."

"I see." The doctor looked at Matt and then at Christy. "I can tell you this. It's a miracle that he's alive."

Christy reached for Matt's hand and squeezed it with all her might.

"The paramedics said they had never seen anyone come out of such an accident alive. Apparently the van rolled three times. The roof and the driver's door and the whole front end were smashed, they said."

"Yes," Christy said nervously. "I saw the van. But how is Todd?"

The doctor looked over the top of his glasses at Christy. "We've moved him upstairs to surgery. My guess is it will be several hours before we can give a thorough assessment. Until then, if you or anyone else you know can donate blood, it looks like he's going to need it. I'll let you know when we learn more."

"Thank you," Christy said. She realized how tightly she had been squeezing Matt's hand. She let it go. "We better tell Katie."

The next two and a half hours floated past Christy in a haze. She found out from the nurse that Todd had type A blood. Christy also had type A, and so did Matt. Katie phoned a bunch of students at Rancho. Sierra and Wes arrived within twenty minutes and had eight other students with them.

They all donated their blood and then sat with Christy in the waiting room. Everyone had questions and speculations. Christy was beginning to feel irritated. They didn't have enough information to come up with so many solutions. She knew everyone was trying to help, but she was glad when her parents arrived, along with her thirteen-year-old brother, David. The three of them looked sick with worry. Christy hugged them and cried on her dad's shoulder.

Two more students from Rancho came, and Christy began to shiver from the chill of the air-conditioned building.

"Will you go outside with me?" Christy's brother asked. He had been standing quietly to the side, listening while all the others discussed the bits of information they had. Christy was glad for the chance to warm up and followed her brother into the autumn afternoon.

"Christy, I'm scared." David was five six, only an inch shorter than Christy. He had big hands and feet and thick, reddish hair like their father. He wore glasses and was now wiping away the embarrassing tears that he had managed to keep back in the waiting room.

"I am, too," Christy said, wrapping her arms around her brother. During the year she had been away, she had communicated with David only when necessary. The wide span in their ages had kept them from ever being close. But at this moment, Christy felt more like David's sister than she ever had before.

David adored Todd. He had for the past five years. Often when Todd came to see Christy at her parents' house, Todd would end up spending just as much time with David as with Christy. Sometimes Christy thought Todd had been a better sibling to David than she had. "Do you think Todd is going to live?" David asked.

"I don't know." Christy held her brother close. "I've been

praying. You heard how the doctor said it was a miracle he was alive."

"If Todd dies, he's going to heaven," David said. It was a statement, not a question. It sounded exactly the way Todd would have said it.

"Yes."

"I know because he told me. He told me lots of times that I needed to give my life to God so that, when I died, I'd go to heaven, too, and then we'd be there together. Todd said we'd build a skateboard ramp if they didn't already have one."

Christy swallowed hard and silently prayed, *Not yet, Father. Please. Don't take Todd yet. Let him build a few more skateboard ramps here first. Let him keep telling kids like my brother that they need to get their lives right with you.*

"I never did it yet." David pulled away and looked at Christy. "I never prayed and turned my life over to Jesus."

Christy had been fourteen when she had realized she wasn't a Christian simply because she had grown up going to church with her family. This was the first time it occurred to her that her brother was almost the same age.

"Are you ready to make that decision?" Christy asked.

David nodded. "I want to. I want to pray right now. Will you pray with me?"

Christy felt her throat tighten and tears rush to her eyes. "Of course," she said in a small voice.

"What do I say?"

"Just say whatever is on your heart. God knows what you're thinking, David. He knows that you're choosing to believe in Him. Now tell Him just that and receive His gift of forgiveness and eternal life."

Christy closed her eyes and bowed her head. David

prayed four or five short, no-nonsense phrases stating that he believed Jesus was God's only Son and that he wanted Jesus to forgive his sins and come in and take over his life. When David ended his prayer with the words "Let it be so," Christy knew David had heard Todd pray more than once.

As she opened her eyes, Christy drew in a deep breath. "You've just been adopted into God's family." A smile came to her tense lips, despite all the trauma of the past hour. "I'm really happy for you, David. Todd will be thrilled." The tears wove their way down Christy's cheeks all over again.

David nodded. "I want to tell Todd I finally did it."

"Maybe they'll let us see him soon. Come on." Christy put her arm around her brother and walked back into the waiting room. She felt stunned and amazed at what had just happened.

"Any word?" Christy asked.

Her mom shook her head. "Your father went to give blood in case they need more."

"I want to give my blood, too," David said.

Mom looked surprised. "You're too young, honey. Even with our consent, you have to be sixteen."

David looked a little disappointed.

"I'm sure your dad could use a little moral support," Mom said. "Let's go find him."

After Christy's mom and brother left the waiting room, Christy thought about what had just happened. She turned to Katie. "My brother gave his life to the Lord when we went outside." Her voice held little emotion because she had so little left to give.

"That's incredible." Katie spoke in a monotone, as well. "How did that happen?"

"Todd has been talking to him about the Lord for a long

time. I guess David wanted to finally make a firm decision. I wish I could feel as happy as I should about it."

Just then a tall, broad-shouldered man with thinning blond hair, wearing a Hawaiian-print shirt, entered the waiting room with Christy's uncle Bob. She had seen Todd's father only once or twice before, but Christy rushed to him and hugged him before she hugged Uncle Bob.

"What have you heard?" Uncle Bob asked. He lived a few blocks from Todd's dad, and apparently the two men had come together.

Christy gave them the rundown and had just finished when the doctor entered the waiting area. He spotted Christy and went to her first.

"This is Todd's dad," Christy said to the doctor.

"Bryan," Todd's father said, shaking hands with the doctor. "Bryan Spencer. How is he?"

"I'm Dr. Johannes. Todd is coming out of surgery right now. We were quite fortunate in that we were able to locate the bleeding right away. He had a perforated colon. The surgeon repaired it and went ahead and removed his appendix because it was swollen. That may or may not be a result of the accident. Everything else looks good. We put quite a few stitches in his hands, and he may need a few more after they get the rest of the glass out."

"He's going to be okay, isn't he?" Katie blurted out.

"I can't guarantee that," Dr. Johannes said. "He's lost a lot of blood, but amazingly, he didn't break any bones. We'll be able to make a better diagnosis in the morning. He'll be in the recovery room for at least another hour or two."

"Can I see him?" Todd's dad asked.

The doctor checked the chart one more time before nodding. "Yes, he's still sedated, of course, so he won't know you're there. But, yes. You can go see him. No more than two visitors, okay?"

Dr. Johannes turned to go and then came back and added in a low voice, looking over the top of his glasses at Todd's dad. "His face is pretty swollen from the impact of the crash. He has a black eye, and they haven't cleaned the blood out of his hair yet. I wanted to tell so you'd know he really is better off than he looks."

Bryan Spencer nodded. Then he turned to Christy and gave her a tentative look. "Would you like to go with me?"

Christy wasn't sure if she was being included because he was hesitant to see Todd by himself or because he knew how much it meant for her to see Todd right away. Christy instinctively linked her arm in his and walked down the hall to the hospital elevator. Bryan's arm was trembling. She knew they needed each other to be strong for what they were about to face.

The nurse on duty in the recovery room led them to where Todd lay on his back with a white sheet covering most of his body. Both arms were on top of the sheet, and several tubes were connected to his right arm. A soft, fluorescent light above the bed flickered on his face, revealing the black eye and swollen mouth as well as the ugly black stitches in his hands, just as Dr. Johannes had described them. Todd wore what looked like a paper shower cap on his head. Christy could see the dark bloodstains in his hair showing through. It took everything within her not to burst into tears at the sight.

"Hey, son," Bryan Spencer's deep voice spoke over Todd. "It's Dad." His voice quavered. He moved closer and touched Todd gently on his left shoulder. It seemed to be about the only part of Todd's body that wasn't bloodied or stitched up or connected to some tube. "The doctor says you're doing good, son. You rest, okay?"

Todd didn't respond.

"Christy's here. She wants to talk to you." He stepped back and let Christy move in next to the bed.

All she could hear were the beeping, ticking, humming sounds of the machines as Todd lay motionless beneath the dull light that kept flickering. Christy wanted to take Todd in her arms and hold him. Her sense of mercy overwhelmed her to the point she had no more tears.

Reaching for his left hand, Christy carefully lifted it. She noticed four places where a series of stitches threaded his skin together. His hand felt cool and heavy. She gently gave it a squeeze. There was no response.

"Todd," she whispered, leaning close, "I'm here with your dad." She raised her voice a little. "We've all been praying for you, Todd. The doctor says you're doing well. They said they would know more after you get some sleep. So don't worry about trying to talk to us. Just sleep, Todd."

Christy drew his heavy hand to her lips and kissed the back of it in between the black suture thread they had used to sew him up after pulling out the shards of windshield glass.

"I have a lot to tell you when you wake up, Todd, so get lots of sleep, okay?" Christy kissed his hand again. She turned to Todd's dad, who stood behind her, pressing his lips together.

"Do you think it would be okay if I stayed here with him?" Christy asked.

"I don't know the hospital rules. Would you like me to ask?"

Christy nodded. "If you need to get back home tonight, I can stay. I'd like to stay."

Mr. Spencer slipped around the other side of the sliding white curtain. Christy could hear him talking to the nurse. She was saying that they prefer not to have people wait in the recovery area, since the space is so limited and the patients often become ill when the anesthesia wears off. She said they would be better off in the waiting room, and when Todd was transferred to a room, the staff would let them know.

Christy kissed Todd tenderly on his swollen cheek and said she would see him later. Joining Todd's dad, she returned to the waiting room, where the two of them reported to the others. After hearing the news, Matt and most of the students left. They told Christy to keep them updated. Katie and Uncle Bob had gone to buy drinks for everyone. That left Christy's parents, Todd's dad, and Christy's brother, David.

"Is he unconscious?" David asked, sidling up to Christy while their parents talked with Todd's dad.

"I don't think so. The anesthesia will wear off soon, and 13I would guess that by morning he will be able to talk to you."

"Did you tell him? About what I did? About how we prayed?" David asked.

"Not yet. Would you like me to tell him or do you want to tell him when he's awake?"

"I heard Dad say that we're going to go now since we can't do anything. I guess you better tell Todd."

"Okay." Christy smiled at her brother. "I'll tell him. And, David?"

He stopped and let Christy put her arms around him and

hug him. "I'm really happy for you." She kissed David on the cheek and said softly in his ear, "You made the most important decision of your life today, and I'm so glad I got to be with you when you did."

He looked like he was dying to wipe her kiss off his cheek but was trying hard to be mature about all this. "Thanks," he said awkwardly.

Then, because Christy felt as if she had made the biggest mistake of her life by not leaving class and running to find Todd to tell him that she loved him, she said, "I love you, David." She decided right then and there that she would never pass up the opportunity to tell the really important people in her life that she loved them.

When her parents were ready to leave, Christy said, "I love you, Mom," and kissed her on the cheek.

"I love you, Dad." Christy hugged him, and he kissed the top of her head.

"Call us in the morning," Dad said. "And if you need anything, or if there's any change, we'll come right back."

"Okay. Thanks, Dad."

"Try to sleep," Mom said.

Katie and Uncle Bob arrived with several cans of soda pop. "Where did everybody go?" Katie asked.

"Home," Christy said. "You can go, too, if you want. I'm going to stay."

"I'll stay with you," Katie offered.

"Are you staying, Bryan?" Uncle Bob asked Todd's dad.

He nodded and took one of the cans of pop that Katie had placed on the coffee table in the waiting room. "At least until he comes out of the anesthesia. If you need to go, Bob, I can make other arrangements to get home."

"Don't think twice about it," Bob said. "I'm happy to

stay. I'd like to." He put his arm around Christy and gave her a sideways hug. "I don't get to see my favorite niece enough these days. I'll take any excuse I can."

Christy wrapped both her arms around her kindhearted uncle and said, "I love you, Uncle Bob. Have I ever told you that? I don't know if I ever have. I love you."

Tears welled up in Bob's eyes. "I love you, too, honey."

Christy didn't know if she imagined it, but Bob's body seemed to flinch when he looked up. Christy followed his gaze and then heard a familiar voice. Then she knew why Uncle Bob had flinched.

"But I am a relative," Christy heard the voice stating emphatically. "I don't understand why I'm not able to see Todd Spencer immediately." No one had as much of an edge to her voice as Aunt Marti did when she was pushing her agenda to the limit.

Christy took off in step with Uncle Bob, and the two of them headed for the front reception desk, leaving Katie alone with Todd's dad. But the two of them followed right behind.

Christy thought she was prepared to face her flamboyant aunt. The hair or the clothes wouldn't shock Christy. Not even Marti's lie about being Todd's relative was a surprise. Marti was a woman who got what she wanted, even if she had to rewrite the rules.

But what Christy wasn't prepared for was the huge man with the copper-colored skin and flowing white hair who towered over Marti as if he were her self-appointed guardian angel.

"Hello, Marti." Bob stood his ground less than a yard away from her.

"Robert?" She looked surprised to see him there.

"Who's that?" Katie whispered under her breath as she stepped up next to Christy.

Christy knew the answer, but she kept her lips sealed. After all, a promise was a promise. It would be up to her very startled aunt Martha to introduce Cheyenne to the rest of them.

CHRISTY AND TODD
THE COLLEGE YEARS

I came as soon as I heard the message on the voice mail."

13 Marti flew to Bob's side and kissed the air next to his ear. She gave Christy the same treatment and then took her by the arms. "How is Todd? Is he going to make it? I was a wreck all the way here."

"The doctor says it looks promising," Todd's dad said. "I'm Bryan Spencer, Todd's father. I don't think we've met."

"Marti," she said, shaking hands. "And don't you look just like Todd! I'm so delighted to meet you." With her left hand Marti made a funny flipping gesture as if shooing away a troublesome gnat.

Christy watched Cheyenne. He stayed back, his expression perplexed. He didn't seem to understand why Marti was signaling for him to leave in her unsubtle way. At that moment, Marti's "aura" wasn't in harmony with anyone else's in the room.

"Hi," Katie said openly to Cheyenne. She waved at him and smiled as if he were just too shy to join them.

That was the only invitation Cheyenne needed to step forward.

"This is my pottery instructor," Marti explained quickly. "I had a class this afternoon, and I was so shaken by the news of Todd that Cheyenne graciously offered to drive me here."

Cheyenne turned to Bob, and the two of them nodded formally, as if they had met before.

"Todd is still in the recovery room," Uncle Bob said with a calm, even meter to his words. "They're going to let us know when we can see him, but it might be a while. If you'd like to go home, I'll be glad to call you with an update once we know something."

"Are all of you staying?" Marti's words were crisp.

"Yes," Bob answered, still sounding controlled.

It seemed that Christy's poor aunt didn't know what to do.

"Has everyone eaten?" Marti asked. Again the words were staccato. The familiar tactic almost made Christy smile. This was the approach to solving problems that Marti and Christy's mother both had learned back on the farm.

Christy had recognized it in herself that night in The Java Jungle when Matt said he had just arrived from Wisconsin. Her first thought was to feed him. Now she realized her aunt could play the role of sophisticated Newport Beach socialite or go completely organic—as was her current state—and play the role of Mother Earth's personal shopper. But the truth was, deep down, Marti was a farm girl from Wisconsin. For some reason, that insight doused Christy with pity for her aunt.

Katie answered for all four of them. "No, we haven't eaten. We bought some drinks out of the machine a few minutes ago, but we didn't want to be away from the waiting room too long."

"Then I'll get food for everyone," Marti announced. "Any allergies or special diets?"

When no one responded, she quickly said, "Good. I'll be back in no time." Turning on her heel, she marched out of the building. Cheyenne nodded at Christy and the others as a farewell gesture before following after Marti and her long, swishing hair.

"Someone better call the laboratory," Katie muttered after they had left the building.

"Why?" Christy asked.

"We need to tell them that their attempt to genetically clone a male calendar model has failed. The escaped mutant is chasing your aunt."

Christy kept herself from smiling at Katie's comment. After all, Marti was her aunt. And Christy's uncle was still standing next to her. She knew that once a person was treated with disrespect, it made it easy for others to jump in and do the same.

The four of them returned to the waiting area. More than an hour later Cheyenne came striding in with several plastic boxes filled with wonderful-smelling Italian food.

"Marti isn't feeling well," Cheyenne said. "I'm going to take her home."

None of them seemed surprised at the announcement.

They ate in silence. Christy had no idea what she was eating.

"I'm going to make a few calls," Bryan said.

"I need some air," Bob said after he had eaten. He left the room.

As Christy sat alone with Katie, a fearful anger began to well up inside her. For years she and Todd had driven up and down the freeways in that beat-up, old surf van. It was a miracle they hadn't both been killed. Christy never wanted to get into another old car as long as she lived.

"Does your car have air bags on both sides?" Christy snapped at Katie.

"What?" Katie asked.

"I'm not riding in Baby Hummer with you anymore," Christy said.

"What are you talking about?"

"Todd could have been killed! His van had no air bags!" The horror of the accident was sinking in, and Christy felt as if she was going to lose her dinner.

"But he wasn't killed," Katie said firmly. "Christy, think about it. God saved him. God isn't finished with him yet. God has a plan. He always has a plan. Some God-things will come from this. Don't freak out on me now. You have to stay strong!"

Katie's sharp words worked like splashes of cold water on Christy's rampant emotions. "You're right. God is here. He's in this. I know He is. He's going to do His God-things."

"Well, duh!" Katie's biting humor rubbed Christy the wrong way. "Look at what happened already. Your brother got saved."

Christy had forgotten. Still, in her pain, she didn't think that was a good enough reason for Todd to have to go through such a terrible experience.

"Chris," Katie reached over and rubbed her shoulder, "we have to keep our perspective here. We're in shock, yes. It's awful. But God isn't pacing the floors of heaven, wringing His hands, saying, 'Oh dear, oh dear, how could this have happened?' He's God. He can do whatever He wants. At this point, it appears God wants Todd to live."

Christy felt the tears on her cheeks. She couldn't believe

she had any moisture left in her system.

"I'm going to get some air, too," Katie said. "Why don't you try to sleep a little bit?" Katie gave Christy a weak smile. "You know that when Todd is ready for visitors you'll want to be as calm as you can be. Try to rest."

Christy closed her eyes and leaned her head back. She drew in a deep breath. All she could smell was ammonia-scented disinfectant mixed with garlic from the marinara sauce. She pushed the food containers aside with her foot and tried to pray.

Peace came over her. She almost believed that if she opened her eyes she would see Jesus seated beside her. He wasn't wringing His hands in fear. Katie was right about that. He was in control. But Christy knew Jesus would feel her pain right along with her.

"Christy?" Uncle Bob's voice spoke into her quiet moment. "Are you okay, honey?"

She opened her eyes and nodded bravely. "I'm okay. How are you doing?"

"Okay," he said with a nod of his head. "It shouldn't be too much longer before they let us see him."

Christy looked at her uncle more closely. "How are you doing, really? I mean with Aunt Marti and everything."

"I'm sorry you had to see her that way. With . . . with him."

"I already knew about Cheyenne," Christy said. "Marti told me about the art colony and her pottery and everything when she came to see me a few weeks ago."

"Did she tell you she's planning to go with him to Santa Fe?" Bob asked.

Christy nodded solemnly. "I promised her I wouldn't say anything to anyone about it. I wish I hadn't promised her, though. I'm sorry I didn't come to you and talk about it."

"Don't apologize. You couldn't have done anything." Bob sat down and put his feet on the coffee table. "Your aunt is going her own way. You can't change her decision."

Obviously Marti's relationship with Cheyenne was no surprise to Bob. Christy wondered if Marti was making plans to leave fairly soon. Gently, Christy asked her uncle, "What are you going to do?"

"A guy I know from church directed me to a verse that relates to my situation," he said. "It's 1 Corinthians 7:15. 'But if the unbeliever leaves, let him do so. A believing man or woman is not bound in such circumstances; God has called us to live in peace.' "

Christy thought her uncle sounded like a robot as he recited the verse. She had to say something. "Are you just going to let her go?"

"I can't fight it." His voice was flat.

"Yes you can." Christy had no idea where the strength to say such words was coming from or why she was saying them. She seemed to have a different well of emotions for Uncle Bob's situation that was separate from the well she had been draining over Todd. This other well was full of opinions, and she drew from it freely. "You can still fight for her, Uncle Bob. Pray for her. Love her. You can't give up."

His eyes filled with tears. Christy didn't think she had ever seen her uncle cry.

"Uncle Bob, that may be a good, helpful verse for you right now, but a lot of other verses about marriage and love are in the Bible." Christy decided to keep talking before this well of strength gave out on her. "If I've learned one thing so far in my Bible classes at Rancho, it's that it can be dangerous to take only one verse and build your belief about a topic around that verse. We have to study everything the Bible has to say on a topic to clearly understand God's heart on the matter."

Bob looked at her quietly before saying, "You're right. I have given up on her without a fight. I was going to let her go off to that art colony, but that might not be what God wants."

Christy had to remind herself that her uncle had only been a Christian for a short time. In his enthusiasm to change everything into a peaceful reflection of Christ's understanding and love, he seemed to have forgotten that this same Jesus got mad, turned over the moneychangers' tables, and openly wept when his friend died. Jesus commanded a dead man to come out of his grave and told the wind and waves to "shut up."

All of these examples were fresh in Christy's mind because she had been getting to know Jesus better by reading the New Testament. She told her uncle about what she had read in the Gospels, and then she suggested he might want to do the same thing.

"It's the Word of God that changes us," Christy said. She had heard that in one of her classes but didn't remember which one.

Bob rubbed the back of his neck and looked up at Christy, his eyes clear. "You know what? I've never read the whole Bible."

"Not many people have."

"But you're right. How can I say I'm a follower of Christ when I haven't even read His life story?"

"He only wrote one book," Christy said. "The Bible. We just need to dig for the answers sometimes."

"You know," Uncle Bob said, "I think I've been depending too much on others to study the Scriptures for me and to pass on their wisdom to me. I don't do that with my investments. Why should I settle for that in my spiritual life?"

Uncle Bob leaned over and gave Christy a kiss on the cheek. "I've missed you, Bright Eyes. You always were my favorite niece."

Christy smiled. "And I've always been your only niece."

"Minor detail, my child. Minor detail."

Todd's dad stepped into the waiting room. "The doctor said we can go see him now. He's in room 302."

"I'll find Katie and be right up," Christy said.

Uncle Bob and Todd's dad went ahead. Christy and Katie joined them in room 302 a few minutes later. Christy could see that Todd's eyes were open, but he didn't seem to recognize her when she came in the room.

With her heart pounding, Christy forced her tears of mercy to stay back. She slipped over to the side of the bed and tenderly took Todd's hand in hers. "Hi," she said.

Todd's expression lit up only slightly, but Christy felt confident he recognized her.

"Da sove," Todd mumbled through his swollen lips.

"What?" Christy leaned closer. He looked awful. "Don't try to talk if it's too hard right now. You can tell me in the morning after you've slept."

"Ar sove," he repeated.

"Sove?" Christy repeated.

Todd nodded ever so slightly.

"Sove. Oh, do you mean stove? Our camp stove?"

Todd nodded. It looked like it hurt him to do so.

Katie stepped in and gave her interpretation. "He's trying to say that he's worried about your camp stove. It must have been in Gus."

Christy gave Todd a smile. "You're worried about our camp stove? Oh, Todd, don't worry about that. We can get another one. It's much more important that you're okay."

Todd closed his eyes.

Christy gave Katie a concerned look. It was hard to know what to do or what to say.

"We're going home for a few hours," Todd's dad said, stepping next to Christy. "I'll be back tomorrow."

Christy felt Todd grasp her hand a little tighter.

"I won't leave you," Christy said. "I'll stay right here."

Todd's grasp released, and he appeared to fall into an exhausted sleep.

"Are you sure you want to stay all night?" Uncle Bob asked.

Christy nodded. "You can go back to school, if you want, Katie. I don't mind staying alone."

"I think I'll do that," Katie said. "I'll come back tomorrow morning. Do you want me to bring you anything?"

"No. I'll call you if I think of anything."

They all hugged good-bye, and Christy was left alone beside the bed. She pulled up the chair from the corner next to the bed and tried to quietly lower the metal bed railing so she could hold Todd's hand more easily.

The first ten minutes Christy prayed. The steady ticks and muffled bleeps of the monitors became the echo of her pleas to God. As long as those ticks and bleeps stayed constant, Todd was stable. He was alive.

Christy looked at one of the tubes that entered Todd's body through his right hand. *He has my blood in him now. My blood and the blood from my family, his family, and his friends. Oh, Todd, you said the other day that you felt so isolated your whole life because you grew up without brothers or sisters. And now look!*

*You are surrounded and supported by a whole family of brothers
and sisters in Christ. Our blood runs in your veins.*

Christy gently traced her fingers along the veins on the
top of Todd's left hand. She studied where the stitches had
been taken, knowing that the scars from those cuts would
be with him for the rest of his life.

*Just like Jesus. That's what you told the youth group last week-
end. When we enter heaven, Christ will hold out His hands to us,
and we will see His scars.*

Christy closed her eyes and imagined Jesus standing
right behind her, His nail-scarred hand resting on her
shoulder. She had felt this close to the Lord only a few times
in her life. With the closeness came peace. She felt calmed,
imagining His hand on her shoulder, her hand in Todd's.

"Can you feel how connected we are, Todd?" Christy
whispered. "God is here. He is in this with us. His presence
is so real right now. Katie was right. God isn't wringing His
hands, asking why this happened. He's reaching out with
those hands. Touching us. Drawing us to each other. Drawing us to Him."

Christy's thoughts spilled into a whispered prayer. It was
a precise prayer, thanking God for His mercy in sparing
Todd's life. She then surrendered to the Lord their future together. Christy ended with the words Todd had used on the
camping trip, "As you wish."

Suddenly Christy opened her eyes, surprised by an insight. *I always want to control and schedule and plan everything.
Ultimately, I'm not in control of my life. Not really. God is.*

Christy thought of how, when Christ was on earth, He
prayed, "Not my will, but yours be done."

*That's what Todd meant when he said, "As you wish." He was
saying, "God, you do what you want, and I'll agree with it."*

She and Todd might never know why this terrible accident had happened. But together they could say to God, "As you wish. You do what you want in our lives, and we willingly will agree with it, even if we don't understand."

Christy wished Todd were awake. She wanted so badly to share her thoughts with him. But he was sleeping. Peacefully sleeping. She couldn't rob him of that precious gift in his long journey to recovery.

For the next few hours, Christy sat, wide awake, beside her beloved, basking in the peace of Christ's presence. The night nurse came in several times to check on Todd. She offered Christy something to eat or drink, but Christy declined. She didn't need anything. Her heart and body were full.

Sometime in the middle of the night, Christy stood to stretch, and when she did, Todd seemed to know she had moved. He stirred, too.

To comfort him, Christy placed her cool hand against his swollen cheek. Todd's breathing returned to a steady pace. With her finger, Christy gently traced the outline of Todd's lips. She ran her fingers across his defined, square jawline and memorized the angle of his face.

"I love you," she whispered. The words tumbled out naturally and unrestricted. A straight path had been cleared from Christy's heart to her mouth. Along that path, those three beautiful words ran unhindered, leaping from her lips and joyfully sprinkling themselves over Todd as he slept.

Christy giggled as she spoke them aloud again and again. "I love you! I really, truly love you! I know you can't hear me, Todd. That's okay. When you wake I'll tell you again with my face in your eye, or whatever Katie's poem said. I will give you the best gift I've given you so far. I will give you evidence of my promise to you. The promise I've already made in my heart."

Drawing in a deep breath, Christy smiled and said clearly, "I love you, Todd Spencer. Forever and ever, and nothing can change that."

Christy woke when she felt someone's hand resting heavily
on her head and slowly stroking her hair. She
opened her eyes, and it all came back—Todd,
the accident, the hospital room.

She had fallen asleep seated in a chair
with her head resting on her folded arms propped against
the side of Todd's hospital bed.

"Hey, you're awake," she said, lifting her head and seeing Todd's eyes were open. She realized she had been drool-
ing. Quickly reaching for a tissue from the end table, she
wiped her mouth. "How are you doing?" she asked.

"Hi." His voice was hoarse.

Christy smiled and touched his arm. "Are you okay?"

"I hurt." Todd moved only his lips and swallowed hard.

"Would you like me to call the nurse?"

Todd didn't answer. He floated back into a fuzzy sleep in-
duced by the pain medication, which was dripping slowly
into his body.

Christy waited by his side another ten minutes, but Todd
was out. So she pulled herself together, washing her face
and going to the hospital cafeteria. Hot tea sounded good.

She also bought an oatmeal cookie and an orange. As she peeled the orange, the fresh fruit's scent brightened the air and revived her.

Todd slept all morning, only waking three times. Katie came with Matt, Wes, two college professors, and Todd's roommate. They laid their hands on Todd and prayed for him while he slept, then they left to hurry back to class. Katie said she would let Donna know that Christy wouldn't be in to the bookstore again that day.

Uncle Bob called Todd's room twice. The second time, the ringing phone woke Todd, and he looked up just as his dad entered the room. The painful grin on Todd's face showed Christy and his dad how glad Todd was that they were there.

A bouquet of yellow roses arrived from Aunt Marti, and Todd's mom called. Christy answered the phone and then turned it over to Todd's dad. From the way the conversation went, his parents sounded as if they were friendly enough with each other. Clearly, both cared a lot for their son. Christy wished Todd had been awake so he could have talked to his mom. But he was oblivious to everything around him, including the second bouquet that arrived with a get-well balloon attached.

Dr. Johannes made his rounds at noon and gave them an update, saying the pain medication would keep Todd in this stupor for at least another day, possibly up to three days. The doctor assured them the critical stage had passed, and everything looked good. Todd was a strong, healthy young man, and his body would heal. It would just take time.

"How long do you think he'll be in the hospital?" Christy asked.

"I'd like to keep him at least a few more days," the doctor said. "You're welcome to stay with him, of course. But don't feel that you need to."

Christy had difficulty deciding if she should stay. She talked it over with his dad and decided she would go back to school. So she leaned over the bed, kissed Todd twice on the cheek, and whispered, "I love you. Sleep deeply. Sleep well. Dream of me."

Todd didn't respond. She didn't expect him to. Yet she couldn't wait until his eyes were open and clear again so she could lose herself in his gaze. Then she would tell him she loved him, and he would be able to hear her and fully understand.

"Would you like to stop for some lunch before I take you back to Rancho?" Todd's dad asked.

"Sure." Since Christy hadn't been around Todd's dad much, she welcomed the chance to know him better.

They were walking out the automatic front doors of the hospital when Christy spotted some of her and Todd's closest friends, Doug and Tracy, coming toward her, calling her name. As they greeted her with hugs, Christy began to cry again. She didn't know why.

"Everything is okay," she told them. "The doctor thinks he's going to be all right."

Doug enveloped Christy in one of his famous Doug hugs. "Katie called us this morning. I wish she had called last night. We would have been here in a flash. You know you always can call on us if you need anything." Doug pulled back and gave Christy a concerned, close-up look. "How are you doing?"

"Okay. Good, actually. I'm tired, but I'm okay." She made her tears stop, and that felt good.

Christy thought petite Tracy looked older than last time she had seen her friend. More mature. She wore small oval glasses, which complemented her heart-shaped face.

"Do you think we can see him?" Tracy asked.

"Sure," Todd's dad said. "He's been sleeping ever since the surgery last night. Don't be surprised if he doesn't wake up or acknowledge you." He went on to give Doug and Tracy an update on the surgery and what the doctor had told them.

"Were you both leaving now?" Doug asked. He was as tall as Todd's dad, but his face still held the little-boy look he always had. His short, sandy blond hair stuck straight up in front, accentuating the mischievous look.

"We were about to eat some lunch, and then I was taking Christy back to Rancho."

"We can take her," Tracy said, reaching for Christy's arm and pulling her close. "Do you mind, Christy? I'd love to spend a little time with you, if you don't have to hurry back."

Christy looked at Todd's dad. She was too tired to form an opinion on anything. "Would that be okay?"

"Of course. Here's my cell phone number. Would you call me if there's any change? I plan to come back tomorrow afternoon and stay awhile."

Christy nodded and took his business card. "Thanks."

Bryan Spencer smiled appreciatively at Christy. "No, thank you, Christy. You're an exceptional woman. Everything Todd told me about you is true." He leaned over and kissed her soundly on the cheek. "Call if you need me for anything at all."

"I will," Christy promised.

Tracy, Doug, and Christy returned to Todd's room. He

was sleeping, as his dad had predicted. Tracy cried quiet tears when she saw his swollen, black-and-blue face.

Doug suggested they pray, and so they did, joining hands with Christy holding Todd's left hand and Doug resting his hand on Todd's right shoulder. When Doug said, "Amen," Christy whispered, "As you wish." She liked those words being her secret message of surrender to the Lord.

They stood close to the bed, talking softly, until the nurse came in and said she needed to take Todd's temperature and adjust his medication.

"Why don't we wait in the cafeteria?" Doug suggested. "I could use some food."

"I wish Todd at least knew we were here." Tracy looked longingly at him.

"We can come back," Christy suggested.

They found an empty table at the cafeteria and talked like the old friends they were, catching up on what had happened since they had seen one another. Christy found herself telling Doug and Tracy that she had come to some conclusions about Todd. Both Doug and Tracy leaned forward, as if they had been waiting as long as Todd to hear what Christy was going to say.

With a self-conscious little shrug, Christy said, "I love him. I love Todd. I haven't told him yet—at least, he hasn't heard me say it—but I know without a doubt I love him."

A charming giggle escaped Tracy's lips. Doug leaned back with a satisfied look on his face and nodded. "It's about time."

Christy gave him a look that said, "Well, thanks a lot!"

"It's just that Todd has been sure of his love for you for so long," Doug said. "I know he never wanted to rush you. This will be good. This will change his life."

"Change his life?" Christy asked.

Doug and Tracy glanced at each other in a way that indicated they both held a few of Todd's confidences. Apparently they were confidences Christy didn't hold yet.

"Should I ask what you two are thinking right now? You look as if you can read each other's minds."

"We can," they said in unison.

All three of them laughed.

Tracy took off her glasses and placed them on the table next to her half-finished turkey sandwich. "Christy, you probably know this already, but Todd has been in love with you for a long time."

Christy had hoped that, but her insecurities had caused her to doubt it many times.

"A long time," Doug said. "I didn't know that until after Tracy and I were married. Todd was over at our apartment one night, and we were talking about when you and I were going out while Todd was in Spain. He asked Tracy if that had been hard on her."

Christy gave her friend a sympathetic glance. Looking back, Christy wished she hadn't caused Tracy any pain by going out with Doug when Tracy was so intently interested in him.

"I told Todd that, back then, we didn't know for sure we were supposed to be together," Tracy said. "Neither Doug nor I was ready to make a commitment. I mean, I was hoping, praying, and thinking things might work out for us one day, but I didn't know for certain."

"And that's when Todd told us that he knew," Doug said. A grin grew on his boyish face. "He said he knew you were the one for him from that first day when we met on the beach. Do you remember, Christy?"

Christy buried her face in her hands. "How could I forget? I was only fourteen years old, and this wave scooped me up and tossed me at your feet all wrapped in seaweed."

Doug chuckled. "Then Todd and I taught you how to ride a body board."

Christy looked up. "You both were so nice to me. I'll never forget that day."

"Todd won't ever forget it, either," Tracy said. "He told us he knew then and there that you were the one for him. The one woman he would love for the rest of his life."

"You're kidding," Christy said. She had heard Todd make comments to that effect before, but she had thought he was teasing. She looked at Doug and then at Tracy to make sure they weren't teasing her. They both looked serious.

"I'm sorry," Christy said, "that is just weird. How could he know something like that when he was . . . how old was he? Sixteen? That's crazy."

"See?" Tracy said. "That's the same thing I said when Todd told us, but Doug got upset with me."

"I wasn't upset with you."

"You told me I shouldn't judge another person's feelings and call them crazy. You said that right in front of Todd."

"What did Todd say?" Christy asked.

"He didn't say much of anything. He didn't defend himself or act embarrassed. He just seemed real matter-of-fact about how he felt." Tracy looked at Doug again before saying, "Todd said he knew he loved you and he didn't have to do anything to prove it. To anyone."

Christy let Tracy's words sink in. She knew she had liked Todd when she had first met him. She had spent plenty of hours dreaming about him and dreaming about what it would be like to end up with him. But love? Forever, true love? No, Christy couldn't say she knew Todd was the one for her until last Saturday during their crazy dune buggy ride.

"You know what?" Tracy said. "I don't think we should have told you all this. This is really personal. It's between you and Todd."

"It's also between Todd and you two," Christy said. "I mean, he told all this to you guys, so he must have trusted you with his thoughts and feelings about me. I don't mind you telling me. It's good, actually, because it helps me to know he started out thinking I was special to him."

"Special?" Doug echoed. "Christy, you were it. You *are* it. No other girls have ever been in his life. It was always you."

"Only you," Tracy agreed.

Christy couldn't believe how quickly the tears found their familiar trail down her face. She never imagined that Todd had chosen to commit his heart to her all those years ago or that he never had wavered from that decision.

"I wish I weren't so bad at making decisions," Christy said between tears. "Why did it take me so long to open my heart to Todd? Why did I ever go out with any other guys?"

"Oh, Chris, don't feel that way," Tracy said. She placed her hand on Christy's shoulder.

"Yeah," Doug agreed. "Speaking as one of the other guys you went out with, I'd like to think you don't regret that time in your life."

Christy quickly sobered. "I don't, Doug. Your friendship and what I learned while we were spending time together were extremely valuable."

"And fun," Doug added. "Don't forget fun. We had some great times."

Tracy said, "What you went through to come to the conclusion that you really love Todd is normal. That's what I was telling Todd that night at our apartment. Maybe it's different for women. I thought I loved Doug, but I wasn't positive until we were in England. Do you remember when I asked to be taken off your team? That was because it hit me so hard that I was in love with him, I couldn't be around him. Especially when I knew he didn't feel that way about me."

"I know," Christy said. "But that's why I feel so bad. I'm thinking of how much I hurt Todd when he was sure about me, but I wasn't sure about him."

"Don't worry about Todd," Doug said. "He's tough. Tough and patient. It's good that you didn't know before, Christy. I think going to Switzerland was a great choice for you. If you and Todd had decided a year ago or even five years ago that you couldn't live without each other, you both would have missed out on so many important experiences. It's all God's timing. There can't be any regrets."

Christy knew Doug was right. It was God's timing. The verse from Song of Solomon about "not arousing nor awakening love until it so desires" was a hidden blessing in her life. Apparently, God now pleased to awaken love fully within Christy.

She composed herself and remembered something Dr. Mitchell had talked about in class on Monday when she had felt compelled to leave and find Todd. He had said something about blessings coming upon you and overtaking you because you obey the Lord's voice. Christy knew she had no reason to regret the way things had gone.

With a little smile she said, "I guess God has been working out the details between us for a long time. A deeper level of love for Todd has just awakened inside me, you know?"

Both Doug and Tracy smiled.

"We know," Tracy said.

"I feel as if God has overtaken me with something new. Something stronger and deeper than ever before. It's so real. I know Todd is the one. He is the one for me." Even as she heard herself speaking the words, Christy ached to go back to Todd's room and declare her love to him.

"You know," Doug said, "some of what you're feeling could be from the shock of the accident."

Tracy swatted her husband on the arm. "Don't try to take it away from her! Christy is in love. Let her just be in love without analyzing it." She turned to Christy and shook her head. "Men!"

"Okay, okay," Doug said. "So it's different for everybody. I'm happy for you, Christy. Todd will be thrilled. And, sweetheart," he said, turning to his pretty little wife, "are you going to finish the other half of your sandwich?"

Christy laughed for the first time in two days. "Some things never change. Doug, you still eat more than anyone I've ever met."

He chomped into the turkey sandwich and said, "And I'm getting the love handles to prove it, aren't I, Trace?"

"Hardly." Tracy shook her head. "You don't slow down long enough to let all that food find a place to stay on you."

"Have things been really busy for you guys?" Christy asked.

Tracy nodded. "Everything is going well, though. Did you hear that we ran into Rick Doyle? He is so changed, Christy; you wouldn't even recognize him. God has . . . what was the term you used earlier? Overtaken? Yes, that's what you said. God has overtaken Rick."

"It's awesome," Doug said with a bite of sandwich still in his mouth.

"Katie heard from him," Christy said. "It sounded as if he was doing great."

"Well, God was certainly tough and patient with Rick," Doug added. "I ought to know—Todd and I were roommates with him when we were in San Diego."

"I remember," Christy said.

"You don't remember half of what I remember," Doug said. "And you don't want to."

"He's definitely changed," Tracy said.

"What's that phrase you were telling me, Tracy?" Doug asked. "Something you read in a book about God pursuing us?" Doug pushed aside the empty plate.

"God is the relentless lover," Tracy said. "And we are His first love. He will never stop pursuing us because He wants us back."

"Yeah, exactly," Doug said. "That's how God is. That's how He was with Rick. I'm telling you, Christy, it's awesome. When Todd's better, we'll have to all get together and go to the beach or something."

"I would love that," Christy said.

"Are you guys ready to go back upstairs and check on Todd?" Tracy asked.

"I am," Christy said.

They returned to room 302, and Todd opened his eyes long enough to recognize Tracy and mumble a few words to Doug. Christy held Todd's hand the whole time, and when Todd fell back to sleep, Doug asked if she was ready to go back to Rancho.

Christy hesitated. "I think I'd rather stay here. I can call

Katie and have her pick me up later. I just don't want to leave him yet."

"Are you sure?" Doug asked.

Tracy smiled and tugged on her husband's arm. "Trust me, Christy is making the right choice."

"Do you need some money for food?" Doug asked.

"No, I have money. Thanks. And thanks for buying lunch."

"Anytime." Doug gave her a strong hug. "I'm serious about our getting together as soon as Todd is ready. You let us know when a good time is for you guys."

"We really missed you while you were in Switzerland." Tracy gave Christy another hug good-bye. "I'm glad you're back, and I'm glad that . . ." She glanced at Todd. "I'm glad that everything is settled in your heart."

"Me too," Christy said.

Tracy whispered in Christy's ear, "And I'll pray that Todd wakes up all the way real soon so you can tell him what you told us."

About half an hour after Doug and Tracy left, Todd woke up.

"Hey, you," Christy said.

Todd's eyes were wide, staring at Christy and barely blinking.

Thrilled to have his complete attention, Christy came close and said, "Todd, I have something important to tell you."

He looked at her peacefully, waiting.

"Todd, I love you. I love you with all my heart."

When he didn't respond, Christy repeated her declaration. "I love you, Todd."

Todd moved his left hand slowly. Christy thought he was

going to reach up and touch her face. Instead, he brushed his fingers across the top of the blanket. His eyes grew wider, and he flicked invisible bits of something from the blanket. His breathing became more rapid.

Christy reached over and pushed the buzzer for the nurse. "Are you okay?" Christy asked Todd.

"There are so many of them," he mumbled. "Look out! They're coming! So many!"

The nurse stepped into the room, and Christy said, "Something's wrong."

"Todd?" the nurse said in a loud voice. "Todd, what is it?"

He continued to flick his hand across the blanket without answering her.

"Do you see something, Todd?" the nurse asked.

"Spiders," he muttered. "So many of them. They won't leave."

Christy's heart began to pound fiercely. *Did the accident affect his brain? What's going on?*

"Okay, Todd," the nurse said firmly. "We'll take care of the spiders. You're hallucinating. We'll put you on a different pain medication right away." She checked the IV bag and detached it from the metal stand.

"The medication is making him hallucinate?" Christy surmised.

"Yes, it's common. We can put him on something else that won't affect him. Don't worry. He'll be okay."

Christy did worry. She stayed beside Todd for the rest of the afternoon. He slept soundly and didn't appear to have any more bouts with invisible spiders. By evening, Katie came to the hospital and urged Christy to return to the dorm with her to get a decent night's sleep.

"You're going to need a shower pretty soon," Katie said, "if you don't mind my saying so. You really should sleep in your own bed tonight."

Christy convinced Katie to stay a little longer. She was glad Katie did because, at about nine o'clock, Todd woke up and talked to both Katie and Christy, telling them how much better he felt. He even laughed a strange, hoarse kind of laugh. The nurse had warned Christy the new medication would make him a little high, and he wouldn't necessarily remember what he said or what they said to him.

Despite the nurse's admonition, Christy nestled in close to Todd and said, "Todd, I love you."

He grinned oddly with his swollen lips and said, "Of course you do."

Katie sympathetically pulled Christy's arm and said, "We need to go. Let him sleep. He'll be able to hear you and process your words better tomorrow. Come on, Chris."

Reluctantly, Christy left room 302 once Todd was asleep again. She followed Katie to the parking lot. When they reached Baby Hummer, Christy stopped.

Katie seemed to read her mind. "I know it doesn't have air bags. Are you nervous about driving with me now?"

"It's not driving with you, Katie, it's getting in a car—any car—and going on the freeway."

"I know. I had the same queasy feelings last night when I left here."

"You did?"

Katie nodded. "I drove extra slow, and I prayed all the way."

"Then let's do that again. You drive extra slow, and we'll both pray." Christy buckled her seat belt. "Only don't drive so slow that you become a danger to other drivers."

"Yes, Mother," Katie quipped.

Christy grinned. "Have you been keeping the room clean while I was gone?"

Katie looked at Christy as if she hoped her roommate was kidding. "Yes, of course. And by the way, Dixie and Daisy are doing just fine."

"Who?"

"Our new goldfish. I bought twins."

Christy shook her head. After working several years at a pet store she knew goldfish didn't have twins. As many as thirty goldfish could be in a tank, and they would all look alike.

"I moved the fishbowl, so they aren't getting heated up from the afternoon sun that comes in the window."

"Good," Christy said.

"Guess what Matt did today?" Katie steered Baby Hummer out of the hospital parking lot.

"I have no idea."

"He found out where they took Gus and went to salvage what he could."

"Did he really? That was so nice of him."

"Yeah, look in the backseat."

Christy turned, and there, on Baby Hummer's backseat, was Todd and Christy's camp stove, still in the box, looking unharmed.

"It was under the backseat. Apparently just about every-thing else was demolished."

"Todd is going to be so happy about the stove," Christy said.

"I know. That's why I brought it with me. I was going to take it into the hospital to show him, but when I got there, I forgot to grab the stove."

"I'll have to bring it with me tomorrow when I go to see him," Christy said.

"Matt pulled one other thing from Gus."

"What?"

"You'll see. It's in our room. On your bed. I even washed it."

"Can't you tell me what it is?"

"You'll see," Katie said.

As promised, Katie drove nice and slow all the way to school, and they arrived in the dorm parking lot without incident.

Christy hurried to their room, driven by curiosity as to what other item had been salvaged from Gus. As soon as she opened their door, Christy felt a surge of warm nostalgia and smiled at her roommate.

"Oh, Katie, I'm so glad Matt saved this. Thanks for washing it." Christy lifted Todd's old navy blue hooded sweat shirt and pressed her face into it.

"Yeah, I thought you two needed each other tonight," Katie said.

She was right. After Christy took a long, hot shower, she pulled on her favorite flannel boxer shorts and a T-shirt. Then, crawling into bed, she wrapped herself up in Todd's sweat shirt, pulling the hood over her head.

For Christy, the rest of the week was filled with trips to the hospital, meals on the run, and the under- standing nods of her professors and Donna whenever Christy explained why she was leaving campus again. By Friday, Todd was ready to leave the hospital. The doctor ordered two weeks of bed rest.

After exploring all the options, everyone agreed Todd would stay at Bob and Marti's, since his dad had a business trip to Canada and Todd wouldn't receive the care he needed in his dorm room.

Matt and Katie had come to the hospital together on Thursday and offered to run the youth group programs at Riverview Heights while Todd was out of commission. Sierra was going to arrange for her friend Randy to bring his band on Sunday for a miniconcert.

On Friday, Bob and Marti arrived at the hospital together to pick up Todd. That surprised Christy. Her aunt showed up with her hair plaited into a single braid down her back and wearing conservative black pants and a simple white shirt. It looked as if she wore a little makeup. Lipstick, for sure.

Christy was glad Cheyenne wasn't there. She wondered if Bob had insisted Todd stay in their home as a way of keeping Marti around and allowing the two of them to join efforts on a project.

A hospital attendant rolled Todd's wheelchair to the parking lot as Marti and Christy followed with the bouquets he had received. Earlier that morning Matt had brought some of Todd's clothes stuffed unceremoniously in a plastic grocery bag, which now rested on Todd's lap as they exited.

Bob had gone to pull the car up to the front. To Christy's surprise, Bob arrived in a blue Volvo station wagon. He got out, all smiles.

"How do you like her?" he asked Todd. Then grinning at Christy, Uncle Bob said, "She's not brand new, but she's sturdy. Safest car on the road, they say. I got a great deal on her."

Christy couldn't imagine why her uncle would be so proud of his "soccer mom" car. It had a rack on the top and peeling surf logo stickers on the back window.

"The car is for you." Marti spelled out to Christy what she obviously hadn't understood.

"For both of you," Bob said. "I put it in both your names. You'll have to sign the papers when we get home. And you'll have to cover your own insurance after the first six months."

Christy was stunned. She didn't know what to say.

"I got a good deal," Bob said again, as if to convince Christy that she should be happy.

"I suggested he buy a Land Rover, but the insurance payments were ridiculous," Marti said. "I know this isn't the brightest and newest vehicle on the road, but when you compare it to that ridiculous death trap Todd was driving . . ."

Christy quickly jumped in. She wanted to preserve dear ol' Gus's memory as positively as she could. "It's wonderful, Uncle Bob. Thank you. You really didn't have to do this. Thank you so much."

Christy wasn't sure if Todd caught all that was going on. He had been much more alert the past two days, but Christy knew he still was on pain-killers. That was why she hadn't attempted to tell him again that she loved him. She wanted to wait until he settled into Bob and Marti's house and things calmed down some. Then he would be able to hear her and to understand.

Leaning over and making eye contact with Todd, who sat patiently in the wheelchair, Marti said, "Well? You haven't said anything, Todd. What do you think?"

"Thank you," Todd said flatly. "Thank you, Marti, Bob. You didn't have to do this. I'll pay you guys back."

"You will do no such thing," Marti said. "If you had any idea how much fun Robert had this week trying to find a car for you, you wouldn't dare rob him of his happiness. Or my happiness, either. I had a small hand in making this choice. It was either this blue one or a drab, olive green one. I said buy the blue one. Don't you think blue is much better than olive green?"

"It's perfect," Todd said. He raised his hand and gave Marti's arm a squeeze. "Thank you."

"Enough of all the thank-yous," Marti said. "Let's get you in the car. We have the den all made up for you, and the sooner you get home, the better."

Christy was amazed at her aunt's caring and efficiency as

she gave directions on how to get Todd into the car as painlessly as possible and where the flowers should be situated in the back of the station wagon. She even insisted Todd sit in the front seat while she and Christy took the backseat. Christy couldn't remember a time when her aunt had given up the front seat to anyone.

The hour and a half drive to Newport Beach went by quickly as Bob told the story of how he had searched for the right car. He had researched the Internet for cars ranked highest in safety ratings. Then he checked for the best year for Volvo station wagons and hunted for one with low miles and in good condition. He was proud of his accomplishment in finding this beauty. Todd and Christy both showered him with their exclamations of appreciation.

Christy felt pretty excited about having a car. She liked this one. In high school she and her mom had shared a car. She didn't need one in Basel, and the way her savings were going, she wouldn't have been able to buy her own for a long time. She smiled as she thought about how she and Todd now shared two possessions: a camp stove and a car. All they needed was a grungy dog, and they could get married and hit the road like a modern American gypsy couple.

Marti was right about having the den all fixed up for Todd. She had moved the leather couch back and set up a rented hospital bed in front of the wide-screen TV. Stacks of videos, magazines, and snack food were arranged on the coffee table, waiting for Todd. She had purchased several new T-shirts and surf shorts and had them folded on the end of the bed with the top sheet turned down, the way a fancy hotel would prepare a bed.

Christy knew Todd wasn't himself yet because he passed by all the food and extras. Instead, he crawled right into bed and fell asleep within minutes.

"I'm going to keep his medication right here." Marti showed Christy a tray she had placed on the end table. A pitcher of water sat ready with a glass and a straw and a thermometer.

Marti, you would have made such an efficient mother. It's really too bad you never had children. Although, what am I saying? After the way Marti always tried to make me into the daughter she never had, how could I wish on her unborn children what I had forced on me for so many years?

"Come see what I've done to your room," Marti said. She led Christy upstairs in their modern beach-front house to the room Marti originally had fixed up for Christy when she came to stay with them the summer she turned fifteen. The decor had been a feminine combination of white eyelet curtains, pink ruffles, and flowers.

When Marti opened the door, Christy couldn't believe she was viewing the same room in which she had spent so many hours during her teen years. Now the motif was southwestern, complete with a stenciled desert landscape painted on the walls. The wall on the far left was covered with a blazing orange-and-pink sunset behind what looked like an actual wooden vegetable cart, complete with strings of red chilies hanging from the top. The mission-style bed was raised from the ground by adobe bricks. Dozens of tiny white twinkling lights were strung from the four wooden bedposts, and a sheer swath of ivory fabric draped the entire ensemble. In front of the window sat an antique table with a brightly painted ceramic water pitcher and washbowl.

The swirl of color and commotion overwhelmed Christy. She didn't know how anyone could be expected to actually sleep in such a room. All it needed was the piped-in sounds of a coyote howling under the moon, and it could be the prototype of an attraction at a theme park.

"What do you think?" Marti asked eagerly. Bob had joined them, and Christy caught his glance before she spoke. He seemed to be cautioning her to think carefully before she answered.

"It's really something," Christy said slowly. It was the most honest phrase she could come up with. She added, "You must have worked very hard on this."

"Yes, I did, thank you. Come see my pottery." Marti marched to the dresser near the adjoining bathroom and told Christy about each bowl, vase, and painted plate that was displayed on the dresser top as well as on hooks on the wall behind the dresser.

"They're really beautiful, Aunt Marti." Christy meant it. The colors and shapes of Marti's pottery were stunning.

"Do you really think so?" Marti asked.

"Yes. I love this small dish, and the way you did the edges in blue."

"I made that as a ring dish. You know, for when you take off your rings at night or to wash your hands. It's a nice place to put them. I'd like you to have that ring dish."

"Oh, I like it, but you don't have to give it to me. I don't want to break up your collection. Besides, I don't have any rings." Christy showed Marti her bare hands. "I mean, I don't usually wear any rings."

"Then use it for your bracelet, Christina." Marti nodded toward the gold ID bracelet Todd had given her, which Christy always wore on her right wrist. "At least until he gives you a ring to wear." Aunt Marti's grin was cunning.

"Thank you." Christy took the small blue dish her aunt had been holding. "I appreciate this very much. I also appreciate all that both of you are doing for Todd. It's really nice of you to let him stay here."

"No problem at all. You know he's like a son to us," Bob said.

Marti looked at Bob over her shoulder and seemed to be softening. She turned to Christy. "There isn't anything we wouldn't do for either of you. You know that."

Before Christy could stop herself, she blurted out, "Then don't leave, Aunt Marti. Don't go to Santa Fe. Stay here where you belong."

White-hot anger flared on Marti's face. But no words spewed from her mouth. Christy pulled back, expecting the lava to come at any moment.

"I already knew." Bob touched Marti gingerly on the shoulder.

She jerked away, as if his touch hurt her. "You told!" she hissed at Christy.

"No, I didn't tell anyone. I promised I would keep your secret, and I did."

"Cheyenne told me," Bob said.

Marti spun around. "Cheyenne? When?"

"Several weeks ago. He came by when you weren't home. I guess he thought you and I had discussed the situation, and he spoke to me about his plans for the art colony and how you were involved."

"Why didn't you tell me?" Marti spat the words at Bob.

Bob paused before answering softly, "Why didn't you tell me?"

"You know what?" Christy said. "I'm going to check on Todd. I'm sorry I said what I did." She hurried to leave the southwestern guest room and paused before closing the door behind her. "But I meant what I said, Aunt Marti. I did keep your secret. And I don't want you to go. I love you."

As soon as Christy shut the door behind her, she heard her aunt yell at her uncle. Christy felt awful as she descended the stairs.

Why did I have to open my mouth? Where did that come from? It just popped right out. I didn't mean to start this war between Bob and Marti.

Christy knew she hadn't actually started anything between her aunt and uncle. Their problems existed long before Christy opened her mouth. She just wished she hadn't said anything. She wished she and Todd weren't here right now. She wished . . .

Suddenly Christy remembered Todd's phrase, *"As you wish."* She stopped at the foot of the stairs. She could hear her aunt and uncle's muffled voices as they argued. Christy sat on the bottom step and prayed for them, concluding with, "And, Lord, I know what matters isn't what I wish would happen. I want things to turn out the way you wish. As you wish. Let it be so."

Tiptoeing into the den, Christy was glad to see Todd still was asleep and couldn't hear Bob and Marti fighting upstairs. Christy smiled when she saw the peaceful expression on Todd's face. All over again she wanted to tell him she loved him. She wanted to kiss him and hold him and tell him that she would love him forever as intensely and sweetly as she loved him at this moment.

"I love you," she said aloud, her voice low and steady. "The whole world and everyone around us might go completely mad, but that won't change my love for you, Todd."

He didn't respond.

Christy padded off into the kitchen and found some apple juice and string cheese in the well-stocked refrigerator. She saw the menu for the weekend written in Bob's handwriting and stuck on the refrigerator door by a magnet in the shape of a sailboat. He had listed lasagna for Friday night. If Christy knew her uncle and his interest in cooking, he already had made the lasagna, and it was waiting to be baked.

Her guess was right. The glass casserole dish was on the refrigerator's bottom shelf. Christy glanced at the clock. It was almost five o'clock. She decided to take the initiative, pop the lasagna in the oven, and put together a salad so dinner would be ready when everyone felt hungry.

As it turned out, Christy ate alone. Todd said he was just thirsty but thought he might eat some toast later. Lasagna didn't sound good to him.

Uncle Bob and Aunt Marti hadn't come downstairs yet, and Christy certainly didn't feel comfortable going upstairs.

Choosing to sit alone in the kitchen, Christy thought of all the meals she had eaten in this house and all the emotions she had gone through in front of her aunt and uncle. She wasn't frightened by the high-pitched level of their emotions she had seen today, as long as everything ended up settled between them.

"Please let them work things out, Father God," Christy prayed. She ate and prayed and then put away the huge quantity of leftovers. She decided to make the toast for Todd, even if he wasn't awake yet. Spreading some butter on the bread, she then drizzled it with honey, the way her mom used to make toast whenever Christy was sick.

For a fleeting moment, Christy wondered if she would make a good mom. She thought she would. She hoped she would. But first of all and above all, she hoped she would make a good wife.

With her heart full of warm thoughts, Christy carried the toast into the den and found Todd sitting up with a handful of tissues over his nose.

"Are you okay?" Christy put down the plate. She noticed blood on the sheets and reached for more tissues.

Todd nodded. "Bloody nose," he garbled. Pulling away his hand, Christy could see his nose had stopped bleeding.

"Can I get you anything?"

"No," Todd leaned back. "Man, all this medicine is messing me up."

"I'll get you a washcloth." Christy returned with a damp cloth and a hand towel.

"I keep thinking one of these times when I wake up, I'll feel normal again, but I don't," Todd said.

"You will," Christy assured him. "One of these times. I'm amazed at how much you're sleeping."

"It's the drugs," Todd said. "I'd take myself off of them if I weren't still hurting so much." He pressed his hand against his side, above his right hip, where the incision had been made for the surgery. He had mentioned before that the area was sore and that he could feel the sutures tugging any time he moved the wrong way.

"I could call the doctor." Christy glanced at the clock. "I don't know if he's still at the hospital, but he might prescribe a different medication. When you were in the hospital, they had to change your pain-killer because you were seeing spiders."

"Oh yeah," Todd said slowly. He wiped his face with the washcloth. "I think I remember that. It's all so fuzzy. They were crawling across my bed, weren't they?"

"I wouldn't know," Christy teased. "I didn't see the spiders. But you certainly did. The nurse said it was common to hallucinate like that."

"Will you call the doctor for me? Ask him if I can take something that won't knock me out or make my nose bleed."

"Okay." Christy turned to go back to the kitchen and then realized she was still holding the plate in her hand. "I brought you some toast with honey."

"Thank you, honey," he said with a teasing grin.

Christy grinned back. That was the first time Todd had called her honey. She liked it.

He called her honey again on Saturday morning when she brought him more toast and orange juice a little after nine o'clock. Todd had turned on the TV and was watching Saturday-morning cartoons. Christy returned to the kitchen, prepared herself a bowl of Cheerios, and made herself comfortable on the couch.

"How did you sleep?" Todd turned to watch Christy instead of the cartoons.

"Not great. My aunt and uncle had a big argument when we arrived last night. I didn't have the nerve to go upstairs since they never came down. So I slept on the couch in the living room." She put her bowl of Cheerios on the floor and stretched out her neck from the kink that was tightening up on the right side.

"Do you think they're okay?" Todd asked.

"I don't know. Todd, I'm worried about them; I prayed for them. Then I got mad at them. I don't know what to think anymore."

"I had a feeling a couple of weeks ago, when I saw your uncle, that things weren't going real great between Bob and Marti."

"I hope they try to work things out. Doesn't it suddenly feel as if you and I are the adults, and they are the volatile teenagers, like we used to be?"

Todd yawned and turned the sound on the cartoons to mute. "I was never volatile."

"Okay, the volatile teen I used to be." Christy went back to her bowl of Cheerios, aware that Todd was still watching her.

"You were never volatile," Todd said. "Emotional, maybe. But not volatile. You always think things through. And you feel everything intensely and honestly. Those are qualities I've long appreciated about you."

Christy paused, her spoon midway to her mouth, dripping milk into the bowl. *Tell him! Go ahead. Look at the way he's looking at you! Tell Todd you love him.*

Returning the spoon to the bowl and composing herself, Christy said, "I've long appreciated many of your qualities, too, Todd. As a matter of fact, I've been wanting to tell you that—"

Before Christy's important words could hit the air, Aunt Marti entered the den with her usual dramatic flair. "How is our precious, precious patient this morning? I am so, so sorry we left you alone last night. Were you able to manage by yourself, dear Todd?"

The sweetness dripping from Marti's words irritated Christy; yet she wondered if the attitude change reflected any changes in her aunt's heart.

"Christy took good care of me," Todd said. "She called the doctor and got a different medication and that seems to be helping."

Marti blinked. "When did you get new medication?"

"Last night. Christy had the doctor call in the prescription to the drugstore over in the Westcliffe Shopping Center. She picked it up last night just before the pharmacy closed."

Marti looked even more surprised that Christy had managed such a feat.

Uncle Bob appeared and asked if anyone was interested in waffles for breakfast. His expression looked more peaceful than it had the night before. Christy hoped all these subtle changes indicated things were better between her aunt and uncle.

"I got some cereal already," Christy said.

"I could go for a waffle," Todd said.

"Does that mean your appetite is returning?" Bob asked. "That sounds like a good sign."

Marti noticed the blood drops on the sheets and immediately made a fuss. When Todd told her it was from a bloody nose, she insisted he go to the emergency room.

"I'm sure it was from the change in climate from the desert to the ocean air," Todd said. "Either that or from the medication. I'm on different stuff now. It's okay, really."

"If it happens again, I think we should go to the emergency room. And we will go immediately," Marti said. "Your health is too volatile right now."

Todd and Christy exchanged glances. It wasn't the last time they read and sent silent messages to each other that weekend. They seemed to know what the other person was thinking. Christy loved this silent, intimate exchange.

Marti and Bob, however, didn't seem to be experiencing as intimate an exchange as Christy had hoped. They didn't offer any information on their conversation the night before. And even though they seemed cordial to Christy and Todd and each other, Christy couldn't tell if they actually had settled anything or if they had put their difficulties aside to focus on Todd. She guessed it was the latter.

Christy spent the weekend indoors, watching movies, watching Todd sleep, and watching Bob and Marti be cordial to each other. Christy felt strange leaving Sunday evening to drive back to school in the new Volvo. She wanted to stay with Todd. That wouldn't have been a good idea since she had missed so many of her classes and work last week. It was time for life to move back to a regular schedule. But her heart wasn't regular about anything.

Christy called Bob and Marti every day and received a full report on how "Marti's patient" was doing before the phone was handed over to Todd. From the way he communicated in short sentences each time she called, Christy guessed Marti was always in the room with him.

Christy's brother called Todd later in the week to tell him he had become a Christian at the hospital when Christy had prayed with him. Christy called her aunt's house on Thursday, and Todd said, "Hey, David called me last night. Can you believe what happened with him?"

"I was supposed to tell you. I can't believe I kept forgetting. I know; it's wonderful, isn't it?"

Her next thought was, *And I need to tell you something else that's wonderful and will make you exceptionally happy. I told you so many times when you couldn't hear me, but now I need to wait until no one else is around.*

During the week, people Christy didn't know stopped her on campus and asked how Todd was doing. By the time she left work on Friday afternoon and loaded up her clothes in the back of the Volvo, she thought she would burst from anticipation.

But the drive to Newport Beach felt as if it were taking hours. The freeway was thick with weekend traffic.

"Come on, come on!" Christy sputtered at the cars in front of her when she entered the Mission Viejo area. The traffic slowed to a crawl at the La Paz exit.

Unless there's been an accident, you people better have a good excuse for slowing down like this!

Christy realized she needed to calm down and slow down before she became part of an accident herself. She breathed more slowly and let her imagination go back to her planning. It had been a week of planning. Planning quietly, when she lay awake unable to sleep at night, planning with Katie when the two of them went to the grocery store on Thursday night and bought eggs, bacon, croissants, and Todd's favorite gourmet mango-papaya jam.

A light October drizzle danced across the windshield. "Oh no you don't," Christy muttered as she switched on the windshield wipers. "You little raindrops are going to be on your way by tomorrow morning, aren't you? Because you aren't invited to breakfast on the beach. I've planned it all out. Breakfast for two. Just Todd and me. No sea gulls. No raindrops. Got it?"

The traffic came to a stop, but Christy's heart raced on ahead to the beach. *Just Todd and me. Just the two of us cuddled close by the fire when I give him those three eternal words that are burning a hole in my heart.*

When Christy arrived at Bob and Marti's house after her aggravating trek on the crowded freeways, she was surprised to see how much Todd had improved. His face was no longer swollen, and his black eye had faded. He greeted Christy at the door with a big hug and told her she was just in time for dinner. Apparently Uncle Bob had been showing Todd how to make chicken enchiladas.

The four of them sat down to eat in the kitchen. Marti eagerly gave Christy a full report on how Todd had improved during the week under Marti's careful attention. Christy and Todd exchanged warm glances and smiles while they ate. In the back of Christy's mind, she continued to plan how her breakfast on the beach would be executed the next morning.

Just before Christy went to bed, she told Todd, "I'd like to make breakfast for us in the morning."

"Sure," he said. "I'll help. Your uncle has been showing me some of his secrets in the kitchen. I think I've learned more about cooking this week than I ever have before."

"Actually, I wanted to make our breakfast on the beach—

at the fire pit we used to go to." She gave him a hopeful, expectant look. "Does that sound like a good idea to you?"

Todd's smile told her it was more than okay. His tender gaze said he loved her idea. "What time?"

"Whenever. What time have you been waking up?"

"Seven. Seven-thirty. Is that too early for you?"

"No, I'll be ready."

Christy was ready at seven-fifteen the next morning. She had packed all the food in Bob and Marti's old picnic basket. It was the same basket Uncle Bob had sent with Todd and Christy the first time they had a breakfast picnic on the beach. She had the firewood, fire starter, matches, blankets, and everything else she thought they would need for a cozy morning on the beach. The raindrops politely had complied with her wishes and hadn't returned with the morning.

The only thing missing was Todd. Her breakfast companion was sound asleep.

Christy considered going to the fire pit, setting up everything, and then waking Todd before she started to cook the eggs. She was trying to figure out how she would carry everything, when Uncle Bob stepped into the kitchen and greeted her by saying, "You sure are up early, Bright Eyes."

Christy told Uncle Bob her plan, and he eagerly agreed to help her by carrying the wood and necessary cooking utensils out to the fire pit. Christy followed him onto the cool sand as she lugged along the blanket and basket of food.

The morning sun hid behind a gray cover of thick clouds. Only a slight breeze ruffled across the sand.

You're just like Todd, Christy thought, looking for the absent sun. *You're nestled under the covers when you should be here, with me. Come on, I'm waiting for you.*

"Could you kids go for some coffee? I could bring a Thermos out to you," Bob said.

"That would be fine as long as . . ." She hesitated, not sure how to say the rest of her sentence politely. "As long as you just bring the coffee and then . . ."

"And then be on my way?" Bob unloaded the wood at the fire pit and gave Christy a curious grin. "You make it sound as if you two want to be alone."

Christy tried not to blush. "I hope that didn't sound rude."

"Oh no, not at all. It sounded to me like a woman in . . . a woman who is in . . . what's that word?"

Christy grinned. "In love."

"Ah yes, a woman in love."

"I am," Christy said quietly. "I really, truly am."

Uncle Bob tilted his head and, with a merry twinkle in his eyes, asked, "Is it anyone I know?"

"Yes, as a matter of fact, it is someone you know. And don't you dare say anything because . . ." Again Christy hesitated, looking for the right way to phrase her thoughts.

Her uncle seemed to know just what she was thinking. "Because, perhaps, you would like to be the one to tell him?"

Christy nodded.

"Then why don't you wait right here? Get your fire going. I'll make the coffee and roust Prince Charming for you. I don't need to bring the Thermos out here; Todd can bring it."

"Thanks, Uncle Bob. You are so good to me."

Uncle Bob brushed off her compliment and hustled back to his beach-front house. Christy made herself comfortable on the blanket by stretching out on her stomach. For several

luxurious moments she gazed contentedly at the magnifi-
cent, endless Pacific Ocean. She breathed in deeply until the
moist, chill air made her lungs ache, and she could feel a
slight tingle of sea salt in her nostrils.

*This is it, Father God. This is your day. You have aroused love
and awakened it in me, haven't you? Thank you for this amazing
gift of love. I know this pleases you. Keep my heart set on you and
on your path.*

Christy thought about how in years past she would have
prayed a testing sort of prayer right about now. She would
have said something like, "God, if you don't want me to tell
Todd I love him and if you don't want us to end up married,
then take away these feelings and make me know somehow
that he's not the one."

However, Christy had come a long way in her relationship with the Lord. She knew God wasn't a "this or that"
dictator. Her life was not about going "this way" and living
or going "that way" and dying. Life was a series of choices
and a process of choosing God and His path and then trusting Him for each step along the way. She knew that God was
her heavenly Father. Her Shepherd. The Lover of her soul.
He wanted what was best for her and had directed her
through the years to make choices that would benefit her
future and strengthen her relationship with Him.

Christy sat up and hugged her bent legs close, warming
her cold nose by wedging it between her knees. She remembered something Todd had told her a long time ago when
they were talking about knowing God's will. She had been
trying to decide if she should go to Switzerland. Todd's advice had been *"Love God and do what you want."*

His statement had seemed flippant to her at the time.
Going to school in Switzerland was a huge decision; yet all

Todd had done was to tell her he would support whatever she decided.

Now Christy understood the wisdom of Todd's advice. As she had begun to fall unreservedly in love with the Lord over the years, her heart was so turned toward Him that more and more she wanted to do whatever was the most pleasing and honoring to God.

"Love God and do what you want," Christy whispered in the gentle morning quiet. She felt complete peace. No doubts. This was right. A smile pressed Christy's lips upward in what felt like a permanent expression. She felt full inside. Full of love. Full of God. Full of hope.

Rising to her feet and stretching, Christy decided she'd better start the fire. The wood caught right away, and the grill she placed across the top of the cement fire ring balanced just enough for her to settle the skillet in the center. She placed the bacon strips in the skillet and waited for them to sing their splattering tune in harmony with the melody that was sizzling in her heart.

The bacon was just beginning to smell promising when Christy looked up and saw Todd coming toward her, Thermos in one hand and two coffee mugs in the other. His steps were slow but steady. Straight. His eyes were set on Christy, and he looked as if nothing in this world could stop him from coming to her.

Christy's heart danced a waltz as she counted his deliberate steps toward her.

Step, two-three-four. Step, two-three-four. Do you have any idea how incredibly handsome you are, my beloved, my friend?

Christy playfully touched her fingers to her lips, kissed them, and tossed her kiss to Todd on the fresh morning breeze.

Since his hands were full, Todd quickly turned his head and stretched his neck, as if to catch her kiss on his cheek. His smile seemed as permanently in place as hers was.

Christy's gaze never wavered from Todd coming toward her. In her mind and her heart, Christy knew she would never forget the sight of this man walking to her in the sand. This man who had brushed up against death two weeks ago and was now very much alive and very much in love. With her.

"Smells good." Todd stopped in front of the fire.

Christy thought it funny that his opening words for this momentous occasion were so common.

"I love you," Christy blurted out. Her hand immediately flew to her mouth. She had meant to say, "It's the bacon," but she was so full of love for Todd that the declaration just tumbled out.

Todd slowly lowered himself next to her on the blanket. He put down the Thermos and mugs and looked at her as if he wasn't sure he could trust his ears. His expression invited her to repeat the words.

Lowering her hand from her mouth, Christy looked at Todd's ocean blue eyes, and taking a deep breath, she dove in all the way to his soul. "I love you," she said slowly and deliberately. "I love you, Todd."

"I thought that's what you said." His voice caught with emotion as he added, "I love you, Kilikina."

Neither of them moved.

The bacon seemed to send sputtering firecrackers into the air while the flames snapped brightly in the fire ring. Overhead, three sea gulls circled and squawked loudly, like trumpeters heralding a proclamation from the King.

Slowly, tenderly, Christy and Todd moved toward each

other until their lips met in a kiss that filled Christy even more full of love. As they drew apart, the overflow brimmed in her eyes and spilled down her smiling face.

Todd wiped her tears with his steady hand. Then he did something he had done when they were in Europe. He pressed his moist hand to his chest, right over his heart. Christy knew that was his way of saying he was holding her tears in his heart.

She touched his warm lips with her fingers. Todd grasped her hand and placed a long kiss in the palm of her hand. Christy let go and pressed his kiss to her heart. In a steady, sure whisper, she said, "I love you."

Todd's grin broadened. "You know what they say about a vow being established. If a declaration is stated three times, that means it's established forever."

Christy nodded. She didn't know if Todd was trying to give her a final opportunity to change her mind, but nothing could prompt her to alter her declaration. He knew what these words meant to her, to him, to their future. Her vow before God was established.

"I love you," she stated firmly, pausing between each word. This time an unexpected giggle escaped at the end. "I had it all planned. We were going to eat, and we were going to be all snuggly and romantic, and then I was going to tell you."

Todd moved closer and took her in his arms. "How's this for snuggly and romantic?"

Christy giggled again. "I can't believe I just blurted it out like that."

"You know," Todd said, his deep voice rumbling from his chest, "I've been dreaming for the past week or more that you told me you love me."

Christy pulled back and faced him. "Those weren't dreams, Todd. I have been telling you. I told you the very first time on the camping trip, but you couldn't hear me over the dune buggy motor. I told you again and again at the hospital while you slept, and also at Bob and Marti's."

"Then I guess I wasn't dreaming." Todd brushed Christy's flyaway hair from the side of her face.

"No," Christy said. "You weren't dreaming then, and you're not dreaming now. This is real. As real as it's ever been for me."

Todd's silver-blue eyes were fixed on hers, filling her, adoring her, speaking to her all the cherished messages she knew he held in his heart for her.

Just then a daring sea gull swooped closer.

"Oh no you don't!" Christy grabbed the spatula and swatted the air. "You guys stay away from the food this time."

Todd reached for the tongs and flipped the bacon. "This is looking like it's almost ready."

"I have eggs and croissants, too," Christy said. "And I even bought mango-papaya jam."

"You are amazing," he said. "How about some coffee? It's strong, but I added cream and sugar in the Thermos, the way you like it."

Christy knew Todd didn't drink coffee very often, but when he did, he drank it black. She thought how considerate he was to remember she liked her coffee spiffed up and to be willing to drink it the way she liked it.

Side by side, heart by heart, Todd and Christy prepared their beach breakfast. The sea gulls kept their distance. The raindrops stayed to themselves on some other corner of the planet while the lazy sun stretched and peeked out from under its thick gray comforter every ten minutes or so.

Todd and Christy's long, slow, private picnic leisurely rolled through the calm October morning. They laughed, teased, kissed, prayed, and ate until they could take in no more. Christy knew she couldn't have asked for a more perfect morning. Everything was more wonderful than any dream she had ever dreamed of Todd.

Yet, as they gathered up the blanket and packed up the cooking gear, Christy felt uninvited remorse come over her. Todd hadn't proposed to her.

She knew she hadn't expected him to. Not really. But after she had opened her heart so wide and felt him responding with equal openness and joy, the next step should have been for Todd to say the life-changing sentence that naturally would follow. He needed to say, "Will you marry me?"

And he hadn't said that at their picnic. He had said lots of other wonderful things. He had told Christy how he had been waiting for her to be sure of her love and to verbalize it. He told her that, yes, Doug and Tracy were right: He had known she was the one for him from that first day on this beach when he had seen her tumble to shore, draped in seaweed. He affirmed to Christy that there had been no other girls for him. She was the only girl he had ever kissed. The only girl he had ever loved. The only one.

But he didn't say, "Marry me."

They walked slowly through the sand back to the house. Todd hadn't taken his medication before joining Christy on the beach, and he was suffering now. Christy carried the heavy picnic basket with the frying pan, dishes, utensils, and leftover jam. All Todd carried was the folded-up blanket and the empty Thermos, but those two items seemed almost too heavy for him.

By the time they entered the warm kitchen, Todd's face was pale, and he had broken out in a sweat. He placed the blanket and Thermos on the kitchen counter and immediately went to bed, where he stayed for the rest of the day.

Christy knew she had no reason to feel anything but delight over their time together. Todd had given her every ounce of energy he had. She reminded herself of that when the nagging thoughts of *Why didn't he propose?* came flying at her the rest of the weekend.

On Sunday morning Bob and Christy went to church together, while Todd stayed in bed and tried to regain some of his strength. Christy and her uncle both invited Marti to go with them, but she insisted Todd needed her.

As it turned out, the message that morning was on baptism, and Christy wasn't sure that was what her aunt needed to hear right now. Marti needed to come to Christ and surrender her life to Him. Christy thought of her brother as the sermon came to a close. She wondered how he was doing and realized she hadn't called home for more than a week.

Her parents would understand. Todd was her top priority right now. She knew they would be supportive of her decision to move forward in her relationship with Todd, too. Yet she felt sad that they were so removed from her life. The separation had begun when she went to Switzerland and had continued even after she settled into school at Rancho. She never had been the kind of daughter who discussed everything with her mom.

Christy had grown up as someone who kept to herself and worked through life's dilemmas quietly, in her room with the door closed.

Now that she had entered this next wonderful stage with Todd, Christy regretted that her mom hadn't been the kind of mom who was a best friend and a pal. But then, Christy's mom didn't have that kind of relationship with her own sister, Marti.

"You know," Bob said on their way home, "I made a decision this morning."

Christy, thinking her uncle was ready to talk about his strained relationship with his wife, positioned herself on the leather seat of Bob's Mercedes to pay full attention. It struck her that sitting in this position in ol' Gus was a miserable experience. But in Bob's car, it felt warm and comfy. She didn't know what it felt like to sit in the front passenger seat of their new Volvo because she hadn't had that pleasure yet.

"I've been doing what you suggested, Christy. I've been reading the Bible. I started in the New Testament with those first four books: Matthew, Mark, Luke, and John."

Christy nodded.

"And what I keep reading over and over is how Christ loved people through their weaknesses. He didn't pretend their problems didn't exist. He spoke the truth in love, but He said what needed to be said."

Christy felt a little nervous. How did her uncle intend to live out his revelation?

"I'm going to speak some truth to my wife," he said firmly.

"In love," Christy added.

"In love." Then Bob paused and said, "Christy, hand me the cell phone, will you?"

Christy handed it to him as he drove. She watched Bob punch in the automatic speed dial number for his home. "Are you going to tell her now? On the phone?"

"No, I'm checking to see if she wants us to pick up some lunch on our way home."

Christy felt nervous about Bob's plan while they stopped at Betsy's Deli to pick up sandwiches and salads. She felt nervous as Bob drove down his street and pulled the car into the garage. She felt nervous when Marti entered the kitchen and asked if the deli had her favorite chicken salad.

To Christy's surprise, instead of Uncle Bob's blasting out to his wife how she needed to make some decisions and some changes in her life, he went to her, wrapped his arms around her, and said, "I love you, Marti. With all my heart, I love you." Then he kissed her soundly on her surprised lips.

Christy couldn't remember ever seeing her uncle shower such affection on her aunt. Bob always had been kind and generous with Marti. But not passionate like this.

Marti pulled back, flabbergasted.

"I haven't told you that in a long time," Bob said, undaunted. "But it's true. It will always be true. I love you, and I always will love you. I'd give my life for you, Marti. Jesus said, 'Do not let your hearts be troubled. Trust in God.' I want your heart no longer to be troubled. I want you to trust in God."

Bob paused in his message of adoration just long enough for Christy to grab two of the deli sandwiches and make her exit, saying she would check on Todd.

He was sitting in the living room by the window, reading one of the textbooks Christy had brought for him, along with a list of assignments from his professors.

"You wouldn't believe what's going on in there." Christy settled in next to Todd and handed him a sandwich.

"Are they arguing again?"

"No, the opposite. Have they been arguing a lot while you've been here?"

"I couldn't sleep the other night because they were yelling so loud about who was right and who was wrong. Bob backed down, as he often does. He apologized, but it didn't settle anything."

"Well, he's in the kitchen right now telling her he loves her and would give his life for her and quoting verses to her."

Todd grinned. "Was the sermon on the book of Ephesians this morning?"

"No, baptism. Why?"

"Ephesians 5 says husbands are called to love their wives the way Christ loved the church and gave himself for her. You know, the way He gave His life for us. It talks about the husband washing his wife with the Word to make her clean."

Christy stared at the unwrapped sandwich in her hand. "That's beautiful. And so poetic. But let me tell you, it's weird to watch."

Todd laughed. "I don't think we're supposed to watch a husband as he washes his wife."

The imagery of Todd's words stirred Christy. She felt herself blushing and turned away. They ate quietly while she processed the concept of being washed clean and made presentable to God by His Word. The thought tied in with what the pastor had said that morning about baptism.

"Todd," Christy said, "I think I should get baptized."

He didn't look surprised by her sudden declaration. But then, she had been doing a lot of declaring lately.

"I was baptized when I was a baby. Or dedicated or something," she said. "I don't remember what they called it at my church in Wisconsin. I have a certificate that says the date and everything. But I want to be baptized now, as an adult, as a way of saying I choose to identify with Christ. To publicly show that I'm His follower."

"Must have been a pretty convincing sermon this morning."

"Not really. Well, maybe. I don't know. I've thought about this before. And that whole picture of being washed and made ready like a bride, well . . ." Christy wondered if she should press forward with her thought. "I see the deeper symbolism of baptism. It's like I said, I want to publicly take a stand and show I have set my heart on following Christ."

Todd nodded. She didn't feel the need for him to say anything. And she didn't need to say anything. She and Todd were moving on to the next level of their relationship, and she had reached a point in her relationship with the Lord in which she was ready to move on to a new level with Him.

"Where would you like to be baptized?" Todd said when he was about halfway through his sandwich.

"I don't know. You were baptized in the ocean, weren't you?"

"How did you remember that?"

"You told me the night Shawn died when we were at the jetty. You said you were baptized on my birthday, July 27."

"That's right."

"I think I'd like to be baptized at Riverview Heights since that's our church now. I'm not really connected to my parents' church in Escondido anymore. This is such a strange era in our lives, isn't it? What do we call home?"

Christy thought about her comment as she drove back to Rancho Corona that night. It was already dark, and she wished she had started back earlier, but she hadn't wanted to leave Todd. She thought about how Bob and Marti's house felt almost as much like home as her parents' house in Escondido—except that she felt as if she were sleeping in a covered wagon every night when she crawled into the raised bed in the southwestern guest room. She missed the pink ruffles more than she would have imagined.

Her dorm room felt temporary the way Basel had felt temporary. What Christy looked forward to was making her own home. A home somewhere with Todd.

She thought about how the weekend had gone. Their breakfast couldn't have been more perfect. Even the way she ended up blurting her "I love you" turned out to be wonderful and thrilling because it had tumbled out.

That Todd hadn't turned around and proposed didn't bother her as much as it had when they were picking up after their breakfast. She could think of all kinds of reasons Todd hadn't taken the next step. The poor guy hadn't recovered from his accident, and the medication made him groggy so he still slept a lot. He probably needed a chance to clear his head and think things through.

Besides all that, Christy thought, as she turned onto the road that led to Rancho Corona, *what would Todd and I use for money to start this new home of ours?*

She smiled at the vision that came to her. She and Todd were cashing all their wedding gift checks and heading for the Bargain Barn. But at least they were driving there in the blue Volvo instead of falling-apart Gus.

Maybe everything will come together little by little.

17

The moment Christy stepped into the dorm room, Katie told her how terrific everything had gone in the youth group that morning. Seventeen students had shown up, and Randy's band was so popular they were playing again at the church Tuesday night.

"Look," Katie said, handing Christy a large get-well card. Pictured on the front was a crowd of funny-looking lions, tigers, and panthers. Inside the card read, *We all miss you fiercely!*

"Every one of the kids signed it," Katie said. "We can mail it to Todd tomorrow. You would be amazed how some of them are getting serious about God. One of the girls stood up this morning and talked about how Todd had said on the camp-out that none of us knows when we're going to die, and then the very next day he was in the accident. One of the guys brought three of his friends to church this week, and they all said they would bring some more friends Tuesday night."

"That's amazing." Christy put the card back in the envelope and unpacked her weekend bag.

"I told you God was doing God-things." Katie turned down her stereo and made herself comfortable on Christy's bed since Katie's wasn't made.

"You'll have to call Todd tomorrow to tell him all this," Christy said. "He'll be so excited. I know he's been praying for the group every day. That is, when he isn't sleeping."

"He's still pretty out of it, huh?" Katie fluffed up Christy's pillow and leaned on her elbow.

"He's doing a lot better." Christy stuffed her dirty clothes into the bag in the back of her closet and flashed a big grin. "Yes, he's doing a lot better."

"What is that smirk on your face, girl?" Katie said. "Am I to read into your comment that Todd is doing a lot better because you finally made your grand confession?"

Christy stood up straight and, with her hands on her hips, said, "Yes, I did. Our breakfast turned out perfect, and my very incredible and wonderful boyfriend should have no doubt in his mind as to how I feel about him."

"Ah, at last you can say, 'I'm my beloved's, and he is mine,' " Katie said with poetic flair.

"Where have I heard that before? It's from the Song of Solomon, isn't it?"

"I guess."

"Have you read that book lately?" Christy went over to Katie's bed, briskly pulled up the sheets and comforter, and then tidied up Katie's pillows, one of which was stuffed in the Little Mermaid pillowcase and the other in the Minnie Mouse pillowcase.

"Nope," Katie said.

"I read Song of Solomon when I was in Basel, and it's the strangest, most exotic, lyrical book. It only has eight chapters."

"Did you read the part that says, 'Your hair is like a flock of goats'?" Katie asked. "How romantic is that? Or that other line, 'Your neck is like the tower of David.' Oh, now, that sounds real attractive! If some guy tried those lines on me, I'm sure I'd fall instantly in love with him."

Christy laughed so hard she had to sit down. "Now I know why poor Matthew Kingsley was checked off your list. He didn't use the right lines on you."

"Poor Matthew Kingsley," Katie said with a sigh. "He never learned the goat hair pickup line back in Brightwater."

Christy laughed again. "Be nice. Matthew is still my dearest friend, you know."

"Oh, I know. Don't get me wrong. I think he's a wonderful guy. He sure jumped in and ran the show Sunday. Matt's a great guy. He's just not great for me. I need someone with pizzazz!"

"Are you saying Rancho Corona is low on guys with pizzazz?"

"Yes, I would say that. But don't read anything into this, Christy. I'm content. I honestly am. My days of searching for the perfect guy are over."

"And why is that?"

"I've decided to become one of those Proverbs 31 women."

"Is that a new club on campus?"

"No, but that's not a bad idea. It could replace the 'P.O. Box Club' Sierra and I started in England."

"And what did that stand for?" Christy asked.

"Don't you remember? The *P* is for 'pals' and the *O* is for 'only.' Sierra and I were the only two members. Our motto was to be Pals Only with guys. But after hearing Sierra's latest report on how she and Paul are getting along, I'm afraid our club has dwindled to one member. Me. So I think I'll start a new club. P–31, for the Proverbs 31 woman."

"I see," Christy said, hiding a smile. "Do I want to ask what the requirements are for entry to this P–31 club?"

"Very simple. We go by the first part of verse ten in that chapter. It says, 'An excellent wife, who can find?' "

Christy raised her eyebrows questioningly as she waited for an explanation.

"Don't you see? It doesn't say, 'An excellent hubby who can find?' It says a good wife. I would say that indicates the guy is the one who should be doing the seeking."

Christy laughed and threw her pillow across the room. Katie ducked, and the pillow hit the wall.

"You think I'm kidding? Believe me, I've thought through every angle of this. From here on out, I'm completely available to God. I'll just keep going about my business, right here, in the very center of God's will for my life now. And if there's a 'beloved' out there for me, then he can start seeking me for a change. I'll be here, an excellent future wife, just waiting for him to find me."

Christy was about to speak when Katie silenced her.

"Don't you dare say anything about how you feel bad that you and Todd are so sure and so close while nobody special is on the horizon for me."

Christy lowered her eyes.

"That's what you were going to say, isn't it?"

"How did you know?" Christy asked.

"Let's just say that you and I are on about verse eighty-four of that familiar song. You know, eighty-fourth verse, same as the first, a little bit louder and a little bit worse."

Christy walked over to sit on the bed next to Katie. "We do sound pretty good together when we sing."

"Not this song." Katie handed the Little Mermaid pillow to Christy for a backrest. "Not anymore. We need to give that old tune a rest. You are about to sing a brand-new song, Chris. Now your duet will be with Todd. Let me sing a new solo now, okay? None of the old verses apply to either of us anymore."

Christy wondered if she had ever admired her dearest friend more than she did at that moment.

"You let God do His God-things in your life, and I'll invite God to do His God-things in my life, and we won't compare ourselves with each other. Okay?" Katie seemed eager for Christy to agree.

With a bow of her head Christy said, "As you wish."

Christy noticed a genuine change in Katie as the week progressed. For one thing, she borrowed Christy's nail file and worked on her fingernails Tuesday night. Christy had never seen her tomboy friend file her nails. Bite them, yes. Pick at the cuticles, yes. But never file them and then rub her hands with cocoa butter lotion.

Katie filed away cheerfully while Christy looked up information on the Internet for her report on Milton, the blind poet. Katie mentioned that she was on the brink of perfecting her latest herbal tea recipe.

By Thursday, Katie was certain she had the mixture just right. To celebrate her breakthrough, she had gone to Bargain Barn to buy a china teapot and enough mismatched cups to host a tea party in their room.

Four of Katie's girl friends came on Thursday evening at seven-thirty. Katie said she would have invited more, but she had found only six china cups at Bargain Barn. Christy had cleaned their room and arranged it so all six "testers" had places to sit. Katie brewed her special tea in a hot pot plugged into the wall. While waiting for the tea to steep, Katie passed around a plate of Oreo cookies.

Sierra was telling the other guests about how her older sister, Tawni, was getting married at Thanksgiving and how Tawni's fiancé had taken a job in Oklahoma.

Christy was interested to hear all the details, but she slipped off into the corner where Katie was straining the herbs from the tea as she poured each cup. "Katie," Christy whispered, "I want to ask you this one more time. Please don't get upset. But are you sure no one is going to break out in a rash after drinking your tea this time?"

"I'm 99.9 percent positive," Katie said. "This is a completely different combination from what I used last spring. There aren't any nettles in this one."

"You used nettles last time?"

"I didn't realize they were stinging nettles, all right?"

"Why do you grow nettles?"

"Because nettles are good for people who have a snoring problem. I just got the dried nettles mixed up with the dried hibiscus. And I only used a pinch. But not this time. This concoction is my Indian summer blend. It's apples, ginger, cinnamon, and other spices. All safe ingredients, I assure you."

Christy would have felt more assured if Katie hadn't used the term "concoction" to describe the tea. Returning to her seat, Christy smiled graciously when Katie offered her a steaming cup of the fragrant brew.

"Katie, this is delicious!" Sierra was the first guest to sip her tea. Her positive report prompted the others to venture bravely where no woman had gone before.

"It is good." Christy nonchalantly checked the skin on

the inside of her arm to see if any spots were appearing. None so far.

"It's a perfect blend," Sierra raved. "I like the balance of the ginger and the spices. Is that clove I taste?"

"Yes."

"It's just right. Not too strong. You've done it, Katie! You've come up with a winner."

Christy and the other guests soon agreed.

Katie beamed. "Then I officially announce the birth of Katie's Indian Summer Tea!"

The group applauded.

After Christy had gone a full twenty-four hours without any spots showing up or experiencing any other adverse effects, she took a small bag of Katie's tea to the bookstore. Donna often drank tea, and Christy thought she might want to try Katie's new blend.

Donna liked the tea as much as Christy, Sierra, and the others had. Later, as Christy was about to leave work to make her weekend trek to Newport Beach, Donna asked if she could get some more of Katie's tea.

"I can bring some in on Monday," Christy said. "Or you could call our room and ask Katie for some more."

"I'd like to pass it on to a friend of mine," Donna said. "He recently opened a bookstore in Murietta Hot Springs with a specialty café adjacent to the store. I thought he might want to add this tea to his menu at the café."

"Wouldn't something like this have to be approved by the Food and Drug Administration before it's served to the public?" Christy asked. She didn't want to discourage such a terrific opportunity for Katie, but she could just see Katie whipping up a batch in a hurry and mistaking nettles for one of the herbs. Christy envisioned café customers doubled over from the tea, and Katie sued for damages.

"I'm sure you're right," Donna said. "The laws have gotten so strict. That's good. But it's also limiting, isn't it?"

Christy felt glad for such laws. She didn't voice her opinion, though.

"If you and Katie have a chance to visit the café, I think you really would like it. It's called The Dove's Nest. They call the bookstore The Ark. Clever, isn't it?"

Christy studied Donna for a moment. She was wearing a pumpkin-colored turtleneck under a cream cable-knit cardigan, and her hair was pulled back in a wide gold barrette. With the rows of books behind her and the empty teacup in her hand, she looked as if she could be a model in an ad for Katie's tea. Donna personified everything that was cozy, welcoming, and warm.

"It sounds like fun," Christy said. "Todd should be able to get out more in the next few weeks. Maybe we could all go together sometime."

"How is he doing?" Donna asked.

"Lots better."

"And your relationship is still strong?"

"Stronger than ever. It's all just about perfect."

Donna placed a hand on Christy's shoulder. "Then remember this time, Christy. Write about it in your diary. Write about this perfect time so you will remember what you know to be true and what you feel bubbling over in your heart. In the years to come, you might experience a season of confusion or doubt. It will help so much if you have this time recorded."

Christy appreciated Donna's words, especially since she seemed to speak from experience. That weekend, Christy made sure she wrote in her diary everything she was feeling about Todd. Part of one of her entries read,

> Right now I can't imagine going on in my life without being partnered with Todd in whatever comes our way. It seems so natural and like such a perfect fit for us to be together.
>
> I know he's going to propose soon. I just know it. Maybe before this weekend is over I'll hear those words dancing from his lips. I wonder how he will ask me. I'm sure it will be creative.
>
> Or maybe not. Todd has a very practical side to him, as well. I wouldn't be surprised if he just turned to me over tacos and said, "So do you want to get married?"
>
> I don't know how he will ask me or when, but I know I'm ready . . . more than ready to say yes.
>
> Yes, yes, a thousand times yes. I will marry you, Todd Spencer, and I will spend the rest of my life loving you with all my heart.
>
> And one more thing. Donna told me to write everything down in detail, so I have one detail to add. I love being in love. I love the way I wake each morning, and as soon as I do, I think about Todd and how I'm wildly, completely in love with him, and I smile.
>
> I've been smiling all the time lately. Nothing gets me down. Katie said I had that mysterious glow of love in my cheeks last week. She said it looked as if my eyes were always laughing about some secret and that even my posture was improved. That made me laugh. She said Todd's love for me had made me beautiful and that my love for him was healing him.
>
> All I know is that love has enabled me to soar higher into the heavens and into my relationship with God than I ever have gone before. Love has given me breath as I have plunged deeper into the ocean of understanding and patience. Love has

focused my eyes to the minutest details, as minor as a ladybug inching across a daisy petal. And at the same time, love has enlarged my embrace so that I can gather friends and family closer to my heart than ever before.

Love is . . . oh, how I wish I had the words. Love is God's greatest gift and His most cherished reward. It is the echo of His own heart, sounded back to Him by us, His children, so that a decaying world might see firsthand the power of resurrection and new life. Love is all I know in my world right now.

I feel like laughing at my own giddiness.

I realize that I'm such a virgin in every way. I have never tasted a sensation as intoxicating as being in love. It has me reeling. Ha! I'm emotionally drunk on God's greatest gift, love. Imagine that!

―――――

Christy reread her diary entry a week and a half after she had penned her "Ode to Love," and she still felt euphoric. Todd had returned to classes and to his position at Riverview Heights Church. A little more than a month had passed since the accident. He was still moving slowly and sleeping a lot, but he had his life back. And Christy had Todd back. Life was rosy.

The report Todd gave Christy regarding Marti and Bob was that Bob was still pouring love over his wife. Washing her with words. Marti had neither pulled away from him nor pulled closer to him. She was stuck. Todd concluded that, for now, that was probably the best place for her to be.

Christy attended the two classes the church required for a person to be baptized and was signed up for the Sunday-evening baptism the week before Thanksgiving. She bought some beautiful ivory parchment cards at the bookstore and wrote invitations to her family and friends. As she addressed each envelope in her best hand-writing, she wondered how long it would be before she was addressing wedding invitations to these same peo-ple.

Todd hadn't proposed yet. She knew it was only a matter of time. They even had talked a few times, in gen-eral terms, about how Doug had gone to Tracy's dad and asked him for Tracy's hand in marriage before Doug had proposed to Tracy. Christy guessed Todd was planning to talk to her dad. But when?

They would all be together in a few weeks for her bap-tism. And for Thanksgiving her parents had invited Todd, his dad, Bob, and Marti to come to their home. Christy wondered if Todd would get on his knees right there, after the turkey and before the pumpkin pie, to ask Christy in front of their relatives to be his wife. That would be mem-orable.

Christy knew the suspense would be driving her crazy if she didn't delight in surprises. That, and knowing she was ready. Any time, any place, in any way, Todd could pop the question, and she knew her answer would be yes.

The day before her baptism, Christy was in her dorm room, trying to finish typing a paper on Katie's laptop, when her mom called. "We were a little surprised to re-ceive your baptism announcement," Mom said.

"You guys are coming, aren't you?"

"Yes," Mom said slowly. "You do realize, don't you, that you were baptized as an infant."

"Yes," Christy said. "And I completely honor that. Please don't think I'm not agreeing with what you and

Dad did in that sacred ceremony. I'm actually trying to demonstrate with my life that I agree wholeheartedly, and that's why I want to be baptized as an adult."

"Both your father and I were baptized as infants, and we didn't feel the need to be baptized again when we were adults."

"I know. And that's what was right for you guys. I feel differently. Can you and Dad honor my choice to do this, even if you don't agree completely?" Christy didn't understand why something like this should unsettle her mom. Her parents were Christians. Why wouldn't they be happy to see her take this step of faith?

Christy and her mom ended the conversation with both of them agreeing to try to see the other's point of view.

When Christy's parents arrived at Riverview Heights on Sunday evening, her mom came into the changing room, where Christy was waiting in a white baptismal gown. Her bare feet were freezing on the linoleum. She wished she hadn't gotten ready so soon. She was the only woman getting baptized that evening, and so she felt especially glad that her mom had come to be with her.

"I'm so glad you guys came," Christy said.

"We wouldn't miss this for anything." Mom gave Christy a hug. "I wanted to make sure you didn't misunderstand my phone call yesterday afternoon. Your father and I have discussed this, and we do honor your decision. We are very proud of you. We always have been. I think you kids today are more emotionally connected to your faith than we ever were. Todd helped us see that you are taking ownership of your faith by doing this. Your father and I can see why this demonstration of your beliefs is important to you."

"Thanks, Mom," Christy said, giving her another hug. In many ways, this moment was a fulfillment of Christy's wish that she and her mom could be closer and more like friends. She didn't know if her mom felt any different right now, but Christy definitely felt as if the two of them had crossed a bridge into a new place where they were both women. As women, they could view each other more as friends.

Her mom must have had some of the same feelings because she gave Christy a tender smile. "Your father and I want you to know that we support all your upcoming decisions. And we're very happy for you. For both of you."

As soon as Mom left and Christy was alone again, with her bare feet tapping on the cold linoleum floor, she wondered what the last part meant about her mom being happy for both of them.

Did you mean you're happy for Todd, too? He's not getting baptized.

Christy remembered that Todd had taken their car all day yesterday and hadn't returned in time for dinner in the cafeteria. He didn't say where he had gone, and Christy hadn't asked because she was so swamped with homework.

Mom also said that Todd helped them to understand why I'm getting baptized. Did he go to their house yesterday?

Christy's heart began to beat a little faster. *Did Todd go there to ask my parents if we could get married? Is Todd about to propose? Tonight?*

The pastor tapped on the door and said she should

come to the baptismal when she heard the music. Christy put aside her dreams and concentrated on the event at hand. She had prepared something to say and knew she would be first. Sounds of a familiar hymn echoed through the closed door.

"Like a river glorious, is God's perfect peace."

Christy smiled. She loved that hymn. It was one of her childhood favorites when they sang it at her old church in Brightwater. It felt as if a part of her childhood had joined her on this important evening. After spending so many years only singing contemporary choruses for worship, Christy loved having one of the oldies there to usher her forward into the built-in baptismal.

The baptismal was a square sort of "hot tub" at the front of the sanctuary and usually was hidden by silk ficus trees. This evening the trees were gone, and Pastor John stood waist-deep in the water, giving Christy a gentle smile and welcoming her to come into the water.

"Stayed upon Jehovah, hearts are fully blessed."

Christy took a cautious step into the water and found it was warm.

"Finding as he promised, perfect peace and rest."

She waded to the center and stood facing Pastor John, not quite ready to look out at the congregation.

The hymn ended, and Pastor John spoke about how Jesus was baptized in the Jordan River. The pastor explained how Christy was responding in obedience to the command found in the book of Acts, " 'Repent and be baptized, every one of you, in the name of Jesus Christ for the forgiveness of your sins.' "

Christy hesitantly looked out and saw Todd in the front row, his face beaming at her. He was surrounded by at least twenty students from the youth group. They all seemed serious as they watched Christy.

What a crowd of witnesses! I had no idea these guys were all going to come!

Pastor John quoted from Matthew 28. " 'Therefore go and make disciples of all nations, baptizing them in the name of the Father and of the Son and of the Holy Spirit, and teaching them to obey everything I have commanded you. And surely I am with you always, to the very end of the age.' "

He turned to Christy, placed a reassuring hand on her shoulder, and said, "I've asked Christy to tell you why she has decided to be baptized today."

Christy realized for the first time that this was a decision. A good decision. And one she had made on her own.

"I surrendered my life to the Lord when I was fifteen," Christy began. She noticed Katie and Sierra sitting with Todd and the youth group. Matt was with them, as well as Sierra's brother and five other students from Rancho.

"Since that day, when I got on my knees and asked Christ to forgive my sins, come into my heart, and take over my life, I have seen Him at work in so many ways." She realized she was speaking fast and tried to calm down so she could slow her words.

"God has changed me, and I know He is always with me. All the time. And I'm learning to trust Him more for all the details." She paused a second, then added, "All the decisions of my life."

The "decisions" part hadn't been in what she originally wrote out, but it was true.

"I decided to be baptized as a way of, first of all, agreeing with my parents' direction in my life when they had me baptized as a baby." Christy made eye contact with her mom. Mom's smile gave Christy all the assurance she needed to know that this was the right decision.

She noticed Aunt Marti sitting next to her mom. Christy hadn't expected her aunt to come.

As she finished her little speech, Christy kept her gaze on Aunt Marti. "The second reason I'm getting baptized is because I see it as an act of obedience. Like those verses Pastor John just quoted. We are commanded by God to turn from living to please ourselves, to come wholeheartedly to God so that we can live the life He has designed for us."

Feeling a burst of boldness, Christy added something else that wasn't in her original notes. "It's like God is the Potter, and we are the clay. He doesn't want us to run off and try to make ourselves into something we weren't created to be. He wants us to stay on His potter's wheel even when we get dizzy sometimes, spinning around and being squeezed and reshaped. He's the One who created us. He knows how to make us into our own person. Or actually, into His own person. The person we were meant to be. He wants us to stay on the wheel so He can shape us with His hands." Christy paused and then added with a final breath, "With His nail-scarred hands."

She realized that everything she had just said was unplanned and that her aunt probably would be upset. But Christy felt clean. Clean and ready to publicly identify with Christ's burial and resurrection by being submerged under the water and coming up new.

Pastor John quietly asked Christy to fold her hands in front of her. She did and she closed her eyes.

Pastor John's deep voice washed over her as he said the words from Scripture, "In the name of the Father, the Son, and the Holy Spirit, I now baptize you, Christina Juliet Miller."

She felt herself being lowered backward by strong hands until her entire body, hair, face, everything, was submerged. For an instant, everything was silent. Dead.

Then those same strong hands pulled her from the water. A rousing burst of applause from the congregation met her as she came back to the land of the living. As she emerged, water dripping everywhere, an unexpected giggle tickled its way from her closed lips.

"Go in peace," the pastor exhorted her. "For Christ Jesus, the Lord of your life, will be with you always."

18 Aunt Marti didn't make a scene about Christy's sermon from the baptismal pool. She didn't acknowledge any of it until that Thursday when the extended family was gathered at Christy's parents' house for Thanksgiving.

Christy and Todd had arrived in Escondido Wednesday night, and both of them had helped Christy's mom make pies. The methods of the three cooks were all different, and the kitchen was small. The four-hour pie-making adventure provided constant laughter and one unauthorized fight between Todd and Christy with small handfuls of flour. But it was enough to put Christy's mom into a cleaning frenzy.

When the pies were presented at the end of Thanksgiving dinner, Todd and Christy playfully boasted about their combined efforts. Mom set the record straight by saying that Christy and Todd had gotten a little too creative with the spices in the pumpkin pie. She suggested that if anyone was interested in a milder dessert, the apple pie she had made would be a good choice.

"Christy does tend to get creative and spice things up, doesn't she?" Marti said. She had been quiet most of the dinner. When she did talk, it was to Todd's dad, who was seated on her right.

Christy took Marti's comment to mean the baptismal message.

"Who wants what?" Mom asked, ignoring her sister's comment. Christy guessed her mom had done that most of her life.

"Did you make mincemeat?" Dad asked.

Christy smiled. He asked that every year. Every Thanksgiving for the past twenty-some years, Mom made one mincemeat pie. And every year, Dad was the only one who ate any of that pie. Yet he still asked, as if maybe she had forgotten this year.

"Mincemeat?" Todd's dad asked. "I'll take mincemeat, if you have it."

"You take yours warmed with vanilla ice cream, Bryan?" Christy's dad asked.

"Is there any other way?" Todd's dad said with a smile.

Christy went to help Mom slice the pies. She was grinning to herself at the way her dad had just bonded with Todd's dad over mincemeat pie.

Whatever it takes!

She wondered what it would take now for Todd to ask her to become his wife. All he had to do was slip into the kitchen, come up behind her, put his arms around her, and whisper in her ear, "How would you like it if we made Thanksgiving pies together for the rest of our lives?"

Christy daydreamed how she would answer with something witty like, "As long as we always keep it spicy."

Or maybe something sweet and mushy would be better, like, "You know I'll always be your punkin."

"Christy?"

She turned to see her mom watching her with concern. Christy had frozen in her daydream with the knife halfway suspended over the first pie.

"I was just, ah, trying to decide how many pieces to cut."

"It doesn't matter. We have plenty. Would you put these two mincemeat pieces in the microwave?"

"Sure." Christy turned from her mom, feeling the blood rushing to her cheeks.

When will I become old enough to stop this crazy blushing? I could understand it when I was fifteen. Or even eighteen. But I'm twenty years old. I'm a woman about to promise herself to a man, and I still blush like a little girl.

Christy wondered if Todd struggled with feelings of shyness. Perhaps that was why he hadn't proposed yet.

After they had eaten pie, Uncle Bob insisted they all gather in the living room so he could take a group picture. He had a remote switch on his camera that allowed him to place the camera on a kitchen chair.

Mom, Marti, Dad, and Todd's dad all squashed themselves together on the couch. David plopped in the middle of the floor in front of the couch. That left openings on either side of David. Christy sat on the right, in front of her mom, and Todd sat in front of his dad on the left side.

To Christy's surprise, David, the nondemonstrative child, put his long arms around Todd's and Christy's necks and let his appendages hang there like thick gray octopus tentacles.

"Everyone say 'hey!' " Bob positioned himself on the couch's arm and leaned over next to Marti.

"I thought *we were* supposed to say 'cheese,' " David said. Christy noticed that his voice was changing. It sounded especially funny since she was so close to him.

"Try saying 'hey' this time," Bob said. "It makes for a more natural smile than a stiff 'cheese.' "

"A stiff cheese!" David repeated and burst out laughing.

Todd and Christy turned their faces toward each other under the mutual lock of their guffawing octopus jailer. They exchanged a look that said, "Oh, brother, tell me we weren't like that when we were his age."

Just then the camera flash went off.

"Take another one," Marti cried. "I had my eyes closed."

Christy and Todd turned back to the positioned camera.

"On the count of three," Bob said. "One, two, three!"

A merry chorus of "Hey!" rose from the couch, and the picture was snapped.

"Now just Todd and Bryan," Bob said, getting into his role of family photo historian. "Why don't you two use this chair here? Let me put you over by the window so I get better light. Bryan, why don't you sit, and, Todd, you stand behind him."

Everyone watched while the father and son took their positions. Christy noticed how much the two resembled each other, and she felt a warmth rush through her.

Wow, Todd, if you look like that twenty-five years from now, I will be a happy woman! What am I saying? I'd be happy with you twenty-five years from now no matter what. But if you turn out like your dad . . .

Christy casually glanced at her mom. She was at least three or maybe four inches shorter than Christy and had a round figure. Her face was round, her body was round. Her hair had gone almost completely gray, and she hadn't colored it or changed the short style. Christy's mom didn't use makeup. She was a simple, uncomplicated, reserved, honest woman. And Christy always admired her for that.

But I hope my looks turn out a little more like Aunt Marti's. Not with the hair extensions or any of that. I just want to keep myself looking appealing to Todd. At least I have some height from my dad's side. Hopefully I'll be able to keep my weight down.

Christy had a feeling that just trying to keep up with Todd for the next twenty-five years would be a thorough workout.

"Okay, that's good." Bob adjusted the camera. "Todd, how about if you put your hand on your dad's shoulder? Yes, like that."

Christy noticed that Todd appeared slightly self-conscious about his hands ever since the stitches had been removed. Both his hands were covered with dashes of white scar tissue where the glass had sliced his flesh. He placed his hand on his dad's shoulder but turned the top of his hand away from the camera so the scars wouldn't show.

For the first time, Christy thought how blessed Todd was that none of the glass had cut his face or throat. Uncle Bob had been severely burned on his neck and left ear several years ago. Christy had gotten so used to how he looked after he healed up that she didn't even notice it anymore. It made her wonder if Marti, who spent her life striving for perfection, found it hard to accept Bob's scars.

Your scars are beautiful to me, Todd. They always will be evidence that you could have died, but God kept you here for a reason. For me. For us. For whatever we do together to further His kingdom.

"Terrific." Bob took the third snapshot of Todd and Bryan Spencer. He proceeded to take shots of Christy's family and then five shots of Todd and Christy together.

"Hey!" Christy said, following Bob's advice for a natural smile.

"Hey yourself, pumpkin pie breath," Todd teased her.

"Are you saying the pie turned out too spicy?"

"I think we should keep the double cinnamon next year but leave out the cloves."

"As you wish," Christy whispered.

Bob snapped a final shot, and his camera began to rewind. "End of the roll," he said.

Christy glanced over and noticed that everyone was still watching her and Todd as they engaged in their snappy exchange.

Marti came closer with a knowing smirk on her face. "Those will make perfect photos for the newspaper announcement."

"What newspaper announcement?" Todd asked.

Marti raised an eyebrow slightly to Christy. Christy didn't need any hints. She knew what her aunt was getting at. The society section of Marti's local newspaper ran engagement announcements complete with the couples' photos. Christy didn't spell it out for Todd.

And Todd didn't spell out any kind of proposal to her that Thanksgiving weekend. Christy thought she was okay with that. Her dreams weren't dashed. A little postponed, perhaps.

It didn't really bother her until she was back at Rancho on Monday, and Sierra came into the bookstore to see her. Sierra was bubbling over with news about her sister's wedding that weekend. Tawni and Jeremy had gotten married at Paul's church in San Diego, where Jeremy and Paul's dad was the pastor. Sierra made an exaggeratedly gruesome face when she described the frilly, mint green bridesmaid dress she was forced to wear. The two friends made plans to meet at The Java Jungle after Christy's class that night so she could hear the rest of the details.

After Sierra left the bookstore, Christy did a little math. Doug and Tracy had been married now for a year and a half. Tawni and Jeremy had met the week that Doug and Tracy got engaged. Katie told her last night about a girl on their floor who had met a guy the first week of classes, and they had gotten married over Thanksgiving break.

Why is everyone else getting married, but Todd and I aren't even engaged? How slow is Todd going to be? He's not waiting for me to say something, is he? No, he would want to be the one to officially do the proposing. So what is he waiting for?

Christy found it easy to come up with a half dozen logical explanations. School and money were at the top of the list. She tried to put it all out of her mind and work hard to complete the class assignments that needed to be turned in before Christmas break. Her only time to study was in between work and classes. Long ago she had discovered that she wasn't a night owl like Katie. Christy reserved her evenings for taking long walks around campus with Todd or for meeting friends to laugh and talk in The Java Jungle.

Weekends inevitably were gobbled up by church and youth group activities, which Christy was beginning to love. The youth group was growing each week. On the Sunday after Thanksgiving they had twenty-four students in the morning session and sixteen of them showed up at evening service. Two of the girls told Christy they had decided to be baptized after they had seen Christy's baptism.

Todd was planning an outreach trip to Mexico the week between Christmas and New Year's since his plans for the Thanksgiving outreach had been cancelled after his accident. It looked as if they might have as many as thirty Rancho students and teens from the church going down to an orphanage in Tecate.

A week and a half before Christmas break Christy volunteered to prepare all the food on the trip, including the shopping this time. She and Todd were sitting at their usual table in the cafeteria with their usual group of friends, when she told Todd she would take care of all the food.

"I'll help you," Todd said.

Christy shook her head. "Oh no you won't!"

In response, Todd kissed her soundly and whispered, "I love you," in front of everyone. He had never been so outwardly demonstrative around their friends before. Christy knew then that if any of them had doubts about Todd and her being an established couple, they wouldn't question it now.

No one questioned anything. They all seemed comfortable being around Todd and Christy even in their new, greatly improved, truly-in-love season of life. Even Matt seemed comfortable and completely himself.

Matt announced to the gang at dinner that same night that he had decided to ask a girl from his earth science class to go out with him on the Friday before Christmas break. He turned to Christy and Katie for their advice.

"You have a week and a half," Katie stated. "That means you should at least ask her by this Friday because it's nice to have a week's notice on a first date." Then she muttered, "Not that I would know."

Christy elbowed her. Katie elbowed Christy right back.

"I'm just saying I would think a week's notice would be nice," Katie said defensively. "That's all."

"Where are you planning to go to dinner?" Sierra asked.

"I keep hearing about this new café that opened up in

Murrieta Hot Springs. It's called The Dove's Nest. There's a bookstore connected to it called The Ark. On the weekends they have live music."

"Why didn't you tell me?" Randy asked. "Our band is looking for more gigs."

"I've heard about that place," Christy said. "Donna at the bookstore said that the manager of the café might want to buy some of your Indian Summer tea, Katie."

"Why didn't you tell me?" Katie mimicked Randy.

"I didn't know if you needed to have approval from the Food and Drug Administration or something."

"Bring the tea with you to Mexico," Todd said. "The people at the orphanage in Tecate would love it. And you don't need any government approvals there."

Katie gave Todd a pained expression. "Yeah, like I'm going to set up a little tea cart under an umbrella and pass out Dixie cups of herbal tea to all the people in the village."

"Do you think The Dove's Nest is too casual a place for me to ask Jenna to go on a first date?" Matt asked Christy, trying to get back on the topic.

"No, I think it sounds perfect."

"Would you mind if I went with you?" Randy asked Matt.

Matt gave him a strange look.

"I mean, I could come up with a date, if I had to. I just want to check out the place."

"What do you mean you could come up with a date if you had to?" Sierra punched her buddy on the arm.

Randy answered her with a crooked grin. "Does that mean you want to go with me?"

"No, you clueless bubble brain. Why don't you ask Vicki?"

Christy knew that Vicki, Sierra's roommate, never seemed to be at a loss for attention from guys on campus.

"Is she still speaking to me?" Randy asked.

"There's one way to find out," Sierra said. "Ask her out."

Randy tilted his head and gave Sierra a timid look. "Will you ask her for me?"

"Wimp!" Sierra spouted.

"What is with all you guys?" Katie asked. "Why are you so afraid of us women?"

"I'm not afraid," Todd said.

"You don't count anymore," Katie said with a coy glance at him.

Todd playfully clutched his chest as if her words were arrows that hit their mark.

"I'm serious, you guys," Katie said. "Why is it no men on this campus . . . no, make that no men in this world, know how to initiate a relationship with a woman?"

"What is she talking about?" Sierra asked, looking directly at Christy.

"I'll tell you what I'm talking about. I'm talking about romance and risk and men who aren't afraid to be men. I'm talking about a man who will walk boldly up to a woman and say, 'Hey, your hair is like a flock of goats. Will you go out with me?' "

Christy burst out laughing, and the others joined in. She didn't know if any of them understood Katie was referring to a quote from the Song of Solomon.

"Flowers are optional," Katie stated over the subsiding laughter.

"You know what?" Matthew said. "You're right. I'm going to go find Jenna right now, and I'm going to ask her out."

"You sure you don't want us all to go with you?" Sierra teased.

Matt's eyes lit up, and he turned to focus on Sierra. "That's a great idea. Instead of Randy and me trying to put together some kind of awkward double date, why don't you guys all come? I could tell Jenna a bunch of us are going, so it won't feel like a date."

"You're hopeless," Katie said. "Here I try to offer you useful advice, and you turn us all into a bunch of decoys to hide behind."

"You're no decoy, Katie," Matt said with an admiring expression. He leaned across the table, and even though everyone could hear what he said, he spoke the words to Katie only. "You are a one-of-a-kind woman, and I'm certain some guy out there will match your wit and your charm. I'm sure you've figured out, though, that it won't be a farm boy."

"Aw, shucks," Katie said. "I thought farm boys were the only ones who knew that flock-of-goats line."

"Not this farm boy."

"No, not you." Katie said the words so tenderly, Christy was certain Matt and Katie had firmly established their friendship.

That night, once the two of them were back in their room, Christy asked Katie, "What was all that between you and Matt and the farm-boy stuff?"

Katie was tapping away on her laptop, throwing together a three-page summary that had been due that day in one of her classes, but she had forgotten about. Katie seemed to forever be turning in papers a day late, but for some reason she charmed her teachers into not lowering her grades.

"We had a talk yesterday. No, the day before," Katie said

between taps of the keys. "It was Monday. Monday afternoon we talked about you and Todd."

"You didn't tell me that."

"You were asleep when I came in the past two nights."

"What did you say about me?"

Katie looked around the corner of her desk to where Christy was snuggled under her covers. "Wouldn't you like to know?"

"Yes, I would!"

"It was nothing big. Just how happy you and Todd are and how totally in love you are and how that's what we all wish for someday."

"Awww," Christy said. "How sweet."

"Yeah, I know. Matt and I also decided that, since chances are good we two would end up in your wedding party, we better stick close so we can help each other out when it comes time to pull those prewedding pranks on Todd."

"Prewedding pranks?" Christy said. "You might be waiting awhile. We don't even have reason for you to come up with pre-*engagement* pranks."

"It's only a matter of time," Katie said. "You know that. I know that. All of us know that. You'll see. Todd is clever and creative. He'll make the moment memorable."

Christy slipped back under the covers and listened to the speedy *click-click*ing of the laptop keys. Her heart was at rest. Whenever Todd did get around to asking her to marry him, she knew she would be ready with the answer.

Katie kept typing but asked, "Are you and Todd going to The Dove's Nest with everybody?"

"I think so. Are you?"

"No, I don't think I'll go."

"Why?"

"Oh, come on, do the math, Chris. You and Todd, Matt and Jenna, Randy and Vicki, Sierra will bring Paul. I obviously would be Mambo number nine."

"But we're all friends," Christy said. "I want you to come. No one would make you feel left out. You could bring some of your tea, like Donna suggested. It's going to be fun. Come on. We'll invite Doug and Tracy. You haven't seen them in a long time."

"Oh, Doug and Tracy. Make me Mambo number eleven, then. Christy, any way you work it, I'm the leftover. I'd rather stay here."

"No, you wouldn't," Christy said. "You would be miserable here, knowing that all of us were out having a good time."

"You know what?" Katie walked to the door. "We weren't going to sing this song anymore, were we? The old chorus about poor Katie. I'm going to open this door, and that old song is going to leave. Ready?" She opened the door, made a few grand whooshing motions with her hands, and then soundly closed the door. "End of discussion. Now, if you don't mind, I have a paper to type."

Christy didn't bring up the subject of going to The Dove's

19 Nest with Katie again. After thinking about Katie's response to the situation, Christy decided to let it go.

Matt stopped by the bookstore late Friday morning to tell Christy that Jenna had agreed to join the outing and to say that the two of them would drive in his truck unless Todd and Christy still had room in their car.

"I think Todd offered Sierra a ride if Paul doesn't come."

"What about Katie?"

Christy tried to make her voice sound causal. "She's not going."

"Why not?"

"You would have to ask her." Christy didn't know if that was too telling an answer or if Matt would read between the lines and drop it.

Fortunately, Christy had a customer and had to cut the conversation short.

"We'll see you there, then," he said.

Christy nodded and waved. When work ended, she went to her dorm room to grab a sweater. The Dove's Nest was only ten miles from Rancho Corona, but going there as a group had become a big event for everyone.

Christy considered leaving Katie a note, urging her to grab a couple of girls from their floor, jump in Baby Hummer, and drive on down to The Dove's Nest. But Christy didn't.

Todd was waiting for her in the lobby. To her surprise, he handed her a single white carnation.

"Just because," he said.

Christy was touched but also curious about where he had bought the flower. She knew no place on campus sold flowers.

"Did you go into town this afternoon?" she asked.

"I went to church for a couple of hours."

They drove down the hill with the windows open and the heater on full blast. It had become a habit because they liked the feel of the fresh air, but it was cold outside, now that the desert climate had settled in to its winter season. The days could still be warm and bright if the sun was shining, but as soon as the sun went down, the thermometer dipped dramatically.

"Were flower vendors on the street corner like at Thanksgiving?" Christy twirled the carnation and drew in the spicy sweet fragrance.

"No." Todd looked at her with a grin. "It's killing you trying to figure out where I got that, isn't it?"

Christy hid her grin. "I'm just curious." She imagined his making a special stop at a florist and ordering a single carnation. Only the flower didn't come wrapped in florist tissue.

"I saw it at church in the Dumpster," Todd said.

"Oh." Christy laid the flower across her lap. Suddenly it

didn't seem so sweet or sentimental.

"They had tossed out the flowers from a luncheon or something, and I saw that lone white carnation, and it made me think of you."

Christy knew it was the thought that counted. She knew with Todd it was always the thought that counted, and it most likely would always be that way.

"Thank you," Christy said. "I love it." Then, leaning over and giving his cheek a kiss, she said, "And I love you."

"I love you more," Todd teased.

"No, I love you more."

"I loved you first," Todd said.

Christy laughed. "Okay, you win. You loved me first. But I still love you more."

"Don't think so." Todd glanced at her as he drove. "I don't think it's possible for you ever to love me as deeply and as completely as I love you. I don't think anyone could ever love another person on this earth as much as I love you."

Christy couldn't compete with that. She didn't want to.

"I talked to your uncle today," Todd said. "Have you talked to him lately?"

"Not since Thanksgiving."

"He said the pictures turned out great, and he's sending them to us. He also said Marti told him last night that she's not leaving."

"Really? What did he say?"

"I guess she quit her art classes and told Bob she was willing to put the effort into working on their marriage as long as he was willing, too."

"Do you think she'll go to church with him?"

"I don't know," Todd said.

"Do you think they'll go to a marriage counselor?"

"I couldn't say."

"I'm glad you told me. That's a big relief. I'm glad she decided to try to work things through. Don't you think that when you stayed with them it helped bring them back together because they had you as a mutual project to work on?"

"Possibly," Todd said.

"I think that helped a lot."

"Are you saying they should have a baby?"

Christy was surprised at Todd's suggestion. "They're too old, aren't they?"

Todd shrugged. "Don't ask me."

There was a pause before Todd said, "How many kids do you want to have?"

Christy thought a moment. "I don't know. Sometimes I liked that there were only two of us, even though David and I weren't real close. When I was younger I thought I wanted to have a huge family with six or eight kids. Then I worked at the orphanage. I think two is good. Four maybe. I think even numbers are better."

A wide grin spread across Todd's face. The afternoon sun was low in the December sky and came streaming in through the driver's window, illuminating his profile. "I want four," he said soundly. "Two boys, two girls. But I'll take whatever God grants. And if they're healthy, so much the better."

Christy was amazed they were talking so naturally about their family. Their future. Although she shouldn't be surprised. They had been having more conversations like this lately. Both of them spoke freely and openly, even though neither of them had yet used terms such as "our children" or "whatever God grants *us*." The understanding that they were discussing their life together was there, under the surface.

Todd reached over and took her hand in his. He glanced at her with a contented smile, then looked back at the road. Christy smoothed her finger across his hand, delicately tracing each scar.

"Do these hurt anymore?" she asked.

"Not really. A few of them are tender."

"I love your hands." Christy drew his hand to her lips and kissed it before pressing it against her cheek.

"You do?"

"Yes, I do."

They both glanced at each other a little awkwardly and smiled. Christy's "I do" had prompted her, and apparently Todd, as well, to think of how those were the words they would one day say to each other at the altar.

Go ahead, say it, Todd. Say, "Will you marry me?" You know I'll say yes.

Todd didn't say anything. He pulled into the parking lot of The Dove's Nest, and Christy felt a mixture of bliss and impatience. If she had a single brazen cell in her body, she would construct a sentence that had the word "marry" in it that ended with a question mark. That would prompt Todd to speak up.

But in the secret place in her heart, Christy was at rest. She and Todd had come so far. They were so close. Everything was just about perfect. If Todd uttered his anticipated proposal to her in three minutes or in three days or in three years, she could wait.

As they walked hand in hand through the parking lot, Todd said, "Isn't that Baby Hummer?"

"Katie came?"

"That's good," he said. "I'd hoped she would."

"Did you say anything to her about it today?"

"No."

Christy was proud of her friend. She must have thought it through and realized she would be happier spending Friday night with her friends than letting the couples part of the event bother her.

When Todd and Christy entered the contemporary-looking café, Christy was drawn to the fireplace, where the dancing golden flames waved to her and bid her come closer.

"Todd, they have a fireplace," Christy said. She noticed Sierra, Paul, Randy, and Vicki all seated near the fire. They had pulled together two small, round tables and had collected a sufficient number of chairs.

"Christy!" Sierra waved to her. Paul, wearing a tweed cap, was seated next to Sierra. Christy had seen him only a few times before, but she hadn't remembered the round glasses perched on his straight nose.

"Have you seen Katie?" Christy asked after she greeted the four.

"She's in the bookstore with Matt and Jenna."

"Did anyone come with Katie?"

"I don't think so."

"Are you guys going to order something to eat?" Todd asked.

"We already did," Sierra said.

Just then a deep voice behind Christy and Todd said, "Did you say *food*?"

They turned to see Doug and Tracy.

Christy laughed as they all hugged. "I should have

known you would show up when food was mentioned," she said to Doug.

"Do you know what you want?" Todd asked Christy. "I'll order for us if you do."

She hadn't seen a menu; how could she know what to order? How could she decide?

"Any kind of sandwich would be fine," Christy said. "Roast beef, if they have it. If not, then whatever."

Todd and Doug exchanged glances as if they were sharing a private insight into Christy's restaurant-ordering abilities.

"That had to be the quickest meal decision I've ever seen you make," Doug said. He punched Todd's arm. "Looks like you two are having a good effect on each other."

"Yeah," Todd said, "she even talks me into putting gas in the car before the gauge registers in the red zone."

"My point exactly," Doug said. "What a team you two make!"

Tracy looked meaningfully at Christy, who read her married friend's expression to mean, "Has he asked you yet?"

Christy closed her eyes slowly and shook her head ever so slightly.

"We'll place the order," Doug said to Tracy. "You might need to pull up another table or at least a few more chairs if all these already are spoken for."

Christy and Tracy figured out how many were in their group and arranged the chairs accordingly. Christy took the seat closest to the fire and let the warmth seep through her jeans. She loved the café's ambience. The fireplace was draped with a fragrant evergreen swag decorated with tiny Christmas ornaments and bright red berries. Glowing white

Christmas lights lined the windows, and a large wreath hung on the front door.

The café reminded Christy of a coffee shop she and her friends used to go to in Basel. The amber-toned lights and dark wood tables, doors, and trim made the café feel homey. Christy liked the large windows and the deeply aromatic coffee.

What she liked most, though, was being with her friends. She noticed a bronze plaque inset on the side of the fireplace that read *Is any pleasure on earth as great as a circle of Christian friends by a fire? C. S. Lewis.*

Christy decided that when she lived in her dream house with Todd one day, they would have that quote engraved on a plaque and displayed by their fireplace.

When Katie, Matt, and Matt's date, Jenna, joined the group, Christy felt the circle was complete. And having the café decorated for Christmas made it magical.

"I'm glad you came," she quietly said to Katie.

Katie sat down in the empty seat beside Christy. "What did you say?"

"I said, I'm glad you came."

"Me too. You were right. This is where I belong."

Christy smiled.

"Is it seven o'clock yet?" Randy asked, getting up.

"It's five after seven," Tracy told him.

"I'm going to see if the manager is in yet. They said he was coming back at seven."

As Randy walked away, Tracy said, "Why does he want to see the manager? Does he know him?"

"No," Sierra explained. "He's in a band, and they want to play here sometime."

Todd arrived at the table with napkins and silverware,

which he handed to Christy. He took the chair directly across from her.

"Do you want to sit next to Christy?" Katie asked.

"No, I'm happy to sit here and gaze into her killer eyes."

Christy hadn't heard anyone refer to her as having "killer eyes" since high school. And that phrase had not come from Todd.

Todd leaned over to Matt, who was seated on his left, and using his hand to cover his mouth, Todd whispered something to Matt.

"No fair telling secrets," Katie said.

"It wasn't a secret," Todd said.

Matt didn't comment. He just left the table. Christy couldn't figure out what was going on. She decided not to try to wring out of Todd the un-secret he had told Matt, even though whatever it was had made Matt leave.

Christy was facing the door; the order window was behind her. She noticed that more people were arriving, and she was glad they had claimed their seats by the fire when they did.

"I ordered you some soup," Todd said. "Beef barley."

"Oh," Christy said. "Did they have sandwiches?"

"Only turkey and ham. I figured the soup had beef in it. It comes with a roll."

"Okay." Christy should have remembered how logically challenged Todd became when he was sent shopping. Actually, the soup was perfect; better than what she had requested. It would warm her up. Todd knew. She slid her leg under the table until she found his foot, and then she rubbed her foot against his ankle.

"Katie, are you trying to play footsie with me under the table?" Todd asked.

"Why would I do that?" Katie spouted.

Christy gave Todd an exasperated look and kicked him playfully. He gave her a slight wink. Either that or he was winking at someone behind her.

A booming voice behind Katie announced, "Hey, your hair is like a flock . . ."

Katie and Christy turned around at the same time and gasped.

Katie was the first to find her voice. "Rick?"

"Katie?"

Rick's voice faltered only for a moment before finishing his line, as if someone had paid him to say it to her. A wide grin spread across his face as he stated loudly, "Your hair is like a flock of goats. Will you go out with me?"

Everyone but Katie and Christy broke into delighted laughter. That had been Katie's wish, her exact words, in fact, when she had said she wanted a stranger to ask her out using the crazy compliment. Only, the tall, broad-shouldered man with dark, wavy hair who was scanning Katie's every detail with his chocolate brown eyes was no stranger to Christy or to Katie.

Katie slowly rose, and he greeted her with a hug. "Okay," she declared wildly. "I'll go out with you since you asked so nicely."

Rick laughed. "Look at you!" He pulled away and examined Katie even more closely. "Wow, when did you grow up?"

"It's my hair. I got it cut."

"Some guy named Matt told me to come over and say your hair was like a flock of goats, but I didn't know it was you. And it's not, you know. I mean it's you, but your hair isn't goat-like at all."

Christy had never seen Rick Doyle fumble his words. He seemed more like a kid than the snobby football star he had been in high school.

Rick pulled his gaze from Katie to see who else was at the table.

"Hi, Rick," Christy said warmly.

"Christy." Rick stooped to hug her around the neck. "It's so great to see you guys. When Todd and Doug walked up to the register, I couldn't believe it. Todd told me you two are . . ." Rick looked at Todd.

Christy looked at Todd.

Todd's expression remained steady.

"Todd told me you two are closer than ever," Rick said. "I'm glad for you. I really am. That's so great."

"I think it's pretty great, too." Christy was glad to know she could sit there and talk to Rick Doyle and know that nothing awkward remained between them from the up-and-down season they had while dating in high school.

Matt returned to his seat, and Katie gave him a hard time for talking Rick into playing a joke on her when really the joke turned out to be on Rick.

"He made me do it." Matt pointed to Todd.

Todd put on his best innocent look and turned to Doug as if it had been his bright idea.

"Don't look at me," Doug said.

Christy realized at that moment that every guy she had ever cared for seriously or deeply in her life was gathered at this table. And none of them was anything like Todd. Her heart turned up another notch in its steady devotion to Todd Spencer. No guy would ever compare.

"Do you want to eat with us?" Katie asked after all the introductions had been made.

"I have to get back to my office. They told me a guy's waiting to talk to me about his band playing here."

"He's with us," Sierra said. "It's Randy."

"Your office?" Katie asked.

"I'm the manager here. Didn't Doug tell you?"

"No, Doug didn't say anything. You're the manager?"

Rick nodded. "My dad bought the place and put me to work. Come with me. I'll show you around." The invitation clearly was for Katie only.

As Katie began to follow him, Christy heard her say, "Have you ever considered serving any gourmet herbal teas here?"

Christy turned to Todd, her eyes wide. "Should I be in shock?"

"Not when God is doing God-things," Todd said smugly.

"With a little help from His friends," Tracy added.

"With a little help from His friends," Todd repeated.

Then the food arrived. The group joined hands around the table, and Doug prayed aloud. When he ended the prayer, Christy and Todd said softly in unison, "As you wish."

They both looked up. Their eyes met. To Christy it seemed as if she were gazing into a reflecting pool. The other half of her heart was gazing back at her, smiling.

Katie's food sat untouched at the empty place beside Christy while the rest of them ate. Randy returned with news about a date in February when his band would play at The Dove's Nest. The soup was good, and the fire had warmed Christy down to her toes. She was happy.

Two guys with guitars, who had been setting up by the front window, began to play. That made it harder for Christy to hear the conversation at the end of the table, where

Sierra sat, but Christy was content to stick with the close conversation between Doug, Tracy, Todd, and her. They were discussing the upcoming trip to the Mexican orphanage when Katie returned to the table, her green eyes lit up like a Christmas tree.

"Can I just say I am stunned? Did you get a chance to talk to that guy? Everything is about how 'the Lord did this,' and 'God took care of that.' It's so fun to be around him now."

"It's awesome," Doug said.

"Yes," Katie agreed, "it is awesome. And you guys are awesome. Rick said you kept in contact with him over the years and sent him letters encouraging him to turn his heart to the Lord. And you know what? He finally listened. I'm just . . . well, I'm stunned and amazed and . . ."

"A bit dazzled?" Christy ventured.

"Maybe a little."

The close group grew silent, waiting for Katie to embellish.

"Well, the guy told me my hair was like a flock of goats, all right? I mean, how can a girl not be dazzled by such poetic brilliance?"

They all laughed with her.

"And look what I found in the stock room." Katie placed a bag of candy hearts on the table. "Dessert!"

"Can you imagine how old those are?" Tracy asked. "I mean, this place is new, isn't it? They aren't selling Valentine's candy anywhere now. It's still Christmas candy everywhere. I don't want to know where these came from."

"Bargain Barn." Todd tore open the bag and spilled the pastel hearts onto the table. "I was in Bargain Barn today, and they had a whole crate of these up front. Now's the time to buy them."

"Buy them, maybe. But eat them? I don't think so." Tracy picked up a heart and read the message. " 'Fax me.' Fax me? When did they start writing 'Fax me' on these things? I thought they said, 'Be mine' and 'Stay true' and . . ." She picked up another one. " 'Kiss me'?"

"Don't mind if I do." Doug pulled Tracy close and planted a big one on her lips.

She giggled as if that had been the first time she had ever been kissed. The sight of her two friends so in love made Christy smile. Doug had never kissed a girl until his wedding day, and when he and Tracy married, their kiss at the altar had prompted the loudest roar of applause Christy had ever heard at a wedding.

"Check this out," Katie said. " 'Page me.' "

They all looked for messages in the hearts. Doug pulled out an "e-mail me" and said, "This must be the interactive bag."

Todd placed a pink heart in front of Christy as if to prove Doug's point. It read, "Marry me."

Christy looked up. "I can't believe what they put on these now. I'm with you, Tracy. I remember when they used to say, 'Be sweet.' "

"Here you go," Katie said. " 'Sweet lips.' "

"I want that one," Tracy said.

"What are you doing, making your own sentence over there?" Katie asked.

"Sure. Try it."

"Here you go: Another 'Page me.' " Christy handed a yellow candy to Tracy.

Todd placed a second candy heart in front of Christy. It also read, "Marry me."

"I think we already have one of those." Christy moved the hearts around and looked for one that no one else had found yet.

Todd was looking, too. He picked up a heart and then came around to Christy's side of the table. He placed the third candy heart in a row with the first two he had given her. "There. Once it's spoken three times, it's established. Forever."

Christy froze. All she could see were the three candy hearts lined up in front of her. All three of them said "Marry me," "Marry me," "Marry me."

She turned as Todd went down on one knee. He covered both her hands with his. His voice washed over her like a waterfall as he stared into her eyes and said, "Kilikina, my Kilikina, will you marry me?"

"Yes," Christy whispered without a moment's hesitation. "Yes," she repeated more loudly. Then a third time, with complete confidence and a cascade of tears, she said, "Yes, Todd, my Todd. I will marry you."

For a moment the whole world stopped, and Christy and Todd remained still. Not breathing. Not blinking. Not moving. Lost in the depths of each other's souls. The only sound Christy heard was her heart beating. But she wasn't sure if it was her heart or Todd's. The two seemed to beat as one.

"What are you doing, Todd?" Katie asked. "Did you lose one of the candies on the ground over there? There are plenty more up here."

Todd didn't move. Christy smiled.

No one knows! Todd just proposed to me, and no one knows. It's our secret.

Christy and Todd's secret bubble was burst when Katie looked at Christy's lineup of hearts. Katie screamed as only Katie could. Everyone in the café stopped talking and eating, and the two guys playing guitars in the corner paused.

"Finally!" Katie shouted. She bounced up from her chair and yelled, "I have an announcement to make! My best friend just got proposed to!"

A rush of hugs and well wishes poured over Todd and Christy.

Katie looked at Christy. "And what did you say?"

Christy grinned confidently. "I said yes!"

"She said yes!" Katie burst into applause, and the rest of the people in the café joined her.

Matt wrapped his arms around Christy and gave her a home-boy kind of hug. "Your grandma is going to love him," he said. "And I won't say eenie-meenie boo-boo to you anymore because it's obvious that Todd is 'it.' "

Christy grinned and giggled. "Yes, he is."

Tracy dissolved into a puddle of tears and so did Sierra. When Sierra hugged Christy, Sierra said, "I didn't cry this much at my sister's wedding! What is it with you and Todd?"

Rick appeared and gave Christy a warm smile. He leaned over and kissed her cheek. "You held out for a hero," he said in her ear. "Good for you, killer eyes."

"Thanks, Rick."

Christy looked at Todd. He was taking in all the well-wishing with the biggest smile.

He looks like a five-year-old, and everyone just showed up for his surprise birthday party.

As Christy thought that, one of the waiters approached the table carrying a round carrot cake with one lit candle in the middle. "Compliments of Mr. Doyle," the waiter said.

"Make a wish!" Katie chanted. "Make a wish!"

"I already did." Todd wrapped his arms around his beloved. "And she came true."

"That is so sweet!" Tracy said. "Todd, I never knew you were such a romantic."

"You haven't seen anything yet," he said. Tilting Christy's chin up with the slightest touch of his finger, Todd kissed her like he had never kissed her before.

As they slowly drew apart, Christy saw the still-burning candle out of the corner of her eye. She had nothing left to wish for. And most certainly not enough breath left to blow out a candle.

"The candle," Katie said. "What about the candle?"

Christy looked into Todd's eyes. He was looking at her "that way." The warm glow seemed brighter than ever behind his screaming silver-blue eyes.

"Let it burn," Todd murmured. He held her cheek gently in his hand. "Let it burn for the rest of our lives."

Christy kissed the palm of Todd's strong, scarred hand, and in a voice so soft that only God and Todd could hear, she whispered, "As you wish."

ENTER THE WORLD OF CHRISTY MILLER
and Find a Friend!

THE CHRISTY MILLER SERIES

A generation of teens have discovered that Robin Jones Gunn's Christy Miller is a teenage girl very much like them. She shares the same worries, hopes, dreams, and joys, and her daily choices to live for God have helped countless teenage girls deepen their own relationship with God.

Beginning with 14-year-old Christy's commitment to Christ, the series follows her high school years as she grows in her walk with the Lord. Throughout, Christy learns about friendship, dating, responsibility, Christ's faithfulness, and God's reward for obedience. She has become a role model for thousands of teens around the world—and more than that, she's become a friend.

From the Secret Place in My Heart: Christy Miller's Diary

Written in Christy's own voice for the first time ever, this unique journal gives readers a chance to hear Christy's deepest hopes, dreams, and prayers.

MEET FREE-SPIRITED SIERRA JENSEN
And Learn Lessons of Faith

THE SIERRA JENSEN SERIES

This fun series introduces readers to a spunky, bold teenager with big dreams and unconventional clothes. Teens will relate to what's going on in Sierra's life— whether it's dealing with school, friends, guys, family, or her faith.

Her faith is what sets Sierra apart. But she soon learns that being different isn't always popular—even during the exciting high school years. Get to know Sierra as she encounters real-life problems and faces difficult choices that take her through unexpected twists and turns.

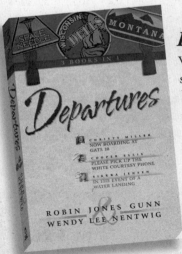

Departures

Written together with Wendy Lee Nentwig, this short story collection features the authors' beloved characters—Sierra Jensen, Cooper Ellis, and Christy Miller—crossing paths and traveling across the country.

The Leader in Christian Fiction!

BETHANYHOUSE

11400 Hampshire Ave S.
Minneapolis, MN 55438
(800) 328-6109
www.bethanyhouse.com